Peace Has Come

Parismita Singh is a writer and artist whose publications include the graphic novels *The Hotel at the End of the World* and *Mara and the Clay Cows*, and the anthology *Centrepiece: New Writing and Art from Northeast India* (2017). She lives in Guwahati, Assam.

Praise for *Peace Has Come*

'In this achingly good collection of short stories by Parismita Singh, each of the eight tales unravels in a part of upper Assam which is also often referred to as "Bodoland" … Through her stories, Singh tells us how common people suffer during "the uneasy, purgatory like time of ceasefire", which is really no better than wartime.'

– Abdullah Khan, *The Hindu*

'Surprisingly, its subject matter does not weigh down this collection or make it a depressing read. *Peace Has Come* allows the reader to experience the kind of the delight that comes from reading about places and cultures she might not know well, and accessing experiences that can only be felt by losing herself and her prejudices in a story well told.'

– Supriya Sharma, *Hindustan Times*

'The imminence of that peace is of course a sinister one, the way the silence in a forest is a disturbing one. It disheartens even as it lends hope. And through the pages, through all the curfews and jeeps and guns and young men that lead up to and mark the ceasefire period in the late 1990s, the reader is compelled to read the individual as a thing both affected and unaffected, touched and untouched, by violence.'

– Sayali Palelkar, *Scroll*

'With tension continuing to brew in Assam, the book is particularly relevant to our times. Rather than taking a partisan stand on militancy, Singh represents diverse ethnic groups that inhabit the space, and ties them together through the shared struggle for rights and identity and an undercurrent of humanity.'

– Kamalika Basu, *The Telegraph*

'Singh's writing is achingly evocative, and her characters, deliciously fleshed out. She doesn't waste words on breaking down her characters; instead, she puts them in a framework – an incredibly spine-chilling, eerie narrative laced with fear and suspicion – and lets it speak for them. Singh barely sinks her teeth into the gore – the secret brutal killings and mass murders – and focuses singularly on the disorder of the human lives.'

– Anshika Ravi, *The Sunday Guardian*

'It is interesting how the writer perceives and translates violence and fear into her stories … Singh deliberately maintains ambiguity and ambivalence that add greater depth to her work.

– Divya Dubey, *India Today*

Peace Has Come

PARISMITA SINGH

First published in hardback by Context, an imprint of Westland Publications Private Limited, in 2018

First published in paperback by Context, an imprint of Westland Books, a division of Nasadiya Technologies Private Limited, in 2023

No. 269/2B, First Floor, 'Irai Arul', Vimalraj Street, Nethaji Nagar, Alapakkam Main Road, Maduravoyal, Chennai 600095

Westland, the Westland logo, Context and the Context logo are the trademarks of Nasadiya Technologies Private Limited, or its affiliates.

ISBN: 9789357768672

10 9 8 7 6 5 4 3 2 1

This is a work of fiction. Names, characters, organisations, places, events and incidents are either products of the author's imagination or used fictitiously.

Typeset by SÜRYA, New Delhi

Printed at Saurabh Printers Pvt. Ltd

Contents

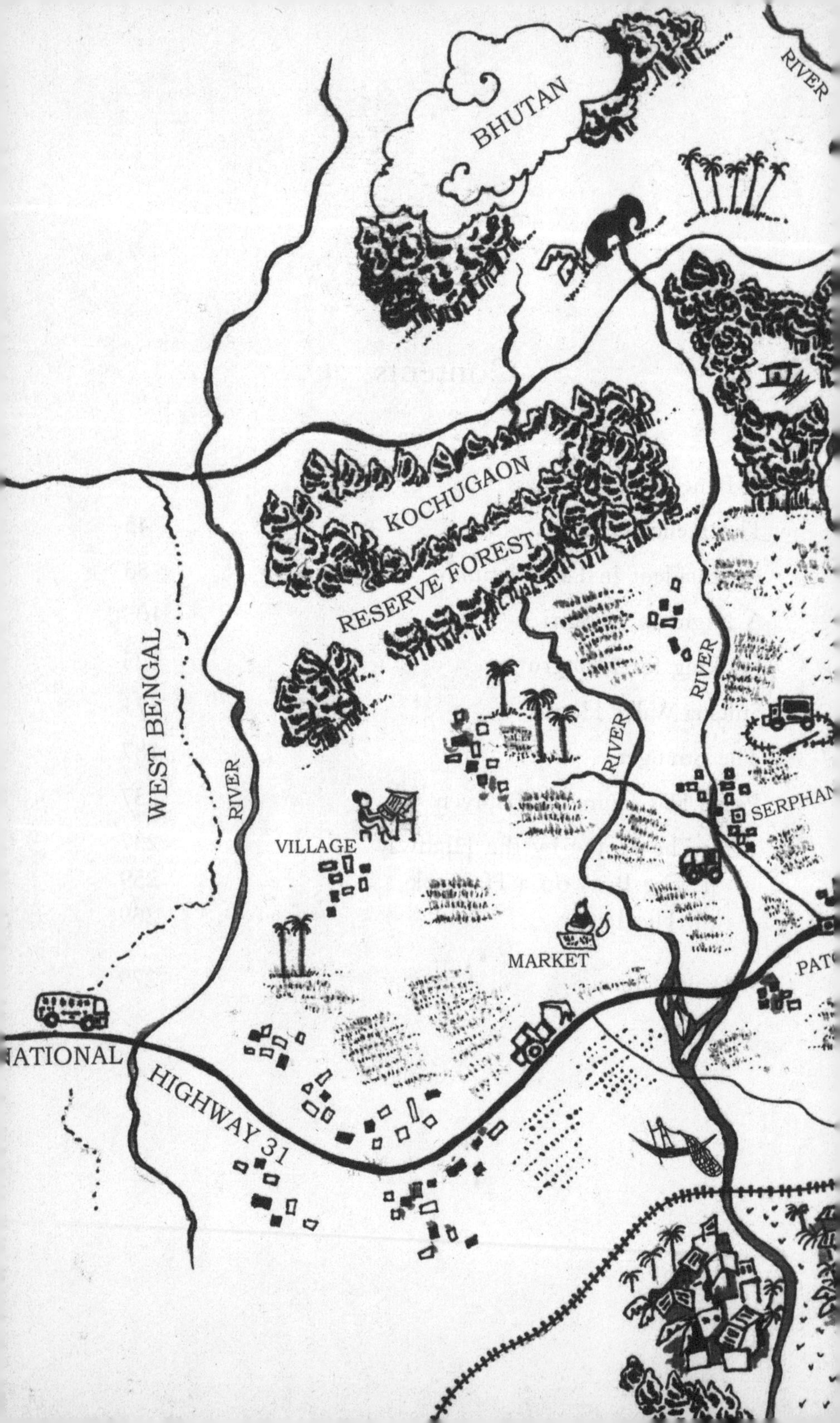
BHUTAN
RIVER
KOCHUGAON
RESERVE FOREST
WEST BENGAL
RIVER
RIVER
RIVER
SERPHAN
VILLAGE
MARKET
PAT
NATIONAL
HIGHWAY 31

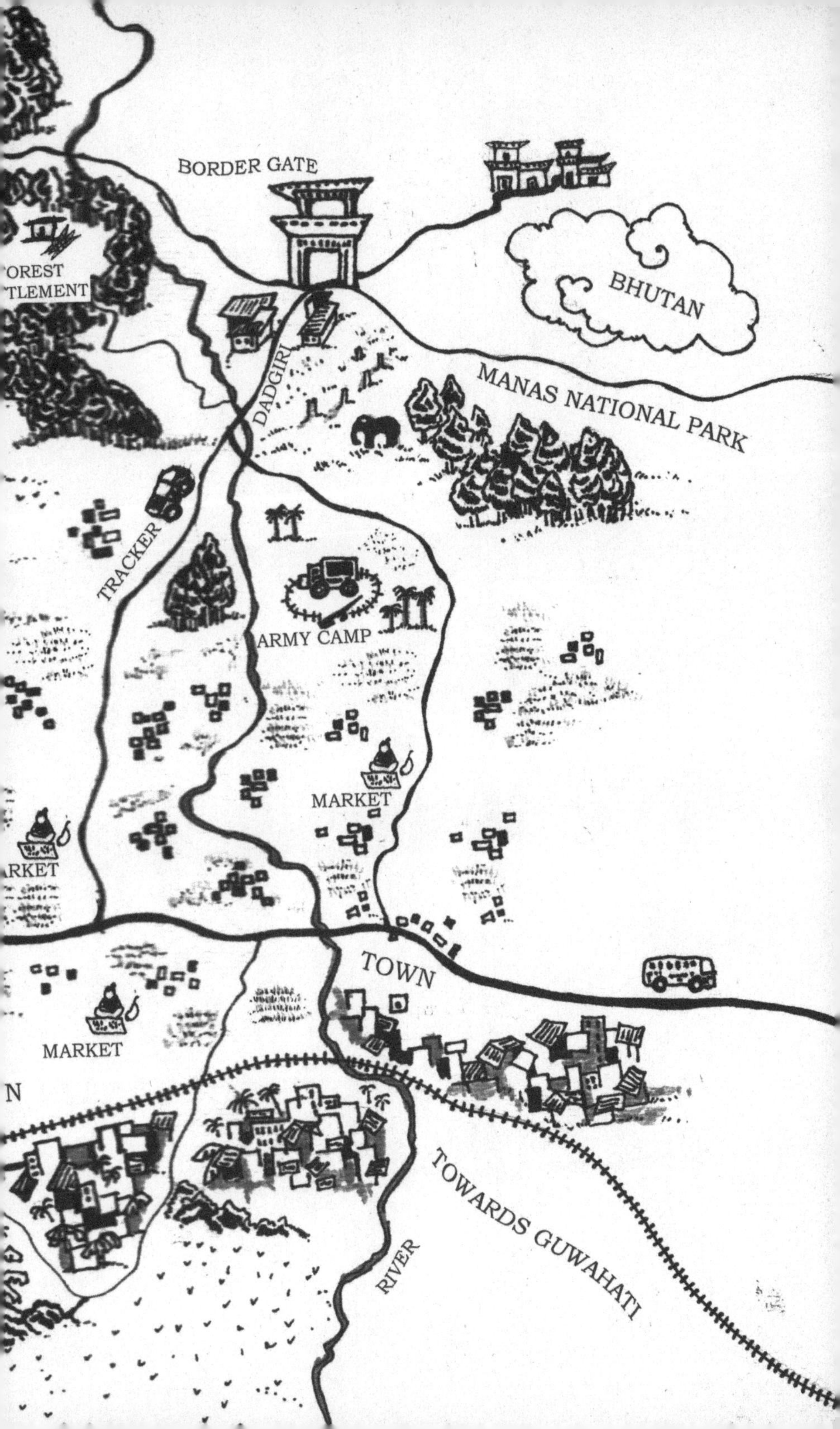
BORDER GATE
BHUTAN
FOREST
TLEMENT
DADGIRI
MANAS NATIONAL PARK
TRACKER
ARMY CAMP
MARKET
RKET
TOWN
MARKET
N
TOWARDS GUWAHATI
RIVER

A Time Made of Glass

She found them at the bottom of the trunk, beneath the yellowed newspaper lining. Two notebooks: a child's copy book, ruled, with a hardback cover; and the other, a longer 'register' book. Someone had placed them there and forgotten about them. She brushed away the rat droppings, and picked up the smaller book; pages and pages of writing in a neat cursive hand. A smell of mould escaped from the pages, so strong she had to hold her breath as she began reading.

With the spokes in his tongue
Dwimalu was still speaking –
It isn't enough
To have your jaw smashed
Nails ripped out
Bones ground into the earth –
It isn't enough to have your heart broken –
Everybody's broken these days.
Everything shattered.

And there was more:

Poetry is not for the heroes
Felled by bullets and betrayal.
They do not need your rhymes
They are at rest.
It is for the other times
For the ones
Who at the end of the fight
Crawl out of their caves
Inching towards the light.
For in every war, there are the drifters
The scoundrels, cheats, the damned, the doubters
Who do not know what they seek.
Their nerves are shot, their flesh is weak
For them I write.

Poetry is not for the heroes.

They looked like poems, in the Roman script, some in Bodo but most of them in English. The register book had more of the same.

She flipped back to the cover, no name or date. Inside, the front page had been ripped out. Bits of pollen from a desiccated, long-pressed flower came off on her fingers.

Her uncle was outside, burning leaves and dead branches at the edge of the garden.

'Here,' she handed them to him, 'are these yours?'

He took them from her, and smiled. 'Oh, these? Where did you find them? I had almost forgotten about them.'

'Someone had secreted them away into the trunk's lining. I was cleaning it out and found them. No names, dates, nothing. I didn't know you wrote poetry.'

'No, they are not mine. A girl gave them to me a long time ago.'

'A girl? You knew girls who wrote poetry?'

He laughed. 'Don't mention that to your aunt. You know her, she has no time for these frivolities, and she'll say I'm a bad influence on you young people!'

'Was this girl in love with you?'

'In love with me? No, no, she wasn't.'

He looked up from the notebooks, taken aback at the directness of her question. She was not looking at him, poking absently at the fire with a twig. His sister's daughter, he had not paid much attention to this niece before, even though they lived in adjacent houses. She was dressed in a homespun dokhona, wore her hair long like the other girls in the neighbourhood. Where were the strains of individuality in the young women these days, he wondered, they seemed to all look the same. It was not simply the dokhonas that they had taken to wearing after the 1980s, or the way they styled their hair or carried themselves, it was something else, something more essential – they were too diffident, too closely wrought into the social strictures of their community even though they had more options with education and careers. This one, his niece, was somewhat of a blur in the family, either rushing to her tuition classes or hurrying through her chores in the house. What did it mean to be young in these times, what were they thinking? He had noted the surprise in her voice, *her uncle knew girls?*

'Oh.' She was not sure how much her uncle would tell her, but she gave it a try. 'This girl just happened to give you her poetry books then?'

'They were her books, yes, and she did give them to me. But she wasn't a poet, she didn't write them.'

'But there are no names below the poems—'

'Well, she wrote them out, she copied them into these books from the scraps of paper that he'd scribble them on. It's her handwriting, I remember that. But the poems, they were written by someone else. She was in love with the poet.'

'Then why did she give you these books?'

'That's a long story. But if you must know, I almost married her.' He laughed.

'Ah, then you did love her!'

'Of course not, I didn't love her. I told you she loved the poet.'

'The poet – he didn't love her?'

'Yes, he did. He did love her. He wrote these poems for her. You're very curious.'

*

It was all such a long time ago, I don't think there's any harm in telling you the story. It was not a secret; everyone knew about it at the time.

I went to college in the town, had to plead with your grandfather. Our families from the villages were not too keen on sending their young people to the town then. Those who could afford to, sent their children outside the state. The colleges barely functioned here; people were apprehensive that their children would turn political and come back as concrete memorials. Even the memorials were getting smaller – and you weren't a proper martyr if it was a fratricidal killing. I think we had begun to look ahead to a time when we would need professionals to run things, not soldiers.

The '90s were a difficult time to be young. It is not like the way it is now – all you people have to worry about is your mobile phone bills! But when we were going out to college, it was different. The Movement had swept across the land – and it was the younger leaders who were able to give it its dynamic form, inspire the masses, give our people hope. Youngsters had laid down their lives when the police opened fire at peaceful protesters, others had picked up guns. Even our women were joining. People all over the world were hearing of our struggle. But fighting is a hard thing, it takes generations to do what our people set out to achieve. What do you think, a few bomb blasts and ambushes, and they would hand over statehood to us on a platter? Assam had already been divided once; they would not give in so easily this time. And our people, they were not clever enough when it came to statecraft, to the wiliness of these non-tribals who had ruled so long. Aie, we fought the Assamese and we knew we couldn't trust them, but it turned out they weren't the only ones we had to watch out for. The leaders from New Delhi were no better! There was a lot of hope when the peace deals of the early '90s were signed, but what did we get? Each ceasefire, each agreement only led to more trouble, more chaos, more armed groups. In the end, we fought our neighbours, and we fought ourselves—

A brief coughing fit interrupted his speaking. He cleared his throat and smiled.

But you know all this, you have heard it before. I must be getting old, beginning one story and telling another, ranting about the past ...

So, to go back to our story, after passing the Higher Secondary exams, I decided to study further. For us in the village, a college degree meant a shot at a job outside, at least till things settled down here. Our father was another matter, of course. He was just like the way you see him now. *Better a farmer's son who can read the clouds than a dead scholar wearing shoes*, he would walk around mumbling. So it didn't matter that I could only manage Janata College, I was more than happy. I simply hoped that I could stretch his munificence to the three years it required to finish the course. But these things didn't bother us students unduly, except toward the end of the month, when the money ran out and we had to smoke bidis on empty stomachs; then, we'd turn philosophical and worry about our futures. But the next day, somebody's money arrived and we would forget all that. We were young and enjoyed living away from our families. Initially, there were four of us living in the same house. The family kept the rooms in front, and let out the rooms at the back to boarders. Our kitchen was a bare shed, where they used to keep cows. But we were an enterprising lot, and soon managed to put together some money for a stove and some utensils. In a year's time, I was a very good cook!

But you were right, I did write poetry, or attempted to in high school. I had a similar notebook of poems, mostly about the revolution and dying young men and romantic yearnings. It must have been very bad, but every boy who read a few books wrote poetry at that age. So, I was thrilled when I found out that a classmate in the hostel, Rwmaii, this boy from Gossaigaon, wrote poems too. He was in the next room. But I knew it was another matter when I saw his bedside. I had never seen so many books before! They were everywhere: stashed under his bed in long columns, piled haphazardly on top of the trunk, under the sheets, a few peeping out from his bathing bucket, photocopies and handwritten notes, old journals, magazines, newspaper sheets, and books and more books. He read in Assamese, Bengali, Bodo and English. When the binding of the old books fell apart, sometimes they would let in pages of other books, other languages. Rwmaii would joke that they read better that way. There was a phase when he wanted to learn Arabic – a friend's brother back from university brought a photocopy of poems by a Palestinian poet. They were in English translation, but for a whole week he chased this madrasa student with a notebook, because he wanted to be able to read the poems in the original! And the Muslims, who couldn't make head or tail of his request, began to suspect he was trying to woo one of their girls. We had a good laugh over it.

Rwmaii … that was not the name his family gave him. His mother was a follower of the Radha Soami group, and they had called him Ram at birth. But he had changed his name to the more poetic Rwmaii, a name more suited to a wordsmith than the old-fashioned one his mother gave him. It's common now, the W in his name. But back then, he had had to explain how the W represented the shortened A sound, unique to our language. He was full of new ideas for our language, for a new literature. The rest of us did not know much about these debates and ideas, about the Movement and other struggles around the world, and Rwmaii would often lecture us. He was going to be a writer; he had already published his poems and stories in local magazines, articles in newspapers. Influenced by him, I began to read poetry and developed a taste for it, and mercifully, I stopped writing my own. We became friends.

Then Rwmaii fell in love with this girl in our class, Sylvia.

Most of us liked one girl or another in those days. But the practicalities of carrying on a romance were daunting. How were things to ever progress from that one look across the hall or the time she asked you for political science notes? It was impossible to drink a cup of tea with a girl in the canteen or walk around with her in those days. You had to be careful. If you loved a girl, or sought to love her, you couldn't risk destroying her reputation in the process. What would be the point of that? The first two years of college were the worst; everybody was keeping an eye on you. An infringement of these social rules could risk you a beating, or worse, get you hauled off to a public bisar by one of the student groups.

That's when Rwmaii decided to use his poetry. (Of course, it also helped that he wasn't too bad to look at.)

I watched his love unfold through his poems. Sometimes I wondered that he let me read them at all. He would describe her hair, her body, and his admiration and desire for them. Not used to reading things like this, I would go all red! He would write about the lover as a martyr to the homeland, touching her like an independence he glimpsed in the horizon, all sorts of things we couldn't imagine. It would make my head spin.

Some of those poems must be in the notebooks you found. They may sound foolish now, but at that time, no one wrote like this. He had something of the old Bodo romantic poets, I liked that about his poems. And of course, he was a brother to all sorts of causes and movements he read about from all over the world, the crazy Americans and the serious Arab poets, a variety of moods and politics. No magazine would have published his poetry at that point. That was the year the Students' Union formally rejected the peace deal. Some of the senior students from college had gone to attend the convention. Already, there were serious divisions among our people about the script and the nature of autonomy we were fighting for. Things were very fraught politically, you couldn't just write anything that came into your head and publish it.

Rwmaii would send her two, three poems every week,

not every day though. I think he kept her waiting, liked to watch her waiting a little longer the days he didn't send her one. He didn't give them to her directly. He slipped them into books that another friend or I left at her desk casually. It was an elaborate courtship, and involved us all; we followed it closely, revelled in it.

That is when we came up with the idea of a literary magazine. Even though there wasn't as much money as you see now, it was not difficult to get a magazine out. Culture was a large part of the struggle, and people were ready to put in a few rupees; we could count on donations from the student unions. Most importantly, it was permissible for young people, both boys and girls to do political work together. Sylvia and two other girls joined us boys. We called it *Gami Gwdan*, The New Village, after Brahma's poem. It was a compromise between those of us who wanted to give the magazine a more radical title, and others who felt the name should reach out to the common reader. There was an English and a Bodo section, someone suggested Assamese and Bengali sections too, but they were shouted down. The Bodo section would contain poems in both Devanagri and Roman script. That was not really necessary, the Devanagri was more or less finalised as the script, especially in our parts, but Rwmaii still felt strongly about the Roman, so we decided to carry both.

Sylvia was not anything exceptional to look at; there were prettier girls in college. But she was intelligent and charming, with a rich, throaty voice, a ready laugh. She knew more of the world than most of us. Her father was in a government job and the family travelled with him to various postings all over the country. She and Rwmaii had decided they would finish their three years here and go to university. It seemed only natural that they would. We all envied Rwmaii his romance, their shared interests, their plans for a future together. And because of the poems, I experienced some of it too, we all did. I would see them and think, this is how a life is to be lived, how one is to love.

*

He stopped speaking, looked at the notebooks.

Then addressed his niece again, 'You are thinking of going to college, aren't you? You should. It's a time when the world treads on you lightly, before the real worries begin. Learning is a luxury, and reading – you have the time to read then. I never kept up my poetry reading after college. Back then, Rwmaii and I had read all the English poems in our Reader, then noted the important poets and found the rest of their collections in the library. Eliot, Yeats, Blake … Have they put any Eliot in your school syllabus?'

'Eliot? I don't know. We haven't finished the book yet.'

'Probably not. Most of them in the syllabus board are political appointees. They must have just reprinted one of the other states' books.'

She interjected, 'About college, can you speak to father? They don't want to send me to the capital, I can tell. Not even for a BSc. They're suddenly talking about money, and the gold they have to make for me.'

He laughed. 'They want to give you gold?'

'Nobody's worrying about money when they're throwing

it on their son's schooling. They don't ask him about his marks, because he barely passes. What do they want me to do here? Spend the rest of my life weaving and cooking or—'

It is as if he has had a glimpse of the way she will look years from now.

She continues to speak, her eyes brimming: 'They're always thinking of their son! They're trying to save money because he won't make it through the entrance and then they'll have to pay to get him into some third-rate engineering college.'

He tries to pacify her, 'You mustn't be bitter about your brother. The poor boy, he doesn't have it easy.'

She glances toward the house. 'I'll have to finish with the trunk, before mother starts shouting. You wait here – I want to hear the rest.'

'Go.'

She reappeared at his side, a little later. She had brought him a cup of tea. He understood this to be a sign that she wanted him to continue the story.

*

Where did I leave off? The end of the first year in college …

We went home for the summer. I stayed on at home a little longer after term began. The rains were late, and we still needed people for the ploughing. That day, I had left for the fields at first light. There was a light drizzle, I urged the cows on, with the mud splashing up my bare feet and arms, streaking my face. I have a clear memory of that morning – the plastic I had wrapped myself in sticking to my body, flapping against the sharp bitter wind, the rain dripping on my eyelashes. I was constantly beating my hands against the flanks of the animals to keep away the numbness. Then I heard my name being called and saw the neighbour's boy at the edge of the field waving his hands wildly. A guest from the town is here, from your college, he shouted. It was a surprise, a pleasant surprise, but not unusual in those days. There were no mobiles, so you often had unexpected visitors, no warning.

I reached home, washed my feet by the hand pump and came in. It was Rwmaii! He sat in the front room with my father. Mother had brought tea. I wasn't alarmed to see him there. Another strike in college, I thought. But as I stepped into the room, I knew something was wrong. Rwmaii looked up at me with bloodshot eyes. He had wiped himself dry, but he must have been cycling in the rain for a long time; he looked exhausted. We greeted each other with the usual joviality for the benefit of my father who was still in the room. The old man must have suspected something but didn't think to intrude. Though he still complained about my college fees, he was at the same time respectful of my educated friends. After he left, Rwmaii and I sat in silence for some time. He seemed to find it difficult to begin, so I waited. Then he blurted it out, *Sylvia*. Something terrible had happened. They had stayed in touch through the holidays. She was in Gossaigaon for some time, and they had met at the market or at a friend's house every few days. After she left for her grandmother's home in the village, they wrote letters. Sometimes, she called him at the local PCO. The PCO man was a friend, so she would call and leave a message if Rwmaii wasn't around when the call came.

'Her family knows about you?' I asked.

He nodded, 'They must have had some inkling of our romance. Word had got around that she had a poet as an admirer.' He smiled a little. 'She told me that they teased her when the letters came. She wasn't worried, she didn't mention anything in her letters, so she must have been taken by surprise when it happened. You see—' He looked up at me with the bloodshot eyes, his face hollowed out by the weight of what he was telling me. 'About three weeks ago, the letters stopped. She would write three or four a week. Then they stopped.'

But since it was only two weeks to college, Rwmaii didn't think much of it. He would see her soon. College began, but she wasn't there. He approached her friends, they said they didn't know anything. Then he started to hear things: this one boy, a relative of hers, was surprised when he mentioned Sylvia – didn't he know, Sylvia was now a married woman. The ceremony had taken place sometime last month. She had married a commander from the ceasefire camp.

Rwmaii stopped speaking, put his hand to his face.

I started to blurt out things I only half believed myself. It couldn't be, no it must be a lie, a misunderstanding. People were like that sometimes, wishing you harm, making up malicious stories to destroy your love. Somebody lies in bed with jaundice for a month and the town is abuzz with stories of her elopement to Nepal.

'No,' he said, 'later a girl from Sylvia's village spoke to

me. It was true, they all knew about it, but didn't know how to tell me. We have to do something. You were the only person I could think of … I need help – I don't know what to do …'

He sat there, hands covering his face, body shaking. It was a terrible thing, to see him like that. I couldn't quite understand it. Why would Sylvia suddenly go off and marry some surrendered guy? I was shaken up myself but I tried to think. We had to do something, at least find out what had happened. Athiabari was close to the Bhutan border. We'd have to make something up to tell my family and go see her parents there. My father wouldn't be happy about it, but we would be back in a day or two. I didn't see what else we could do. We couldn't go on with our lives as if nothing had happened.

'There must have been a letter she left me,' he was sobbing, 'something …'

We left home when the rain let up for a while. I packed a bag with some clothes for both of us. Rwmaii had left in such a hurry he didn't think of carrying anything. Later he confessed to me that he had felt such darkness inside him that he had tried to shake it off by cycling furiously down the road. He had cycled blindly without direction for miles and, when he found himself on the highway going towards my village, he had decided to come see me. He must have cycled for a good five hours to reach here.

In the bus, his exhaustion caught up with him and he dozed off. I was glad of that. It was a futile exercise, conjuring up images of Sylvia coming to greet us as we approached her house, or finding her at home, recovering from some sickness.

I realised then that I had liked her, I had liked them together. I was not envious of their happiness as I very easily could have been, with no romantic or other prospect in my life at that time. People said that about girls, of course, that they left you for money or family reasons, but I couldn't imagine Sylvia doing it. I didn't quite know what to believe, so it was easier to make a plan and have something to do.

We broke our journey in the evening and stayed at my cousin's place. Rwmaii was still brooding, subdued, but did not look as upset as before. He brought out a small notebook and started scribbling. I was glad to see this; he would have to come out of this somehow. It was like that in the lives of so many poets. We had often spoken in the hostel of how a poet must be open to melancholy and devastation in order to write more fully of the emotions and the world. We had spoken of childhood grief, of changing seasons and unknown longings, of death. But this was different. Rwmaii's despair and helplessness had alarmed me. I barely recognised my friend.

My cousin accompanied us to Sylvia's village. He knew the family. Normally, the father would have left for the city by now, but with the marriage and everything, he had extended his leave. There was an old grandmother and some relatives who stayed in the village house through the year. The mother divided her time between the village and the various accommodations of her husband's postings. Sylvia had two brothers and a sister. The younger boy was in junior college, the sister in school. There was something wrong, they said, with the older brother – he was never quite the same after a childhood fever. He lived in the village with his grandmother. The cousin didn't want to say too much but he hinted that the family was not happy with the marriage; that it was a very hurried affair, and nobody had quite expected it to take place.

We didn't know what to expect. It was not a customary thing to visit the parental home of your beloved after she had married someone else. If she had eloped, they would take their anger out on us. Or they may take us to be troublemakers. Nobody liked to have the past come back in this manner, and even though it was barely a month ago that Sylvia was making phone calls and writing letters to Rwmaii, it all felt like a very long time ago.

We found them at home, the mother and the father. They were puzzled to see three boys walk in. They recognised my cousin, but he introduced us and quickly left. Then the younger sister spoke up, and asked if this was the same Rwmaii who wrote the letters. We had imagined that the family would be hostile or reluctant to speak to us. We were prepared to be persistent, to leave only after having discovered what had happened to Sylvia. We had not expected kindness.

The mother and the sister had tears in their eyes, and when the father spoke, his voice shook, *Forgive me, son, she had told us about you, she didn't want to go, but there was no choice. We made her go.*

We were taken aback by this, and sat there in silence for a while. The sister brought tea.

It was the mother who finally spoke. 'We had dreams for Sylvia, she had done well in school, did not give us any trouble. We knew she wanted to study, at least an MA. All the girls were doing that, maybe she would look for a job after. Nowadays, nobody gets their daughter married off like this, in the middle of her studies. When the proposal came through a neighbour, we didn't take it very seriously. I had known him as one of the many young men in the village who left to join the groups when the fighting began. They said he had set his mind on Sylvia then.

'It became a difficult situation, people around gave advice: that it would not be wise to say no in these times, that he was a good man, and now after the ceasefire, they would lead a normal life and so on.

'But Sylvia ... you know how she can be—', the mother broke off with a sigh.

'She was adamant, she didn't want it, she told us she wanted to study, but ... it was difficult, we had to find a way to say no without insulting him or the people from the group. Then these young men started to drop by for a cup of tea. Nobody said anything, but it became more and more difficult. Her father decided to speak to the elders. You see, we have been living outside the village for a long time now, because of my husband's job. But a community, it has its rules and regulations; it is what holds us together. It was a simple thing to do: we wanted to refuse a proposal – but how were we to do it?

'So her father, he goes to the elders for advice. But as it turns out, the world has changed a lot. These old men were just that – old men in a world now run by the young. They suggested we go to the other group and ask for their protection. But that would be involving too many people. And how were we to know how that would turn out, what new problems that would bring for us? We have two sons, one of whom is, you know, he is not quite right in the head, he stays in the village here. We have to be careful. Someone can say something and have the Army pick him up. He won't even be able to find his way home. Our other son is too young, what could we do? There was a lot of talk, mostly village gossip. And these boys, they never threatened us, but we didn't know which way to turn.

'People told us to consider the proposal, after all he was a good man. That's when we realised there was nothing we could do. Sylvia cried and threatened to kill herself. She shut herself in her room for a day. But after that, what was she to do? We persuaded her to go.

'You see', the mother had said, with the measured calm of a woman who had known regret but also a way back into life, 'he is not a bad man. He comes from a good family, he will take care of her. And when things settle a bit, she can rejoin some other college. It's just that these boys have become accustomed to getting what they want. They have been away from society, they have known death and fear, they have suffered. It would not be right to disrespect their sacrifices, would it? Do you have any brothers who went to the jungle? No? Then it may be difficult to understand …

'My older brother left home to fight. We lost him a few years ago, but the one time he came home, he was already another man. It's hard, what they set out to do, the people they become. And then to come back to heed the old rules, that's hard too …

'Now, they are in ceasefire, they deserve the fruits of peace time.' She ran her scarf over her eyes, but she no longer had tears. The talking had done her good, unburdened her and us.

She continued to speak once she realised nobody else was stepping in. 'It will be a while before they settle, these boys. And we were not afraid of the man who is our son-in-law now, we did not give her away for fear, you understand? It was the others around him. It is the time we are in. We are simple people, we have no part in politics … we wanted to stay away from this … this marriage—'

She was smiling now. 'But it has turned out well. Sylvia did not look sad the last time I visited her. He is a good man, he'll look after her. Otherwise we wouldn't have given her away like this. But we share your sorrow, son. You are so young yourself, you will find another girl, but we are sorry …'

And then, there was nothing more to say. They wanted us to stay for a meal but we declined. It was noon when we left their house.

After the rains, the sun had reappeared in the sky, and the heat was oppressive, clawing at our skin, leaving us breathless. The cousin was waiting outside. He took us to the old bazaar, to the women who sit at the end, near the butchers. He got us a glass of jou each, and said, drink, it will be good to forget all this.

⋆

Sylvia, now more than ever, became a constant in Rwmaii's poetry and in our lives. We moved to a new hostel, and a corner of the desk we shared turned into a shrine to Sylvia and their time together, with a greetings card she had given him, a passport-size photograph, tickets from a bus ride they had taken together, a few books. On the wall, he had pasted a piece of paper with a line neatly inscribed in ink: 'I fear for a time made of glass.' I recognised it. It was the Palestinian poet.

The mood in his poems became darker. Reading them, I would have tears in my eyes. Let me see if I can find a poem from this period in his notebook. Here, yes, something like this –

In HER absence

I leapt across wild rivers
walked walked walked this wasted land –
the fields of rice water rock and sand
This land of mine – from moon to moon, hill to hill –
Could not my bruised tongue starved heart fill
I look for you –
For a glimpse of your face
I will give everything – this fierce heart, this hard land –
I will give it all away
But your face –
over the horizon – there!
Crumbles into chalk dust empty space –
It's a curse! the old women shout and pray
Turn back – look away! Look away!

Perhaps, they don't sound so raw read out today.

But yes, soon we were busy with college. Work resumed on the magazine. Initially it was hard, sitting together with the team without being hit by Sylvia's absence. Especially for Rwmaii, but his grief was slowly subsumed by his writing and reading. I was glad I had made that impulsive decision to travel to Sylvia's village and that I had met her family. Sylvia had not betrayed her love, no – they had been separated by time and fate. They became the thing that true love was made of in literature: the star-crossed lovers.

So, no one expected that phone call. Not me, not Rwmaii. And least of all, the PCO man in Rwmaii's village. The call must have made an impression, because he shut the shop and changed two buses to come to our college looking for Rwmaii. He found us at the canteen and, over a cup of tea, delivered the message. It was Sylvia. She was in Soraidaka, a forest village close to the Bhutan border. One day, when there was no one around, she had left the house. She walked for two days along the river, till she reached Soraidaka to make the phone call. That's where she would wait for Rwmaii to come for her.

Rwmaii looked like something had hit him. He started to stammer out his gratitude to this PCO man, as if he had brought her back with him. He was a good man; he took Rwmaii's hand in his, and said, 'Look brother, in life the good things that happen are so few, especially when we have given up hope. I had to make sure the news reached you. That's all. But please hurry, you boys, do something, she can't be safe there all by herself. It's been two days since she fled, so they must already know, they will find her …'

We got to work immediately. First, we started a fund, with everyone putting in a contribution including two of the teachers and the college guard. It was only a matter of time before the news spread. We couldn't wait for a bus, a motorbike would be too risky. A friend's older brother drove a taxi, we persuaded him to drive us. In less than an hour's time, Rwmaii and I were driving out of the college in Bhupen's taxi. Despite the frantic energy with which we had organised things, I was afraid we may have taken too long. Sylvia had called in the morning when the PCO opened. Now, it was noon. Where would she have spent the day? What if someone had spotted her and informed the local unit there that this was the runaway wife of a commander? All sorts of people could take advantage of this. What if someone informed the police? They could not be trusted in such a situation.

Rwmaii voiced the fear in all our hearts: what if she is no longer in Soraidaka when we get there? Where do we go then? Who do we ask?

In those days, there were several Army and police checkposts on the outskirts of the town. We were fortunate to have Bhupen, who was a familiar face and used to dealing with checkings and the Army jawans. It had also been a relatively peaceful week with no news of clashes or bomb blasts in the area. This in itself was a lucky chance. Militant attacks on police stations and ambushes were common in those days, and there were regular Army operations in the villages. The other fear was, of course, the steady build-up of tensions between the Bodo and Santhali communities, with reports of clashes in the areas around the town.

A lot of things could have gone wrong at a time like this. But it went smoothly enough. Maybe they were going on leave soon or had been served tandoori chicken for lunch, but the jawans at the checkpoint merely glanced at the car and waved us through. Bhupen didn't even have a chance to give them his story of a medical emergency, of having to ferry a sick relative from the village to the town. That, he assured us, was a rare event. This raised our spirits, if only for a while. In those days, as soon as you left the town, it was miles and miles of paddy fields and jungles. With the dark settling in, it was a desolate, lonely journey. At least the town would have its nominal few hours of electric light in the evening, but here there was no electricity at all, the transformers having been blown up or destroyed as the agitation intensified. This was a region where the power equation shifted constantly – often the security forces would patrol these areas by day, only for the insurgent groups to hold by night. But Bhupen had good relations with the groups operating here. We had nothing to fear, unless news of our connection to Sylvia had become known or some such complication arose.

The daily market in Soraidaka would soon be winding up, people making their way back home before the light disappeared. Commerce and life are dictated by daylight. We were all nervous, and we had to ask Bhupen not to speed too much, the roads were bad and a punctured tyre would cost us more time.

When we finally reached, evening had descended, and only the skeletal remains of the bazaar greeted us: the bamboo sticks that held up the cloth roofs of the vegetable stalls, dogs sniffing around where the meat seller had sat. The dark was moving in fast. Here and there, we could make out the hazy, slumped figures of drunks, and men on their way out, lingering by their cycles over a last cigarette or snatch of gossip. The women who came in from the villages with vegetables, dry fish and rice had all left. Only the papor buri remained. She would sit there a little longer, in case people – mostly drinkers – came by. Her makeshift stall was by the shacks at one end of the bazaar.

A group of boys by the side of the road were watching us intently. The scarves around their necks looked like they were Kocha, but we could not be sure. They did not approach us, and we chose to ignore them.

I sat down on my haunches, near the papor buri's stall, watching the wafers sizzle in the oil. It was a warm evening, and she sat upright, majestic on her low stool, whisking away the mosquitoes from her bare shoulders with her blouse. She reminded me of the old women in my village; like them, she wore her dokhona without a blouse for some relief from the heat, and there was a whiff of jou around her. There was an old man in the shadows, but he had had his evening's share, and nodded off as he sat, mumbling incoherently.

'Abo, any chance of a cup of tea with the fried stuff? Is there a tea shop that will serve us at this hour?'

I thought she looked at each of us a little longer than necessary, as if to ascertain something.

'Has there been any trouble today? You sold enough papors?' I asked her, and then casually mentioned that we would have to drive back to the town late in the evening.

'No, no, it was the usual,' she said, 'didn't sell as much. But then business has been bad for a while now. They all want these packet things. A cup of tea, you said?' She looked towards one of the shacks at the back. 'Let's see.'

The door of the shop was shut, but we could see flickers of lamp light through the thin bamboo sheath of its walls.

'Try those people – out there – they are usually gone by now. But they seem to have stayed on longer today.' And she brought the oil lamp closer to our faces, where we crouched around her, as if to look at us better. The flame flickered at our noses. Then she asked, 'Have you come from the town?'

'Yes, yes,' we said, 'from the college in the town. We are students.'

Then Rwmaii blurted out, 'Abo, a friend was supposed to … we are looking for a friend, she was—'

The woman nodded, picked up a piece of newspaper from her side, put a handful of pakoras on it and handed it to Rwmaii. Deftly tucking in the hem of the dokhona around her waist, she stood up and with the lamp held up in one hand, she said aloud, 'Let me see if I can get you boys a cup of tea.'

She walked up to the shack she had earlier indicated, and called out, 'Hey, there are some boys here, have to go all the way back to their college in the town. Get them a cup of tea, will you?'

The door opened, a woman's voice. 'Only tea, mind you.'

'Yes, yes, thank you, a cup of tea would be fine.'

The papor lady went back to her spot. We entered the tea shop. A few uneven slabs of wood served as benches and tables, and we settled down there. The cooking area was apportioned off with a straw screen and a curtain. The wood-fire stove was lit and we could make out the forms of two women behind the screen.

The lady serving us spoke, 'How come you boys are out so late? You aren't from this area, are you?'

We first gave her the story about the sick relative. Then Rwmaii changed his mind, and spoke quietly, 'I had a phone call from a friend and have come looking for her.'

He took out his college ID and presented it to the lady. She seemed a little puzzled, so he said, 'Show this to her, so she will know it's me.'

Oh, the woman said and went quiet, and peered at the ID card.

Rwmaii then took out a notebook and held that out. 'Give her this as well.'

She placed them on a tray and disappeared behind the curtain.

Both Rwmaii and Bhupen were sitting very still, but I was suddenly apprehensive. What if this was a trap? *They* may have heard of our visit to Sylvia's home and wanted to teach us a lesson. If so, this would be the perfect place, miles away from people we knew, not one knife or gun between us. Then we sensed a movement behind the screen, the tinkling of cups. Our tea was coming.

And there, half lit by the shadows of the kitchen fire, slowly brushing aside the curtain, stood Sylvia with a tray of tea in her hands.

*

After driving out a kilometre into the dark, we stopped by the side of the road and waited there in the darkness. It was only the three of us in the car; Sylvia was not with us. The women from the tea shop thought it unwise for us to walk away from the market accompanied by her. So we were to go ahead, drive two kilometres down the road and wait. We sat in nervous silence, but seeing Sylvia and talking to her had made us feel better, kept the fears somewhat at bay.

Points of light emerged in the far darkness, they were coming.

Bhupen started humming a Hindi song. 'Brother, this is like a film, no?'

'Better than a film.' Rwmaii grinned.

We laughed, the relief washing over us.

The lights reached us, Sylvia slipped in and we were gone, speeding into the night. I don't remember much of the rest of the trip. Yes, we stopped for a meal at this dhaba for truckers, run by a Nepali woman. I had never eaten there by night, but she knew us, and did not seem surprised or curious about why we were travelling at night. She even offered us beer with our food. I realised the world was changing for us. We declined, though Bhupen looked like he would have liked some. Sylvia had cried when she saw us at the tea shop in Soraidaka. She could barely speak. But after the car ride and a meal – she ate six or seven rotis – she had cheered up. It was like old times; she had her smile back, and laughed and teased us. She and Rwmaii held hands when we walked back to the car. I remember that, because earlier, since we were mostly around friends, they were careful not to make the rest of us uncomfortable. It was still uncommon for girls to walk with boys in public.

Bhupen did not want to risk the Army and police checkpoints on the way back and took a longer route, avoiding the highway and driving instead through dry river beds and rice fields.

Once we reached the hostel, Sylvia went in to rest. She would stay in our room with Rwmaii, while I would find a bed for the night in a friend's room. Rwmaii and I went out into the veranda for a cigarette. I had a plan: they couldn't risk staying for too long in the town, they would have to go away, at least for a while till things cooled off.

'Go where?' Rwmaii asked, fiddling with the pen in his hands.

'It's a big country. You can go anywhere you want.' I tore out a page from his notebook and started making a list.

'But where? I've only ever been till the capital here,' he sighed.

'That would be okay. You can go to the capital or another town, if you don't want to go too far.' I scribbled the names of some places on the paper.

'How long do you think we will have to hide? Be away from college?'

'For some time, till they let it go. Even if these guys find out you are there in the capital, what can they do? You have to get out of here – anywhere else is fine.'

'Do you think we'll be back before the half-yearly exams?' Rwmaii seemed distracted. 'And the magazine, there is so much work left …'

I could see that he was tired, but we could not afford to lose time. They would have to leave in a day or two, and that would require a lot of planning. I continued, 'You'll need to rent a room, maybe get a job—'

'A job? You want me to get a job?' He raised an eyebrow and sneered. 'As a waiter in a tea shop? Washing dishes, cutting onions? I hear that the restaurants in the city only want BA-pass waiters now.'

'You could look for work in a school, something like that. Or you could both give tuitions.' I stopped speaking. He was right, what was I thinking? Then there was only one thing. 'Tomorrow morning, you will have to go see your older brother at home and explain things to him. You can take a transfer and enrol in a college in the capital. It will be the same as studying here, your family will support you.'

He didn't say anything. He sprawled back on the floor, his hands behind his head. It was a warm night, and I kept shaking my feet and slapping at my arms to get rid of the mosquitoes. But Rwmaii lay absolutely still, even the insects seem to leave him alone.

I said, 'You should take the train out tomorrow evening. I can do the reservations ...'

'Why are you always telling me what to do?' He spoke quietly but his voice was hard.

That took me by surprise. I let him be, and went to a friend's room to sleep. I must have dropped off immediately, because I did not hear Rwmaii come in and draw out another mat. He didn't go back to our room either.

Next morning, Rwmaii was already dressed and preparing to leave, when I opened my eyes. He got me a glass of tea and murmured, 'I'm going to see my brother.'

I sat up and took the tea. I knew he was sorry about his remark the previous day. He stood there, waiting for me to speak. The first thing that came to my mind was, 'Sylvia?'

'She's sleeping. Let her sleep a little longer, she must be tired. I should be able to get back by late afternoon if I take the morning bus now.'

'You go. I'll see to things here. I'll keep your tickets for the evening train ready, in case you are late.'

Rwmaii left.

I leant back against the wall and finished my tea. There would be a lot to see to. Perhaps even accompany them. I have a cousin and another friend from the village studying in the capital. We could spend the day in one of their paying guest accommodations. Or we could go to the hill station town a few hours away. I'd always wanted to go there …

In the midst of all the excitement, I managed to slip away to college for a while and sit through a class. If there were any rumours, I would catch them faster there. A few people inquired, but I made noncommittal answers, and nobody was interested enough to pursue the matter.

By the time I got back to the hostel, it was noon. I opened the gate to find Sylvia sitting on the veranda steps.

I had forgotten she was here, and got a start. All the boys had left by then. She had washed her hair and was drying it out with a gamsa, with the sun in her face. I had never seen her with her hair left loose. It was long, almost reached her waist. Her neck and blouse were damp where the water from her hair had settled. Maybe she sensed my uneasiness, because she looked up and smiled, then deftly wrapped the gamsa around her head, gathering her hair into a low bun.

The fragrance of her shampoo or talc, a touch of jasmine still lingered in the air.

I was awkward, somewhat unsure of what to do next, but didn't want to embarrass her by rushing into my room and making her feel unwelcome. So I stood there. I noticed she had changed into a new dokhona, and felt an absurd pride seeing her in the purple-and-yellow dokhona. That had been one of the things on my list that morning, fresh clothes for her.

'Did you go to college?'

I told her I had attended a class, and that it was alright, there was no talk that should alarm us. Speaking of our shared adventure made me feel more confident. I sat down on one of the steps.

'Rwmaii must have reached Siyalmari by now,' she said, looking at her watch.

It had a gold-lined dial with a delicate strap, looked expensive. It must have been a gift. These things would be important if we had to arrange extra money.

'Yes. Enough time for him to eat lunch and take the bus back. Two hours and he should be here. You must be worried …'

'No, no, I'm just …' she struggled for the word, then found it. 'Happy. I'm happy to be here.

'I never thought I would be able to come back. The commander—' She referred to her husband as the commander, as did we. 'He was not a bad man. He was very good to me. He was willing to give me time to settle there before—'

She broke off in some confusion, and then began again. This time she did not look at me, she gazed ahead at the wall, impassive, and continued, 'I was very homesick – for everyone, mother, my sister and all of you. I cried a lot. He didn't know what to make of it, what to do. It was not the way a new bride should be, but he didn't mind. He was willing to wait. He kept trying to find ways to make me happy. One time, he brought me a whole lot of books.' She smiled.

'But not being able to come back to college was terrible, it … it ate into my being. All the time, I thought of Rwmaii, I read and reread the poems, I wondered what you all were doing – till I didn't live there any longer. I was here. In my mind, I was here all the time. If someone called out, asked something, I had to switch back, get back to that other world. I created this world in my head with all of you and college. I spoke to people who weren't there … I thought I would go mad. We kept moving from one house to another, he didn't want me in the camp, though he lived there himself. I was happy to be without him. But there would always be these two or three women in the house, and the guards for my safety. Then one day, they had to go to the bazaar, one of the women fell sick. And I was alone. I don't know what came over me, I didn't want to let go of all of this …'

She gestured with her hands, *all of this*, it contained us all.

'I didn't think of the consequences till it was dark. I had walked along the river for a few hours. My slipper broke, I tied it up with string. I wasn't sure where I was going. I didn't want to give my family any more trouble. I thought if I found a PCO somewhere, I could speak to Rwmaii. But it was miles away from anywhere. I realised then what I had done.'

I glanced at her bare feet, where her dokhona stopped, the skin was lined with cuts and sores. Walking along the stony banks of the Hel river in those thin slippers must have been punishing. I wanted to ask her if she needed Band-Aid or lotion for her feet, but couldn't find the words. I made a mental note to buy some and give them to Rwmaii.

'I was lucky. More than wild animals, I feared coming across the Army or police, you know how that area is … I joined a group of people crossing the river, going to the market. Then, I met a young Santhali couple on their way to a relative's place in Soraidaka. They had run away but their families had come around and accepted their being together. Their wedding was fixed for when the families manage to arrange the money. I told them my story, and they walked with me. When we got to Soraidaka, it was dark and I had nowhere to go. I knew people in a nearby village, but I did not want to go to them. So, I went with the Santhali couple to their relative's place. Their people were puzzled to see me. They rushed us in and shut the door. They were all arguing, speaking in their own language, but the aunt broke in now and then, addressing me in Bodo. They said that violence between Bodos and Santhalis had erupted and people were fleeing villages closer to the forests. It was especially tense in villages like theirs with a 'mixed' population of Santhali and Bodo people. *What if news got out*, the aunt said, *that they had a Bodo girl in their house who had run away from her husband. People could make all sorts of trouble.* She looked very worried, and suggested I stay in their Bodo neighbour's house. But I refused. I would be safer here. They finally gave in; they could hardly have turned me out in the dark. The aunt left the room and came back with a lungi pansi, asked me to change out of the dokhona. Once I had changed my clothes, they all laughed. *That should be okay*, the aunt said, *good thing you aren't as fair as some of your people.*

'I spent the night there, and left at daybreak for the market dressed in a lungi pansi so the neighbours wouldn't think anything amiss. I knew the Soraidaka market area, I had attended a wedding there a few years ago. At least, I knew where the phone booth was ...'

She stopped, took a long breath

'Then you called the PCO near Rwmaii's house.'

'Yes, but by then, I was tired, scared,' she said. 'All along, the thought of reaching a PCO and sending Rwmaii a message had sustained me, and then it was done. I hadn't thought of how long I would have to wait for him to come. I called again after a half hour to check with the PCO man. The phone rang and rang but he didn't pick it up. I finally made my way to the tea shop where you found me. I don't know why, perhaps the stupidity of my decision was slowly dawning upon me, I told the women there my story. They were two sisters who ran the shop together. The Santhali couple I had met earlier had been sympathetic to my story. But watching the hardened expression on the faces of these two women, I knew I had done something foolish. They had heard similar stories before. The sisters were quiet for a while. Then the older one spoke: so the PCO man in the village who you spoke to will go tell your friend in the town, and he'll come here and take you away before your husband reaches here? I nodded, I could tell that she believed my story, but did not think it would turn out well. She sighed and said, in that case, you will have to stay in Soraidaka till either of them decide to find you, or else you go home. I told her I couldn't go home. She nodded, she wasn't surprised. Then the other sister pointed at my dress and laughed. 'Were you trying to fool your husband by pretending to be a Santhali woman?' I changed back into the dokhona I carried in a plastic bag, and they let me stay and help in the shop. If anyone asked, they would say I was a visiting relative.

Sylvia stopped to catch her breath. Though I knew we would reach a few hours later in the story, the suspense was still compelling.

'So you worked in a tea shop for a day!' I laughed, teasing her. Rwmaii's remark from the night before came back to me.

She was laughing with me. 'I'll have to learn to cut vegetables faster though. I must have peeled a hundred potatoes that day! And then, just as I had given up hope, at the end of the day, you boys came.'

Her story was over, and we sat in silence, looking at the gate. I remembered the oranges in my bag. It was still too early in the season, and they were dry and sour, but we ate them slowly. I peeled off the covers and removed the dried veins before passing them to her; it gave me something to do. Somewhere above us, from the shaded branches of the high trees, cries of *la-fa-sai-kho* punctuated our silence. It was a kind of peace.

We could not see the road from where we sat on the veranda. It used to be a girls' hostel earlier, and a high tin wall surrounded the house. But sounds from the outside made their way in: the clatter of the occasional rickshaw or cycle wheel against the pebbles of the road, or the horn of a scooter passing by. The gate creaking open, however, took us by surprise.

We both looked up, half expecting to see Rwmaii, though it was too early for him to be back.

Instead, it was one of the hostel boys. Jonathan came in with his cycle, threw it against the wall and called out my name.

'What happened?' I had begun, when he cut in, still trying to catch his breath. In his excitement, he had started to stammer.

We made him sit down, take a deep breath: 'Who were "they"?'

It was what I had feared. He told us that some men had come on motorbikes to the college. They were asking around for Sylvia, if anyone had seen her, if she was back in the town.

There was no time to lose. I picked up my bag and one for Rwmaii, threw in some essentials: clothes, toiletries, a few books, whatever I could lay my hands on. Sylvia had her bag with her. I asked Jonathan to wait here for Rwmaii, to let him know that we would be waiting at the train station. He was to look for us on the platform or by the stairs of the overbridge where we went to smoke.

I thought of leaving a note for him, but what if the men came here next? It was likely they would. They must know about Rwmaii, they could be looking for him as well. We left without a note. Sylvia worried about it, but I made Jonathan promise that he would not leave the house till he had delivered the message to Rwmaii.

It was not a busy station, and saw long periods of calm, especially during the afternoons, when the long, open corridors and benches provided a refuge for the elderly, the romancing couples and the young men with nowhere to go. Fortunately for us, the crowds for the evening trains were beginning to pour in, and we would not stand out. A military contingent had spread their trunks and holdalls, and made themselves comfortable in the middle of the station. Then there were the villagers who stacked their piles of bananas against the wall. Add in the regular office crowd returning home, and a bunch of art students with sketch pads, and the station was quite crowded. I found Sylvia a place to sit with our bags.

'Don't worry. You walked to Soraidaka, this will be far simpler. And Jonathan is very reliable …'

'No, I'm not worried.' Her face looked strained and she kept twisting the ends of her scarf. 'But this has been so much trouble for you. And now, coming all the way with us …'

'No, no. I'll be back in college soon—' I said, trying to stave off her gratitude.

Sylvia sighed, looked away. I regretted mentioning college. It was true, my life would get back to normal in a week, a month, but for her, it would not be so simple. Her morning exuberance was draining away. She sat bent over in tension, nibbling at her nails. It must have been an old childhood habit that had resurfaced. From what I could remember, she had had long, painted nails when she was in college, now they were bitten down to the edges.

She smiled, straightened her shoulders. 'Come, I'll wait here with the bags. You get some tea with salty biscuits.'

I'd been pestering her to eat something for a while, and jumped at her suggestion.

I had almost made it back with the cups of tea and biscuits when a sudden downpour hit the station. The noise of the rain was all around us, hammering at the tin roof, sweeping pools of water through the floor. The tube lights spluttered, then shut down, leaving only the emergency lights on, their red glow permeating the station, making us a little more miserable. She sat with her scarf pulled tightly around her shoulders, shivering, and held the tea in its soggy paper cup, without sipping from it. I stood next to her, leaning against the pillar. There was place for me to sit, but I hesitated. She was too lost in her thoughts to notice.

The rain gradually died down, but each time a train thundered past, it would shake loose a fine cold spray of water that would envelope us momentarily.

Then, just as electricity flickered back to life, I saw Rwmaii walking towards us. Ah, at first I was so relieved, I wanted to run out and hoist him on my shoulders.

It was a while before I realised he was not smiling. Sylvia had held out her hand in an instinctive gesture, but he had stood there awkwardly, not responding.

I slapped him on the back or some such. 'Oh, you got the message from Jonathan? Sylvia was scared he would go to piss and—' I laughed in relief. 'Did you get caught in the rain? So sudden, where did it come from! There has been so much action here. How … how did it go at home? Another ten minutes and we would have started to worry.' I carried on blabbering.

Rwmaii sat down heavily on the bench. 'Wait. Please, I'm trying to think. Why are you so excited?'

I went quiet, looked at Sylvia. She had caught Rwmaii's mood before I had. He brought out a handkerchief from his pocket and was wiping his face.

'They reached before me. They visited my home last night. My family already knew.' He didn't have to tell us who 'they' were; I presumed it was the same men on motorcycles who had come looking for Sylvia in the college this morning.

'Then?' I interrupted, 'Did they threaten your family? Did they do anything?'

'No,' he said bitterly, 'they didn't have to. They came and had a meal at home, spoke to my brothers, told them about Sylvia. They said I had a good career ahead of me, and they hoped that I was not foolish enough to get involved, because peace would come soon and they would need people like me in the university, to build our new nation …'

I tried to follow his argument: where was this going?

He said, 'My brother who is supporting me, he is a contractor. He does timber, some small-time construction, irrigation work. His business runs on connections, on keeping people happy. Without that, he is nothing. He was very worried about all this. They were happy I had come, because in a day or two, he planned to come and see me in college. It was not good having these boys come home and speak about me.'

I glanced at my watch, the train was going to come soon, the crowds were swelling, but I couldn't see where this was going, 'You told them about the plan? What did they say? Did you explain that it would only be for a short time?'

I was talking without thinking, and tried to stop. Sylvia was silent. She had sat down, the paper cup was still in her hand.

Rwmaii shook his head. 'I – I couldn't tell them. There was no point really …'

I waited for him to continue. He had worked something out, I could tell.

He finally looked at Sylvia, and spoke faster, 'I have a better plan. We'll go to the capital now, all three of us. You said you have some relatives there? An aunt? We will leave you there, we'll explain to her about your studies, and you can enrol in a college. Or …' and he was faltering, but continued to speak, 'we'll find you a hostel. We spoke to your parents in the summer, we visited them. If they know you aren't happy with the commander, they'll support you. We'll speak to them again if there is a need, and you can study in a college there.'

He had recovered his flow, he spoke persuasively now, even smiled. 'See, this is a better solution, more practical, don't you think? I need some time to get my mind around all this, finish my studies, then—'

He looked relieved to have finally said aloud what

was on his mind. I looked away, trying to avoid meeting Sylvia's eyes.

Now, it was Rwmaii who couldn't stop speaking. 'It's just that I need some time to think, it's all been so rushed, and the magazine we've begun in college, the first issue has to go to press soon, I can't just ...'

The magazine again. I couldn't understand why he kept bringing that up. I don't know how long he continued to talk. I wanted to yell at him to stop, to shut up.

It was Sylvia who finally spoke. 'Yes, I understand.'

She looked very calm: there were no tears, the tension in her face was gone, her hands rested on her lap. At least, it stopped Rwmaii from going on and on. The gong rang, our train had been announced.

Rwmaii started to speak again, but Sylvia gestured with her hand to silence him, then spoke slowly, deliberately, 'Yes, it is a good solution. I'll go. I have family in the capital. You two need not come. What is the point in going there and coming back? You must be tired after all this ...'

The bastard looked relieved. 'Are you sure?' he asked. 'We could go, it's no trouble. How will you take an auto by yourself in the night?'

She smiled. 'Don't worry about it.'

The train came into the station, thundering past us, drowning out all conversation. Sylvia picked up her bag and began moving towards the train. Rwmaii stood up looking uncertain, his earlier confidence had vanished. I wanted to punch him. As the crowd pressed around us, I finally managed to shout out to Rwmaii, 'I'll go drop her. I have already told my cousin.'

Sylvia and I boarded the train.

As we pulled away from the station, I struggled to find the words. Outside, there was no landscape, nothing to hold on to, just a dense black that roared past the bars of the train windows, swallowing up the occasional speck of light that blinked in the distance. It came to me then, in a rush, in the blank faces of the strangers jostling around us, in the shuddering of our bodies, in the feverish rhythm of the train's wheels: *I should have asked her earlier, I should have known. I didn't mind giving up my studies. I could work and support her, do night college, both of us could do night college …*

But I couldn't find the words.

Instead she was the one who spoke. 'I'm not going to the capital. I'll get off at the next station, I'll go home. I want to see my mother. She'll know what to do.

'Here.' She handed the two notebooks to me. 'You keep these.'

The words still wouldn't come.

All I remembered to do before she got off at the next station was to give her the tube of antiseptic cream for her bruised feet.

*

The story was over. He expected the niece to ask questions. *And then what? What happens to all these people? What do they do? How do they live the rest of their lives?*

But she doesn't. She is watching the last of the fire. He is tempted to read a few more poems, relive those days. Then, deciding against it, bends down to gently slip the two notebooks into the embers.

The Relief Grant

Runa was slowly returning to the world: she felt the crease of the mat where it had twisted under her, digging into the flesh of her back, a damp, slight itch trailing the inside of her thighs and on to her stomach, the sweat in her hair meandering down her neck. A mosquito had made its way into her stupor, humming maniacally in her ear, calling for blood. But she did not want to move. No, not yet.

Somewhere in the distance, she could hear the faint sounds of the marriage song.

The oil lamp had died away, and they were lost in the darkness of the room. He lay motionless by her side, face down, lying heavily on his stomach. Occasionally, she was tempted to move her cheek closer to his face and feel him breathing. She felt such an overwhelming tenderness for this sleeping boy that she could almost love him. She was glad, of course, that she did not. She did plan on eventually settling for love, but not now, not as yet. (Not that she intended to be one of those washed-out women who kept their suitors waiting too long and then had only their cold beds to themselves, no.)

But where she came from, keeping away from love for as long as possible was making time for the world.

The boy lying next to her (Runa thought of him as a boy, though they were of the same age) – that was special, and she smiled to see herself so vain. She was not good-looking like the other girls. She was short and timid, her figure indistinct in its curves, and she did not play her features to her advantage, often creasing her forehead and mouth in thought instead of letting them repose in grace. Her mother had seen that and trained her to manage without beauty, trained her well. She was a good student in high school. Her parents would send her to college, despite their current troubles.

But she would not think of all that now. Instead she looked at this beautiful boy she had thought out of her reach and, caressing his hair, felt pleased with herself. It's unlikely he would want the relationship to go further, or offer marriage; boys are good that way, it's the girls that cling to them. Even if he did, she would make the usual promises. She had seen too many of these young men go sour, the fighting and drunkenness that follow. And what would he do, this boy, in the future? He had left school after class nine. His skin was too radiant, unmarked – she couldn't imagine him working in the fields or in the jungle for long. Neither did he have that edge of violence you could see in some of the boys, to make money doing the other work, the little that there was of it. But not being in love with him, she didn't have to concern herself with these matters for long, and continued to absently caress his hair. She felt content, water-buoyed weightless in the dark, like the tiny floating specks of light she could see hovering somewhere in the depths of the room. Fireflies, where did they come in from?

The thundering at her door, like a low rumble … then deafening. Her first thought was for the door latch, even as she scrambled for her clothes and tried to rouse the boy. She hoped desperately that she had fastened it well, that it would hold till she was able to hide him away, settle her clothes and reach the front room. Breathless with panic, panting, she was at the door, having pushed him into the cowshed from the back and run back in, even considering for a second if she should fold the mat away, sweep the floor – and then letting it go: it was too dark to see. She was behaving like a fool, and what had gotten into her parents to come back so soon? A deep breath, rubbing one eye (as one pulled rudely out of sleep at this hour should do), she reached for the latch.

Her mother was not annoyed at the time she took to come to the door, did not ask her sharp questions, or cast out rebukes before bustling in. Instead, Runa saw these two people, her parents, standing there smiling, their faces glinting in the moonlight. Her father had one arm around her mother's waist, his eyes were dancing. She realised with a start that she had forgotten they could look like this, be so free of care. The moon shadowed the creases in her mother's face, and she had flowers tucked into her bun, a radiant smile. It made her look much younger, a person from another time.

Her father pulled up a stool, and her mother sat on the mud plinth of the veranda. 'It's so much cooler outside, get us some water. We'll catch our breath before going in,' her mother said.

Runa went in to light the lamp, and make some tea. The moon had emerged from the clouds and the courtyard was illuminated by a grey-blue underwater sheen. You could trace the light where it fell, through the veins of a leaf or the lines of a fence or bamboo stalk. It was that kind of night, the world divided evenly in light and shadow. She hoped the boy had the sense to wait in the cowshed till dawn; even if her parents didn't catch him, the villagers would and, taking him to be a thief, they would thrash him first and ask questions later.

Waiting for the water to boil, she watched her parents sitting outside. The elation she had glimpsed on their faces had slipped away, and the folds of skin sagged into their earlier downcast shadows, the fatigue creeping back into the lines of their faces. But it was still unusual for her mother to grant her father this companionship – sitting by his side, instead of hurrying in, and getting the beds ready or the water boiled, or tending to one of the hundred chores that beckoned her, even in the middle of the night. Runa would wait till the tea was ready, give them some time before she asked them the inevitable question: what had happened at the wedding, what was it that had so delighted and exhausted them?

As it is, their lives had changed so much in the last month, with the announcement of the Relief Grant. Was it only a month? It felt much longer. Like every story around here, her father would have traced it back to 1997, to the time of the ethnic clashes, or gone further back, since that's when the madness began. But she was tired of all that. For the younger people, the camps were already a part of the past; they did not date their stories or hold their memories from so long ago.

News had come that the relief money from almost seventeen years ago would be given for the houses destroyed, people killed, livestock lost, in the violence of the late '90s. The people from the government had come and surveyed the losses a few months after the incident – Runa had been a child, newly weaned – and they had been told to have patience and wait for the reports to be compiled and processed so the money could be released. But the money never came. For years, people waited.

The community leaders who had survived the '90s didn't fight hard enough, and those who did, were picked off one by one. That teacher, for instance, of whom her mother still spoke, who had turned politician after the riots and eventually joined the government: he was ambushed on his way back from a wedding, his convoy sprayed with bullets. Runa had seen the abandoned car by the side of the road before they took it away.

There was little else to do, people moved on. From the camps back to their old villages or to new ones, to rebuild their hearths, churches and shrines, plant their crops and learn new trades where no land remained. As Runa's family had done. Along the same foundation, they erected another house where the old one had been, the walls of knit bamboo, then tin – now, it was as close to the old house as it could be. (Though her mother still complained that they had moved the kitchen from its earlier, more auspicious position, and the rice never boiled well in this one.)

Every few years, the rumours of this relief money would creep back. Nobody gave them much attention this time around either. Then people started showing up from near the town who said that this time the money was real, the officers said so, even newspapers were reporting it. There was a renewed interest; it would be a substantial amount, almost fifty thousand rupees.

In Runa's mind, this news was always connected to the 'guest house' that they crossed on their way to high school. It was a few feet from the shops selling biscuits, tea and paan under the adel dari, a great big simolu tree. This was no ordinary house, though it had all the appearances of one, with its tin roof, mud walls and papaya trees in the yard. It used to serve as a camp for surrendered militants, before they were shifted to a bigger one in the town. After that, it continued to serve as a transit house for various groups when they wanted to take refuge in the village. Runa was not sure how this worked, who controlled it, who could stay and who couldn't, and their alliances shifted often, making it difficult for common folk to keep up. But the boys staying there would hang around the shops, and this created some excitement in their group of girls walking to high school.

Runa was not bold enough, but when her cousin Lupsi had been around, walking by those shops was quite an event. Lupsi was her age, and had stayed with them for a year, going to school with her, while the family tried to decide if they should move back to the village they had had to flee seventeen years ago. Lupsi was tall, with skin like sandalwood and a playful smile; boys noticed her easily. And her eyes – pale green-brown, so unusual here – flitting like a sunbird, made the older women uneasy, and the men a little more attentive. Runa missed Lupsi. The other girls were too meek to respond to the teasing, the compliments shouted out or the music playing from the shops – a glance at the guest house and they would scurry off, giggling. One time, Lupsi had plucked the ripe red flower off one of the lower branches of the polas and fixed it in her hair, right in front of the shops, with the boys watching. Runa and the others had giggled in shock. Whoever wore this ungainly red-orange flower in their hair?

They didn't care which group the boys came from, if they were underground or in ceasefire. For the girls, it was a welcome distraction on their way to school. They hurried by, though, if Army trucks or jeeps were parked there. Sometimes there would be Army men in conversation with the boys; probably ceasefire groups, the girls whispered.

Around the time the news of the money was coming in, the number of people by the shops increased. Runa recognised only one or two boys from her village, the others were from different areas, though they were from her community. A classmate spoke of seeing a gun but, when pressed, the girl admitted she hadn't seen it herself, her brother's friend had. Everyone agreed that there was an increased traffic, an unusual amount of coming and going, more new faces and, with it, the inevitable rumour that something was going to happen.

Runa mentioned this to her father on her return from school. She had continued talking about other things, but he caught on to that: *new boys in the guest house?* This surprised her – it was not the kind of thing her father usually noticed. 'You saw them, did you? And all new faces, boys from other areas, heh? Narayan, Sylvanus … I haven't seen any of them around in the village. I need to talk to them, but no one seems to know where they've gone.'

He was wiping his brow repeatedly. 'There is something I have to tell you both, it is important. You see, the money—'

Both Runa and her mother stopped what they were doing to face him. After the news of the compensation came in, every family had had to face this moment: what was one to do with the money? They feared that her father in his recklessness might give it away, or buy a battery-run television, or some such extravagance when so much else needed attention around the house. Runa had also spoken to her mother about putting aside some money for when she went to college, so she could live in the town. Her father had already paid for her older sister's education, and this money would take the burden off them, at least for the first year. They looked at each other: has Father already made up his mind about what to do with the money?

Instead, he was rambling in a distracted manner, '… money, I have always tried to tell you women, is not a good thing. This new money that you are all so happy about will create more problems. I knew it the moment I heard of the relief money, felt it in my bones, my digestive process, so sure I was—'

Was this a prelude to a declaration that he would give all the money away? Was he in debt? Her mother must have been thinking a similar thought because her lips had settled into a grim straight line. She looked at her husband, unblinking, stern.

'The boys came around to see me the other day. They didn't come home, they called me to their office. They were very respectful, yes, they accorded me the respect due an elder. But they say we have got this relief money because of their efforts, their sacrifices …'

Oh, that was it then, Runa knew what would follow.

'I know you people are getting tired of these young boys doing their politics. But, you see, these are the rules now. We need people who will represent us, negotiate for us with the police, the militants, all that … So, I understand their point of view … To keep a group running, there are all these costs, and where will the money come from? How many businessmen or officers do we have to make contributions?'

He coughed, smiling. This was a sore point in the family. Even after all these years, Runa's father still believed that they needed their young men to mobilise, to yield some strength, protect the community in case of trouble. Runa was impatient: what did they do, these boys, but hold meetings and feasts, and drive around on bikes? Times had changed. No one was going to attack them now.

'It's not wrong on their part to ask for a contribution from the money we are going to receive. We should be happy to give them something, so they can build their group and protect us. So that another '97 does not happen. But they say they don't want to collect it from individuals. As gaonbura, they want me to collect the money and give it to them on behalf of the village. It will be my responsibility to deliver the money.' He was looking down at his hands.

Runa's mother, her mouth still set in its sternness, whispered, 'How much?'

'They want twelve thousand rupees from every house, a few lakhs from this village. They want this as soon as the money arrives, a day or two, so people don't have the chance to say they have spent it.'

They had sat in silence after this, Runa remembers. Not the companionable silence of today that her parents shared sitting out in the moonlight. But one of bewilderment and disarray, what impossibility was this, what was to be done? Theirs was a village of sharecroppers and migrant workers who had spent years in relief camps and rebuilt their houses with their own labour, even the land was barely enough for them all. They were good people, their fellow villagers. But this money would be the kind of windfall they only ever dreamt of. How on earth would Runa's father be able to convince them to part with it? No cause would move them enough.

Over the next few weeks, Runa's father spoke to student associations, teachers, unions, representatives of the armed groups, other village heads, government officials (of their community), members of literary sabhas, everyone he could think of. Every morning, he would step out of the house with a list of people to entreat. After a month of these negotiations, the group brought down the amount to ten thousand rupees per household. It still meant more than three lakh rupees from their village. Her father had decided that if there was to be a solution, it would have to be arrived at before the money reached the people. He was right about that.

The money came, but when he went from house to house, people gave a thousand, two thousand, maybe five. Some people locked their houses so as not to face him. His back a little more bent, face haggard and ashen, he walked from house to house. Ever since the relief money had been announced, he had not had a night of undisturbed sleep. If he managed to convince a husband, the wife would object, and if a mother agreed, the son would not permit it. Times had changed, Runa's father finally accepted, people were more concerned with a new TV set or house repairs than their community's student groups. The money collected was nowhere close to the amount demanded. If her family were to put the entire amount of their relief money into the fund, along with what had been collected from the villagers' contribution, it would still be short of a lakh, while he was to deliver three. Where was this money to come from?

Runa's parents were respected in the village. Her father had been village headman for a few years now. To be a village head in these forest villages was no mean task. He routinely handled the paramilitary and the police on their excursions into the village, the forest department people, the poachers and the timber mafia. Then there was the administrative work for the villagers, building a school room or overseeing the food grains for the school meals, a collection for a boy whose own parents couldn't afford to send him to college, or for the bridge that got swept away every year, and so on. He was a well-respected man and seeing him in this situation made people uneasy. Initially they avoided discussions on the relief money when he was around, preferring to confer sympathy. Eventually they conceded that the problem would not go away.

The school teacher had accosted her father on the road one day. 'What is this I hear about you giving up all your money? That will be foolishness! We are all looking for a solution. You have been asked to deliver the money, but it will not fall on your head alone if there is no money to give. We will work something out.'

They did not hold a village meeting though. They were wary of the boys who were hanging around the village these days, the new faces in the 'guest house'. Instead they met informally in small groups, often coming over to Runa's house for tea and handi, talking by lamplight, night after night. A solution would come up, surely. Then this distant relative of theirs, Elison from the neighbouring village, came to invite them for his nephew's wedding (the one they had returned from today). Their conversation had turned to the money problem. This man was younger than Runa's father, and had in his youth been an influential member of a group himself. Like her father, Elison too had tried to speak with people here and there about this amount, people he knew from the days when he had shot arrows together with them (he said arrows instead of guns as a metaphor, they suspected, because he was an eloquent, well-spoken man). It had come to nothing, the negotiations; the gaonburas were stuck between the obstinate villagers who would not pay and the boys who would not listen.

'We are responsible for them having turned out this way, our people coveting every bit of cash, the poor devils, and these young men refusing to listen,' Elison had complained.

Runa's father had nodded in agreement. He was never bitter about these boys. It was the generation that grew up after the riots. *Look how we failed them, we could not protect or nurture them. We let them go*, he would often say, *us and the times.*

But the visitor had swatted aside his sympathy, 'All that is well, but now we must prepare to tell these boys firmly what amount we are able to give them, and they must manage with that.' Elison's words put some spirit in her father's steps.

There were more meetings and discussions. Her father made several visits to the neighbouring village on the pretext of helping with the festivities. On the day of the wedding, Runa did not go. She had exams in a few months' time, and her parents were happy to let her stay back.

And that is where we were, Runa boiling the water for tea, her parents having returned much earlier than anticipated from the wedding festivities.

Runa joins her parents outside, and the three of them sip their tea. Her father lights a bidi. Runa decides it is time for her to ask the question: what happened?

Her father sighs. 'It was such a long evening. Why, I can hardly believe it happened at all. You know how it has been – all we have been thinking about is the money, the money, the money. It has been a week since the day they wanted us to deliver the amount. All the village heads in this area, we are all in this situation now, people refused to give more than a few thousand if they gave anything at all. So, the boys, they decide to teach us a lesson. They come to the wedding, seven, eight of them, and request us to accompany them out, all four of us village heads who are there. It was about five in the evening, the celebrations were underway. Elison insists we should not go. There is a scuffle, they push him away and escort us out. I don't think they meant any harm, these boys – just to give us a bit of a scare.' He smiles. 'But you should have seen your mother …'

His wife glares at him. 'Me? You should have seen your father! A brave one, he becomes now, but then, being pushed around, dropping his glasses …'

Oh lord, Runa thinks, with a tinge of irritation, these two. They can't even get a story straight without pecking at each other. Fortunately, her father lets it go and continues, 'These boys, they were not the leaders. I don't know if they had instructions from above or they thought they would somehow scare us into handing over the money. I don't think they had planned this properly. They were a little surprised at the reaction – the scuffle, women wailing, angry people shouting everywhere. They made us walk to the guest house. There the four of us, village heads, we sat on the bench inside and waited. One of them began to talk to us, first saluting us and taking our blessings the traditional way. He apologised, then tried to explain, "Please understand, dear uncles, this is a small contribution. You are respected in the village. People will listen to you—"

'Just then, another man came in, looking angry and took this fellow out. They sounded like they were having an argument, their voices rose and fell. They must have realised we were listening, so they moved away. We were not alarmed. There seemed to be some misunderstanding amongst them, and having brought us there they didn't know what to do with us. Lakhan, the old man from Hansipur village, had had too much to drink already, and he found a corner and went off to sleep, would you believe it?

'They brought us some tea. We sat drinking it, quietly, when we heard some loud noise in the distance, like thunder …'

As if on cue, Runa's mother steps in. They are enjoying this. 'Ah, if we had known these old folks were sitting at the guest house sipping tea, and having a good sleep, we wouldn't have bothered, but when they were taken away, a terrible fear seized us. It felt like the old days, men being taken away and not coming back … you young people … as the boys are, too young to have known the past, will not understand this. You did not live through it. We were seized again by this old fear. I was crying and shouting. Then, I calmed down a little. We talked, people from eight, nine villages, we took a decision, and all of us marched out—'

'Can you imagine, it was all these people, the thunder!' her father exclaims.

Is that what she had taken to be the sound of the marriage songs? And, suddenly, Runa's thoughts turn to the boy in the cowshed. She hopes he will stay there long enough for the story to end. And then her attention turns again to the march of the people. She should have gone to the wedding instead.

Her father says, 'There was no fighting, thank god. But our people came with bows and arrows. Someone said they saw a gun among the boys at the guest house, but what would you do with one gun in such a situation? They didn't do anything, just picked up their bikes and fled. As the crowd came in – some having had quite a drop to drink, this adding to their courage – they fired some arrows at the house, so we stayed inside till they reached, and opened the doors. Then they carried us away on their shoulders, it was like winning a football match!' He laughs. 'We had to hurriedly awaken Lakhan so he wouldn't miss it.'

He smiles. 'You should have seen it, all of them shouting, we won't give any money, and singing the wedding songs – oh, it was a big festival. Then your mother said, let's go home, though everyone was returning to the wedding. It is too much for one day, for old people like us. She thinks she is old, ha!' He winks in her direction.

This time, she does not retaliate, her jovial mood fast diminishing. 'Yes, and so are you an old man. Enough, let's go in.'

Runa laughs with her father. He puts a hand on her shoulder on his way in. 'We don't have to worry about this anymore. Go get some sleep.'

She follows them back into the house, and goes into her room. She doesn't want to risk the creaking of the back door just then; after all this excitement, her parents may take some time to fall asleep. Especially her mother, who is the kind to come out to see what the noise is about, even if she knows it is Runa stepping out to relieve herself. She lies on her bed. Another ten minutes and she will go and open the cowshed door, release the poor boy. She feels an urge to giggle at the thought of him cooped up with the brown cow. Another ten minutes and she'll get him out, she thinks, as she drifts off to sleep.

*

For the second time that night, Runa sat up to loud, insistent knocking on the front door, and the sound of the latch threatening to give way. Was she dreaming, no, she wasn't. It was her mother shaking her by the shoulder, and speaking in a large, loud voice, like the beating of wood. No, that wasn't her mother. Her mother was dragging her out, and she followed ... it was only as she passed the kitchen that the thought came to her: her father! He must have already reached the front door, because now there was no sound of knocking, only loud voices. What did she expect to hear? Gunshots, cries? Her mother's voice *run run run*. And she pushed Runa away till she was half scrambling through the vegetation in the backyard, through the groves of banana trees. Maybe this was in the dream itself. It happens that you wake up in a dream, drink water, walk out of the gate and only later see that you have not done any of that – shoulders, face, knees scratched through fields of rice stalks, her naked feet beating on the ground, lungs breathless, struggling for air.

The full moon trailed her, like a giant torchlight in her tracks, as she struggled to escape it and them.

It was only when she reached her aunt's door post in the next village, held on to it with one hand and threw up, that it came to her: the boy, she had left the boy behind.

★

The next afternoon, both the boy and her father were in the police station. Runa had returned home to see her mother, distraught, putting together a bundle of things for her husband. *They are going to take him away*, she kept repeating.

There were many people outside the police station, scrambling to be heard, trying to get someone to answer their questions. Inside, the men squatted on the floor. Relatives crowded the entrance, with little children running around the stairs. Runa tried to push her way through this crowd to ask the policemen under what charges they were arresting her father and the boy. The policemen refused to speak to her, trying to keep the crowd in order, using their lathis, shouting in Assamese and Hindi.

Her mother was too distraught to think of anyone except her husband. But her aunts were suspicious. 'This boy, was it anything to do with you? Was he hurrying back from some theft when he hid behind your house? Isn't he Soren's son? What was he doing so far away from his home?' And so on.

A neighbour had added, 'The CRP followed a trail of blood, black in the moonlight, to the house, and found the wounded boy fleeing after a murder attempt. Is that true?'

Despite the fear in her stomach and the bewilderment, Runa found herself retorting, 'And the people he killed? Surely they found them too in our house – under the beds, no?'

But Soren's son in their cowshed was only one of the many strange, inexplicable happenings of the night before, and soon people moved on to other things. There were bigger worries. They stood outside the station, trying to peer in through the iron bars of the window and the shabby curtain that fluttered over it. She had never seen such filthy cloth, Runa thought. Then one of the policemen came out and asked the crowd to leave, to make way for the law and go home. Two others followed with their canes in action, women and children scattered, crying out and hurling abuses. Some of them tried to run to the van where the men would be taken and were beaten back. Twelve men were marched to the van (two had been let off, it was unclear why), with the policemen swinging their lathis and shouting. Runa stood at the edge of the veranda, holding her mother back, to stop her from running to the bus like the other women. Her father was there, he was looking out towards the crowd. Runa waved, trying to indicate where she and her mother stood. Then he disappeared into the bus. A few paces behind him was the boy. Then he too disappeared.

The boy didn't have much of a family: a father who was a known drunk, and didn't take responsibility for his children; a married sister who had too many problems of her own to spare time for anything else; no one knew about the mother. That was a good thing for Runa, because nobody rushed to her wanting to know what their boy was doing in her house (or behind it or in front of it, as the various stories went), how he got caught up in this incident. People must have talked but she was not worried.

The events of the night were very hazy. Both her parents had been so focused on sending her away from the house, their minds alert to the sound of her voice (in case the men had seen her) that they did not seem to be more than mildly puzzled by this other boy who was pulled out from their cowshed. In a few days, when the FIR became common knowledge, then the public's story would change. Surely this boy had been brought to the house by the CRP and planted there as evidence, as a pretext to catch the old man for not paying up. Everyone knew the CRP was going to get their cut out of this. It seemed a credible story; Runa could have believed it. It was definitely more credible than the one told by the FIR.

But what had happened went something like this (or what Runa was able to piece together, not knowing too much about the inner workings of these things). After the villagers had attacked the 'guest house', the boys there fled to another village. The high command of their group had been alerted. These boys were not from an underground group, they were on ceasefire. So they didn't have to do anything dirty themselves, they had the Army and CRP for that. They put down the names of the four village heads, and the others who had incited the villagers against them (including Elison from Batabari, the man whose nephew got married that night) and passed this information on to the CRP battalion in Serphanguri. The younger men were put down as members, the older, frailer ones as sympathisers, weapons suppliers and link men of a splinter group that remained underground. The CRP raided the houses, supported by some of the boys who had fled the village only a few hours ago. In Runa's house, when they found the young man hiding there, they decided to put him down as a hardened anti-ceasefire cadre. He was charged with inciting violence earlier in the evening and also had a murder charge from another case pinned on him, one where the shooters had not been identified. Runa's father was thus guilty not just of rioting and attempted murder (for the attack on the guest house) but also sheltering an accused. The CRP transferred them to the police the next day for charges to be framed, and for them to be sent to Goalpara jail. This too happened through the intervention of the gods that Runa's mother had entreated all night, the various pantheons, including Jesus, though they were not Christian. The men picked up from the village had been in CRP custody for only one night, or what was left of it, and for that, her mother thanked the gods, all of them, again and again.

After that, a series of reconciliation meetings were held in the village. Runa and her mother attended them. The misunderstanding between the public and the groups was sorted out. The problem was between the groups, those who chose to fight on in the forests and others who had come back, but were now without work or money. Some of the hot-headed ones had run crazy and pulled the village headmen out of the wedding. The leaders accepted that it was a mistake, there was even an apology. But what was done was done, and now that the police and the CRP were involved, it would take some time to sort things out. A few months at least they should be prepared for. As a part of the compromise, the leaders said they would get a lawyer and work out regular visits for the families of the jailed.

The jail was in the next district, a few hours away by bus. Runa pestered the leaders till they got her dates for a visit. At least twice a month, she was promised.

The final exams were around the corner, and Runa tried to study at home. She would open a book and lie down on her bed, but her mind wandered or she fell asleep. Sometimes, when her sleep broke at two or three in the morning, and she had to lie there waiting for the dawn, she worried about her studies, the impending examinations and the long absence from school. Finally, she decided she would not take the exams that year.

Runa's life now centred around her visits to the jail. The day before, she would wash her long hair and choose a lungi pansi. In the village, she wore long skirts with a scarf thrown over her shirt, and for the occasional trip to the town, one of the two salwar kameez suits she owned. But for the trips to Goalpara, she had instinctively picked the lungi pansi, the dress of women who have come of age. This was to become a rule. She was careful to stretch out the pansi over her blouse, tucking the ends in securely, so she did not show any skin. It was more suited to this sombre task, her need for respectability. Through this careful preparation and grooming, she was determined to put herself above and apart from the situation she was in. She chose the colours with care: the coarse bottle green and pale blue; the dull gold ochre of Assamese mekhalas; sometimes the lungi in the commonplace blue and green checks with a white plain pansi. She put aside the red and gold brocade, the purples and sunflower yellows. She looked older, more solemn, like a woman with a purpose. Runa regarded her reflection in the small mirror, held at an angle so it captured her body in the grown-up clothes, with more than a little satisfaction.

That first trip was a disaster. She and her mother had gone all the way, only to be told that the court had not issued the letter and they would not be able to visit. So, they stood outside the jail for a while and then took the bus home.

Runa was surprised by how upset her mother had been. There were the old stories, of the '90s, when her mother was a young woman with two infant daughters (and a dead son); she'd carried them through burning villages, survived the camps and, most importantly, she had been one of those few women able to protect her husband. Runa's father didn't come out of the camps bitter and drinking, though he had lost so much. He had had a lot of contact with the Bodo community before the trouble, having grown up in a mixed locality, speaking their language better than his own. He had lost his business, home and friends; almost lost his mind. But her mother had somehow held him together.

Now, as Runa stood by the road waiting for the bus, she looked at the woman by her side, snivelling and wiping her eyes, and wondered at those stories. Later, in the bus, her mother would mumble through her tears: 'Look around you, there is peace. People leading their daily lives. The past is gone for them ...'

Runa was barely able to discern the words in her choked voice.

'Why now? Why has this happened to us now, when everything is fine?'

She had held her mother and whispered to her till she calmed down. But she didn't understand her mother's anguish.

*

Today, she had time for her reflections, as she waited at the Serphanguri bus stand.

They had left home at first light, walking the few miles from the village to Serphanguri, from where they would take a bus to Kokrajhar. Runa avoided the main road leading out of the village, walking across the fields instead. It was a shorter route but a rougher one. Their sandal-shod feet tripped over the uneven ground, and weeds clung to the ends of lungis, the hooked bristles chaffing their feet for the rest of the day. It would take a whole morning to pluck each minute hook off the clothes, these wretched plants with no other business but to spread their seed, no matter what other calamities felled the world. When she looked up, Runa could see the tall adel dari tree that stood over the guest house, the flecks of bright red in the branches, towering against the blue sky. It was one of the few trees that flowered in the dry season, and the flowers, they would fall heavily, petulantly, so that the road near the shops would be littered with their rotting red carcasses. It was too early for the shops to open, or for anyone to be around, but Runa could not bear to walk by the road near the guest house, especially on days she was going for a jail visit.

On reaching Serphanguri, they faced a new predicament. It was 6.30 in the morning, but the vehicles did not move, even the early morning ones. The bus drivers had arrived, so had the passengers, but everybody waited for the all-clear. It was still uncertain if there would be Rajbongshi mobilisation for a bandh later in the day.

Runa and her mother waited at a roadside hotel, settling down over cups of red tea while keeping a lookout for the bus. It was still early; the tea-shop women were beginning their day. They had started the fire and put the kettle on, and one of them sat sorting vegetables and the other pounding the rice for steamed breakfast pithas. The older of the two Bodo women knew her mother, and they began a conversation over the rhythmic pounding of the dheki.

'Sister, how is your old man doing? We heard they took him away—'

That would be enough to get her mother going.

Runa took this chance to slip away. Outside, it was a morning like any other, and despite the rumours of a chakka bandh, the shops and small hotels around were bustling. She took a deep breath: the sharp acidic petrol fumes mingled with the aroma of rice and meat and wood fire, the splatter of frying fish and hissing curries that seeped through the bamboo matting of the kitchen next door, the sound of engines revving and the call of the bus boys – the smells and sounds of the world in motion filled her soul.

She spotted a face that looked familiar. He was stepping out from a hotel, a friend of her older sister's from school. She struggled for a moment to recall his name, what did they call him – Gongor or Bhutiya, or something like that. That wasn't his real name; he was Bodo and had nothing to do with Bhutan. He acquired his nickname because of his white-and-rose complexion that would not darken even after working in the fields during harvest. He owned a tracker jeep and plied the route from Serphanguri to the town.

She didn't know many of her sister's classmates, but this fellow she remembered from the time her mother had cooked snail curry. Her father had brought back a bag of snails from the river one evening, which her mother soaked overnight to cook for lunch. It was an unexpected mid-week treat. Runa had rushed back from school, only to find these older children in the house. Her sister had boasted in school, and these three had decided to join them for lunch. Runa's heart sank. She had cursed them as she put the second pot of rice to boil. But this one had come into the kitchen and insisted on pounding the chilli and fish for a chutney. Runa smiled at the memory. And when they all sat together to eat, the boys had joked and made her laugh. It had turned out very well.

She could see him now, standing with the other drivers. He would know what was happening with the bandh, and then, maybe, she and her mother could get seats on his vehicle. He would inquire, of course, about where they were going and why. Runa felt no shame in visiting her father in jail, why, Gongor may have even heard of the incident. But she suddenly felt a great exhaustion at the thought of answering the questions that would follow, narrating the whole incident to him. Besides, it would provide her mother with another chance to break down. She would probably hold his hand sobbing; the memories of a simpler, happier past had become unbearable to her these days. The thought of these possible consequences mortified Runa, and she turned back.

Back at the hotel, she saw a circle of women around her mother. They sat dabbing at their eyes, their cups of tea going cold, surrounded by bags of vegetables for the market, while her mother narrated her story.

They did not go that day. Her mother was so weak with the crying and cursing, Runa thought it better to take her home. And she knew then that her mother would not go to see her father in jail.

The next trip, quite by accident, she acquired a new companion for her journey. She was getting ready to leave when she saw Matla drinking tea in their courtyard. He was the neighbourhood orphan, about eight or nine years old. (Though he had a married older brother with his own family, they did not do anything for him; he was always hungry, his clothes torn.) Runa's mother had served him tea in a copper bowl with some muri thrown in, and he had sat in his torn shirt, slurping it noisily.

Runa teased him, 'Aie, Matla, want to come for a bus ride with me?'

Matla had looked up at her with his big brown eyes and nodded. Finishing his tea, he stood up expectantly.

She found something for him to wear (from the time her sister's son had been with them), and took him along. His older brother didn't care if Matla lay in somebody's courtyard all day, so what would it matter if he accompanied her, she reasoned.

He was a good child. Runa bought him a packet of biscuits and it kept him quiet. She suspected he had never been outside the village; she watched him in the bus, holding the window and looking out as the landscape flashed by. It was better than having her mother sighing over her fate and weeping.

There was also the added advantage of walking into the jail with a young boy by her side. The policemen and guards stopped to pat his head or smile at him. It softened them. They would often be mistaken for a family – that she, the boy in jail and Matla, they formed a unit. (But on their return, in the dark, she had to be careful. She discovered that there was something wrong with Matla's eyes. He couldn't see after dark, not as much as she could, or maybe nothing at all.)

Other people from Runa's area had come, and they were all herded together into the jail, and moved to the visitors' area. The imprisoned men were behind the windows, waiting and craning their necks to see the people outside, while the visitors stood two feet away, a bamboo railing demarcating their boundary.

Runa stood leaning against the bamboo, while her father moved across the window to face her. He looked thinner. The food was adequate, he said, but he had not been well. He smiled and spoke softly, joked with her, but it was hard seeing him there, and she couldn't hold back her tears.

No, no, don't worry. There are some good people here … Soren's son takes care of me. When the malaria returned, he got the jailers to provide medicine. Don't worry, and don't tell your mother.

That's when she noticed him. Standing by her father was the boy. Despite their escapades, they did not know each other well, and he was awkward at her gratitude and tears. So they spoke of other things. The standing and straining at the window tired out her father, and he went in after some time. She spent the last ten minutes speaking to the boy. Nobody from his family had come.

This is what they would do each visit. She would come to the jail accompanied by Matla, spend the first few minutes speaking to her father, and then once he retired, she would talk to the boy.

One visit, he asked her to bring him some books.

'In the village, there were so many things to do, most of us boys were too busy to attend school,' he laughed. 'But here, I have a lot of time on my hands. I got thinking, if I spend two-three hours studying the books every day, I can take the class nine exam again. After that, who knows, I could get my high school degree ...'

For some reason, this had pleased Runa. For the next visit, she prepared a package with a pen, notebooks and a math and social science text book. Then she made notes for a few lessons, to make it simpler.

But a month was a long time in jail for the boy, she found. She had managed to get the packet to him through the jailer, but the books and pens genuinely puzzled him, he couldn't remember what they were for. In fact, he had moved on to a new plan.

'You are thinking of going to college in the town for a degree? I've been talking to people here, and they are useless, these degrees. Half the thieves in here have a

BA. And it didn't get them anywhere, no jobs, wives, nothing!

'So many years of studying, and for what? There is no guarantee of anything at the end of it. For me, it will be almost six-seven years of studying to finish college. By then, I'll be an old man ...'

Runa was relieved to see that he could do his simple calculations quickly. And the new plan? Yes, he had a plan. His eyes were gleaming with excitement. It was a bright day, and the enclosure where he stood had natural light streaming in. She could see him clearly. He flicked a lock of hair from his forehead, lowered his head, pressing his nose to the wire mesh.

'You remember, Laxman and the others who were always speaking of the Ol Chiki script, they were right! I am going to learn the script, and then do the class ten exam in Ol Chiki board. They have an office in Gossaigaon. Then, I can go to Jharkhand to do a BA there. And no one cares for a simple BA these days, so an MA after that. It's easy to do in Jharkhand. All the colleges will admit you there.'

His eyes flitted away for a moment and then back to her.

'And what's the point of going alone? There are so many boys in the village, sitting doing nothing. I can organise them and we can go together. We will be a big group. This way, living there will also be easy ...

'Then, after our studies, when we come back, all of us, we will go to the government here and demand our rights. Seeing so many educated boys, they will not be able to ignore us. Who knows, maybe we will be able to convince them to give us tribal status.

'The problem with us young people is that we are all like those guest house jokers in our village. They want to do something for the community, but instead they land up taking our money, pushing people like us into jail. They have no education, no plan for the future, nothing, so what is one to expect?

'When I get out of here, I want to do something different …'

He trailed off.

Runa had been nodding in agreement, in encouragement all through, and now smiled broadly at him. But she had only been half listening. The bus ride had tired her and she was distracted by his proximity. Her eyes wandered off to his face, the texture of his skin, smooth and iridescent, the scar by the neck like a scratched out etching of a wing, a half-bird in flight. She wanted to reach out and touch the mark, the disturbed skin.

He was a little abashed by his own brilliance, and added shyly: 'You know, you should come to Jharkhand too. You're good at studies, if you study Ol Chiki, you can become our general secretary!'

They both laughed and stood there for the few more minutes permitted them.

As they bid goodbye, he called out to her, 'Can you get me the Ol Chiki alphabets, someone in the village must know. I can start my preparations …'

Matla had stood quietly by her through the visit. After leaving the jail, Runa decided she would reward him with something to eat in one of the small hotels that line the road outside. They would both have a cup of tea and a sweet.

As she bent over the glass cabinet in a shop, selecting a sweet, Runa heard people enter and looked up. A group of Bodo people had come into the shop, and standing next to her, placing orders for bottles of water and cold drinks, was a tall lady in a dokhona. She was speaking on her mobile phone and placing orders at the same time, occasionally holding her hand over the phone's mouthpiece to address the shopkeeper. Runa stepped aside and let them finish. They had the countenance of people who mattered. The men wore sunglasses and pressed trousers and shirts that stretched tight over well-fed bellies, the women were in dokhonas. The shopkeeper addressed the lady as 'madam' and was cloying in his deference. He insisted on carrying the bottles to the vehicle even though they were enough people in her group to do so, offering tea and paan, maybe they would like to taste the fresh singaras, and so on.

The group did not sit inside the dingy hotel, carrying the snacks and glasses of tea outside. Runa went back to the shop front to pay for her tea. The shopkeeper spoke to her in Bangla, his eyes still lingering at the door as the last of the group left, 'Sister, you didn't recognise her, did you, the lady there?'

Runa shook her head.

He looked surprised. 'Not even from TV? She is there all the time, speaking about this and that. Look closely.'

Runa blinked, tried not to look in that direction. Had she seen this lady before? She didn't have TV at home.

The man continued, as he handed her some change. 'That was the NFRP chief's sister.'

Runa froze. Was that her? She knew that the underground

group's leader had been arrested in Bangladesh and brought here, but was he in this jail?

'Is that so?'

And the shopkeeper grinned, bending his head and leering, as he spoke, 'Don't think she is very different from us now, looking all high and mighty as she does. They have put 500 cases on her brother I have heard, and they are dragging him from one district to another to register all the cases. They will hang him or kill him in jail. One sister killed last year, now this fellow in jail.' The man continued to smirk, his shoulders shaking in silent laughter.

Runa took Matla's hand and quickly walked out of the shop. She didn't like this man. Did he know she was returning from a visit to the jail; was it so easy to tell?

The group was still there, finishing their snacks and stretching their legs. They looked like they had a long way to travel. The lady, her spectacles pushed up on her head, was still speaking on the phone, leaning on the bonnet of the Bolero. Though she was no longer young, her face was bright, unlined, her eyes sparkled. She had a way of filling the space around her, commanding respect. She seemed to be amused at something the other person on the phone had said. Then Runa realised the lady had caught her eye and smiled. In a panoramic sweep, that lasted a moment, the eyes took her in, took in Matla and the stray dog rubbing himself against a tree, the cigarette seller beneath it, and the passing pedestrians, acknowledging, greeting them all.

She must be an important lady, Runa thought, if what the shopkeeper said was true.

*

Then one day, they received the news they had been waiting for.

Elison's son stopped by their house, shouting out – 'Kowki! Our people are coming back!' – his cycle propped against the jackfruit tree, not even stopping for a cup of tea.

Runa and her mother came running out into the courtyard, pestering him for more information.

'Seven underground groups, including anti-ceasefire factions are going to surrender in a grand ceremony next month. They say ministers from Delhi will be there. As a goodwill measure, they are releasing people from jail connected to the groups, including all the people from our village. The union boys are handling the bail and other official things. They should be home soon.'

Soon. How soon?

'In a week's time. It's in the newspapers and the people at the police station said so too. I have to inform three houses in this village before I can tell my own mother, so I have to rush! Kowki, no more tears. Why are you crying now!'

Runa and her mother sat out in the dusk for a long time. Her parents had not seen each other in six months.

'Do you think they will create some new problem and stop him from coming home? I had thought your father would be free in one, two months, then three months, and now it has been so long …'

Her mother looked around the courtyard.

'There is so much for him to do …'

The fence around the vegetable patch had frayed in places, with openings big enough for a goat to squeeze through and the cowshed needed repairs. In one corner, lay a block of wood, split in half. Her father had planned to make a bench. They did not ask anyone else to lend a hand because he was always going to be back, if not next week, then the one after that.

'He will need some rest first—'

'Oh, don't worry about that. Your father is a strong man. He will be able to look after his home.'

Mother and daughter had kept things going, having harvested the bor dhaan in the hot months without him. They worked with the neighbourhood women, first on their own fields, then for a share of the adi crop.

'I knew he would be back by the time the rice was in the fields, he will see it ripen. When the harvest comes in this year, we'll put together what's left of the money and have a feast, offer thanks …'

They now talked of the things that needed mending, buying a new goat and waiting for the sow to fatten, planting the mustard and sesame for the winter crop, a feast of thanksgiving when the new rice comes in. Neither of them mentioned the boy.

On the bus a week later, there were so many people going to bring back uncles and sons and nephews that it was as if they were on their way to a festival. Her mother agreed to go. Matla had stood hopelessly by their gate, so Runa had taken him along too.

Outside the jail, there were more people waiting, from other communities as well. Then the door opened, and the jailed people started walking out, looking around for relatives. Runa held her breath. And he was there, her father, in the group of people who came out of the jail gate.

The boy was not.

The union boys were walking around, looking officious. One of them had a list with him, and was speaking to a set of relatives. People directed her there. No, not everyone was released. Those on serious charges like murder were being transferred to the jail in Upper Assam, didn't she know? Where? Dibrugarh? She called out the boy's name, what about him? Nobody was listening.

Then Matla pulled her aside. 'There, on the other side, the vans are going.'

They held hands and ran together. There were a few police vans with people inside. She moved from one to the other, desperately peering at the shadows behind the wire mesh windows. A Bodo man noticed her, knew who she was looking for. The boy came to the bus window; he smiled and waved at her, saying something she could not understand. Then the van started and they were gone.

She stood there, shielding her eyes from the waves of dust the departing vehicles left in their wake. There were two more vans and a jeep full of police, then more vehicles, more police, all leaving the jail premises.

When the dust settled, she noticed someone else. The tall lady in the dokhona she had seen at the sweet shop. She stood by herself, a little apart from the others. Wiping her eyes with her scarf, her mouth downcast, twisted, she did not look ahead but above. The easy grace of her movements, the assured posture, had crumbled away. She looked smaller, somewhat diminished, standing in the dust of the departing vehicles. She reminded Runa of her mother.

It was getting dark. Runa slowly walked back with Matla.

'Tell me when you can't see.' She reminded him. 'Don't fall'.

He grunted.

What?

Matla was holding up a piece of paper to her, crumpled up in his fist. She unfolded it to see pages of a notebook with the Ol Chiki alphabet copied out. *Oh that.* In the rush, she must have handed the pages to Matla. She had taken them out of her bag to pass on to the boy, if she managed to get close enough. Now it would have to wait till next month. Dibrugarh – it sounded far.

'Matla, you want to go to Dibrugarh with me?'

He nodded solemnly, making her laugh.

Halfway through the bus ride home, she had planned it all out. She would get work at the road construction site. The GREF was giving good money. She would be able to go to Dibrugarh once or maybe twice a month. It was twelve, fourteen hours by train, they would cross Kaziranga. The landscape is different from here; upper Assam looks beautiful in the pictures. Then she closed her eyes, leaned back against the bus seat, and felt the night breeze against her face and neck. *We'll go by train. Matla, you've never seen a train, have you?*

Dibrugarh. She wondered if the tall lady in the dokhona was going to be there too.

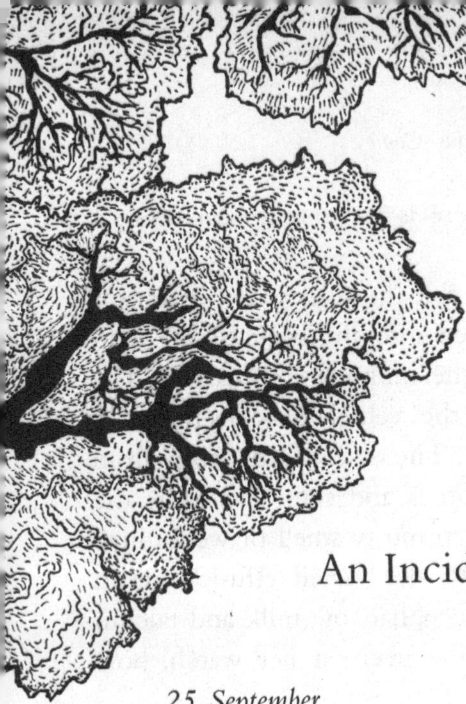

An Incident in Late Autumn

25 September
4 p.m.
On the highway from Ambari towards the town

THE THREE OF them are pressed together on the left side, leaning forward, their bags crushed on their laps, peering at the mobile phone in the man's hands. The man with the phone, a Hindi-speaking travelling salesman with henna-dyed hair, has arranged his rolls of carpets and mats around the muddy floor and made himself comfortable. The passengers are packed tightly into the back of the jeep, on the ledge seats on either side and on the floor – and they are the lucky few, the ones who have been able to run up and storm in as soon as the police jeep stopped to offer help. The others are still standing by the road, waiting for the bus tyre to be repaired.

Now, they all gather around the Hindi-speaking salesman's phone.

'Here, I'll play it. But there is no sound, something is wrong with the speaker.'

For a moment, Rosi is able to forget her irritation. They are eight people packed into the back of the jeep, along with the carpets and the milkman's containers. The canvas flap at the back of the vehicle has been pulled down to keep out the rain. The sweat and damp from the rain courses through clothes and skin, and coats the entrails of the jeep. It is a deep musty smell of wet animal fur and rot, and, mixed with the varied effusions from her co-passengers – the tobacco, hair oil, milk and talcum powder – it is unbearable. She peers at her watch, how long till they reach the town?

But now, as she watches the screen, she feels the breath sucked out of her. *That? That was the girl who was killed?*

She cannot believe she hasn't heard anything in the village. This was all over the news, they said. Not that Rosi had the time to discuss politics with anyone or watch TV. As it is, electricity had been so irregular the last month that even her sister-in-law had stopped putting on the television set. But if she had even an inkling of this trouble, she would have stayed home. It would have been a good enough excuse to miss the teachers' training in the town. Anyway, now that she is already halfway there, there is no point in turning back, it will be near impossible getting a bus back from here.

To compensate for the absence of sound in the video, the carpet salesman is providing the voice over, in Hindi mixed with Bangla:

'That's the girl,' he points out, as a photo of a girl shows up on the screen. It is a pleasant face, a girl smiling into the camera for a formal photograph; her hair is tied back in a bun, she is dressed in a yellow-red striped dokhona. Another image follows: this one shows her body in the field after the shooting. Her face has been blurred by the news channel, but you can see the loosened long hair, the body's slightly tangled, unnatural position. The photos make the incident somewhat more real to the people around. They gape at it, tut-tutting, *What a thing to happen, to anyone, especially a girl so young, about to appear for her class ten examinations.*

'Her body is still out there. The police are too scared to pick it up. They don't dare go there.'

Everyone turns to the policeman, who is squeezed into a corner of his own jeep. The senior policemen are sitting in front; the crowd has already guessed that he must be a lowly constable, a lathi wielder. *Is it true, then, that the police let the body lie there?*

Babulal, the policeman, sighs. 'These are not matters for small people like us – we wait for orders. We reached Ambari yesterday. But the village is still further away. Two rivers in spate and forests, no proper roads. We were waiting for orders. What can we do?'

The Nepali man travelling to the town with his aluminium milk cans, warms up at the policeman's discomfort. 'Oh, the police must have confused these militants for the ones in that film!' He chuckles, and then goes on to explain, 'A few years ago, there was a Hindi film about Bodo militants – hei … what was it, some Sharl … Sharlie—'

The college girl next to Rosi pipes up. '*Tango Charlie*. I saw it on TV.'

'Ai yes, yes. In the film, the Bodo militants ate the fingers of their enemies' – he breaks off to laugh – 'and when they injured an Army man, they put bombs in him, so that when the others came to help him, he exploded and killed them!

'Maybe the police thought our militants are getting inspired by their filmy versions. And on top of that, there is no money to be made in picking up a body!'

There is some laughter but they do not press the joke further. The salesman looks uneasy. 'It is not easy, doing a policeman's job—'

The Bodo student picks up from him. 'My brother-in-law is in the police. He has duty even on holidays, has no time for family ...'

That is wise, thinks Rosi, after all, they were travelling in a police jeep, better to not take it too far, even though the constable has smiled through the exchange.

The news video is played again. It will play a number of times before they reach the town; there is nothing else to do.

The girl on her way to college sitting beside Rosi has placed her elbows on Rosi's lap to stretch across for a better view. There is a faint stench of sweat that merges with the film of talcum powder Rosi can see clinging to her neck, under her thick, plaited hair. 'Is that the leader? The leader of the group?' she demands, her eyes glinting.

'Yes, see ...' The carpet man freezes the frame and passes it around for everyone to take a closer look. The leader of the militant group is young, so are the others. None of the men in the video has their faces covered; they speak to the camera, challenging the world. Funny, Rosi thinks, the security forces are at them like dogs. Every day, you hear of an encounter, somewhere or the other, and no arrests, just killings. But here they are – showing their faces to the world, what must they be thinking?

The leader is filmed more often, in close up, then as he holds his gun at the waist, poses and shoots, the bullets blasting away the dust and grass into pieces. There is no sound but it is as if she can hear the tat-tat-tat, feel the explosion in the blown-away sand, the bits and pieces in the air. The rest of the cadres stand behind him, they march up and down and pose with their guns. Like a second row of dancers, she thinks, but doesn't say so aloud.

There are pictures of the village people who look like they are attending an ordinary bisar, then the girl's body lying in the field, and finally, the leader again in close up. He speaks into the camera but they can't hear him. The carpet salesman resumes the narrative: 'This must be after the killing. He is giving the reasons for her killing. That they had to punish her because she had leaked information to her lover, who is a surrendered fellow, and who passed on this information to the Army.'

A short man hunched near the door adds in a slow rasping voice, 'The money? Does he say anything about the money? They say there was 12 lakh with the militants when they were killed, and the security forces reported recovering only 6 lakhs. Which means the informants or the Army or someone made off with the remaining money – or maybe they shared it together.'

The carpet salesman referred to the leader as 'Terannam'. First Rosi thinks it's his name, but no, it is a reference to his straight shoulder-length hair, parted in the middle. It is a style made popular by the hero of a Hindi film, *Tera Naam*. The rest laugh.

She is beginning to tire of this, and edges her shoulders away from the tight huddle. They have opened the canvas at the back to let in some air. She leans forward to spit out her tamul. Outside, it is still raining, she cannot see much. Just the endless expanse of the highway stretching behind them and the smudged horizon.

The others are engrossed in the video, and she finds herself drawn back into the circle: *Did they film the firing as well? Or did they kill her elsewhere and then bring her here? Was she still alive when the leader was talking into the camera?*

Then in a flash, she spots this other image of a young man, a brief second before the camera pans back to the leader of the group. Unlike the others, he is not a part of the choreographed marching and posing, though he is dressed like them in an olive-coloured shirt, a black cloth around the head. There is some white bandage on his hands, and he seems to stand a little apart from the rest, looking away from the camera. Perhaps an injured cadre, she thinks.

The jeep rattles through the afternoon, clanking the aluminium milk vessels wedged between bundles of cloth and the passengers' bodies. Rosi is still absently watching the video but thinking of other things, the things that matter – of the high-school teacher who has been paying her a lot of attention and if he will be around, the rising price of tamul this year and how many days to the puja holidays …

II
24 September
2 p.m.
Ambari Market

'Dada, dada, can you hear me?' His sister finally managed to snatch the phone from his mother's hands. Her voice was more controlled, but he could hear his mother bawling in the background. The mobile network was restless, flitting this way and that; her voice came in rushes, then gave way to static.

Babulal pulled his raincoat cap over his police beret and climbed out of the jeep, into the rain, hollering into the mobile. He caught some network and his sister's voice returned. '… it's no use lying, Babu, please! We know you aren't at the station. Your phone was out of reach all morning, so mother called Raju. He said you're out on duty, going to the village where the attack has been … I had to rush back home from school during half-time. Mother is going mad with worry—'

He sighed, wondering if he should shout 'hello, hello' into the phone a few times, and switch it off. What was he to do, check in with his mother each time he was called out on duty? His sister was usually level-headed about all this, but she seems to have lost her mind too. Did she really leave her teaching halfway to come home and make a phone call?

Static again. '… hello … are you there?' Her voice returned. 'It is in the news on TV. They are showing the militants firing guns and marching. If they could kill such a young girl, there is no knowing what ... You come back. Leave the job, or say you have loose motions and come back, Babu—'

He felt the rain trickling down into his shoes, making his toes damp. *So they know.* The TV people have aired the footage. They will play it again and again, non-stop for days now, shouting like crazy, till the whole place goes mad. He had heard at the station that the SP had given orders to confiscate the footage and arrest the two cameramen who went to the village after receiving a call from the militants. But he was under no illusion about the power the force had over these things. They'd pick up a few guys, lock them up, but what good would it do? All it required was a memory card wedged between the fingers to be passed on. You can't stop these things.

He tried to reassure the women at home. 'We are two dozen policemen here. Nothing will happen. We haven't reached the village yet. We're still—' The rain has picked up pace, he stepped back into the refuge of the jeep, and the network snapped of its own volition. He glanced down at the mobile, not a single stick. There was nothing he could do and he felt the better for it.

They were on the way to the village where the girl had been executed to pick up her body, but it was still an hour from here. It would have helped if the news was not all over TV channels. And frankly, let them portray the police as a pack of spineless asses, he didn't care. *Better to be cowards than to die like a bunch of fools.*

The body had been out in the open for a whole day now, if the reports of the killing were true.

Nobody was clear on what was to be the next step, though. In truth, they were only five of them in the jeep, and they had been waiting at the market crossing in Ambari for reinforcements. To reach Dabrubil village, they would have to cross two rivers and drive through miles of reserve forest, a rebel stronghold.

It had been two hours, but they were not in a hurry to get anywhere. The driver played Hindi songs on his mobile, the station officer Arup bought a few packets of chana from the shop and passed them around. Nobody talked much. They were content to sit in the jeep, watching the rain. In another hour, dusk would fall and they would have an excuse to return.

III

23 September

2.35 p.m.

Dabrubil Village

'How much longer?'

'God only knows. It looks like they're waiting for someone.'

'Hmm.' Jwngma nodded.

The other cameraman said, 'Better to be careful, these people are not like the militants of the past. That was a different era. These ones now …' He let the sentence hang in the air.

Jwngma had been asked to stand there by the armed men, along with this other camera man from NS TV. But it had already been an hour, and the waiting was making him restless, his hands getting so sweaty he had to keep taking them off the camera and rubbing them against his trousers.

Would this be interpreted as a threatening gesture? He had no idea; well, better to be careful.

He didn't know the other cameraman personally but had seen him once or twice in office. He was a senior guy, who did work for a media house in Guwahati and directed Bodo films on the side. When he was younger, he had tried his hand at acting, and Jwngma could see that something of his good looks remained, the eyes and the sharp nose, though the wrinkles had arrived, and parts of his face sagged with what he guessed was regular, if not excessive, alcohol intake.

They had both been standing there for a while now. An hour, perhaps longer. Initially, they had been wary of looking beyond their cameras, but now they relaxed somewhat and talked in whispers. It was mostly the older cameraman holding forth: 'It's all this factionalism. The minute the government is able to split them along lines of ceasefire and no ceasefire, all this happens. I have no sympathy for this lot. But the way the security forces are pitting brother against brother, that's not right, I tell you … Did you see the morning news? You saw what happened here yesterday?'

'Yes,' Jwngma lied. He hadn't watched the news or heard of the incident. Militants dead in an encounter in some distant forest village, it was hardly something people discussed in the town. As a friend had commented the other day, the days of middle-class revolutionaries are gone. Now, no one cares.

Jwngma had been glad to be near the older cameraman, whom he addressed as 'da'. He expected the man to be more knowledgeable about situations like this one, with some experience in dealing with them. But now Jwngma suspected he was as nervous. The man couldn't stop talking.

'… there was a joint operation, Army and police, before dawn. They shot down three top leaders of their group as they ate dinner, blew out the door and just blasted them away. Then they were off, dragging the bodies back with them like trophies. By morning, the Army had left, and now these guys are back to seek revenge for their brothers' deaths. Someone must have informed …'

Hmm. Jwngma turned away, fidgeting with his machine, shifting his weight from one leg to another, pretending to remedy a cramp in his leg.

The office felt very distant even though it was only this morning that they had called him in, taken him aside and told him about this 'important work' he had been selected to do. (That was a lie and he knew it: the senior cameramen were all away filming, so they didn't have a choice but to ask him.) The main editor looked so excited, it was as if a plate of roasted pig was being held a few inches from his nose; he was smacking his lips in anticipation of whatever it was Jwngma was going out there to bring back for the TV station. The phone call from the group had stipulated one cameraman only, no journalists, so he was to go alone. *It was nothing, not a big deal*, they kept repeating, *a normal shoot. Just go film them marching near the jungle, then a close-up, a sound byte or two – that's it! No need to panic*, and so on.

There was no way he could have wriggled out of it, but he should have negotiated a regular salary in return or something of that sort. Most of the older guys in office had their tall stories: some of them had been to insurgent camps in Bhutan, reported live on bomb blasts and shootings, all part of the job. Often, he wasn't quite sure what to believe of their stories.

There were quite a few people there. The villagers had been ordered out of their homes and were sitting around the grazing ground, a clearing in the forest. A few cows and buffaloes calmly chewed grass at one end. In another corner stood a football goal post made of wood. It was one of those small settlements edging its way into the reserve forest. There were no government facilities – on paper, the settlement did not exist. He had no idea how long the villagers had been waiting, but noticed that people were beginning to relax despite the tension.

Meanwhile, the six or seven militants walked around with their guns, watching over things. The cameramen had been told that they would be given a sound byte by the commander himself, but before that, there was to be an 'event'.

He tried to keep the camera's lens from travelling in that direction. It was inevitable, though – there was only one direction in which the afternoon was heading. At the edge of his lens, a little apart from where the villagers sat, a middle-aged man and his young daughter were kneeling on the ground. The girl was wearing an informal maxi dress with a scarf placed around her shoulder. It was as if she had been caught unawares, in the midst of some domestic chores, on her way to wash her hair in the river, or to bring back the washed clothes put out to dry on a bamboo pole. Both their heads were bowed, her face covered by her long unbound hair. They made no sound, not a whimper, even though they had been beaten and the man's face was bleeding.

Jwngma decided to take a break. No one was paying the cameramen any attention. He gently lowered the camera, heavy on his shoulders, to the ground. Then he sat on his haunches, looking down, pulling at bits of grass, in the posture of indefinite patient waiting.

He need not have bothered. It would not be long now.

Heads were turning towards the edge of the fields. Someone was walking out of the jungle. The gun-bearing men turned towards the figure, some raised a hand. He emerged from the jungle foliage surrounding the fields, a crutch under an arm, hands bandaged, limping and supported by another comrade. He looked ragged and bruised unlike the other young men from the group, with their tense postures and aggressive mien, their sheathed knives neatly by their side and automatic rifles along their chests. The injured man was in the same uniform as the others, a black cloth around his head. As he came closer, the cameramen could see that he was as young as the others, perhaps a little older than the girl kneeling.

The man's arrival set off something in the air: a nervous tremor passed through the watching people like a murmur, though no one spoke. The armed men positioned themselves around the grazing ground. They were to move to the most important part now: the bisar. Though, not many were in doubt of the judgement.

The other cameraman had edged himself closer to Jwngma, and whispered, 'That one – he was the sole survivor of the operation, managed to drag himself away despite one shot in the leg. He is the one who is going to pull the trigger today.'

IV

23 September
1.30 a.m.
Outside Dabrubil village

The ground is still damp, with pools of water and muddy in places, thanks to the rain that beat down earlier in the day. He has rolled into a ditch at the edge of the village and waits, face down, on his stomach, his body stretched out, trying to stop the breathing. The blood is loud in his ears, and he tries to control these enormous heaves of panic and pain that escape his mouth. They terrify him. He has dragged himself the length of the village from the house where they had been eating dinner a half hour ago.

The mud that swathes every part of his body would camouflage him in the dark, but he will have to do something about his breathing. He is surprised they haven't found him yet, haven't sniffed him out from the rasping sounds his lungs force out, like the breathing of a desperate animal. Now he must decide whether to continue into the forest or wait here till daybreak. The Army or the others, they won't wait in the village long; he can see the brightly illuminated spot where their vehicles wait. They are carrying away the bodies, preparing to leave.

When the light broke, he could count on someone from the village to help him. *Or could he?* They had felt safe here, this was a village with no schools, no communication, nothing. Then how did the security forces find them?

He is tough, but he must not take any unnecessary risks. A small mistake was the thin line that would yield him to death; he is still alive but it is possible that he has run too far with his luck today. There is a bullet wound on his left leg, below the knee. It may not be serious but he cannot crawl or run, the pain radiates through the length of his calf and thighs and will not stop. The ankle on the other foot took a sprain of some sort when he leapt away from the water pump.

At the sound of gunfire, he had not waited for anything, knew it was all lost. He leapt blindly into the dark, crashing into the stone ledge around the well and hitting the fence before scrambling away from the house. Behind him, the dark had been sprayed by gunfire.

They had thought that an ambush was impossible in these villages. Even if the Army received some information, it would have had to be very specific. Their group had arrived that morning and they were to leave the next day. He didn't think anyone else in the room had made it out: three of their top leaders, four cadres and money. Yes, he thought in anger: maybe it was the money that they really came for, the fifteen lakh in the backpacks in the room. But how did they know? Were the gunmen from the Indian Army, or were they his old comrades with their faces covered? He had received information that they were using surrendered rebels to force their group out. Could it have been them, hired to kill their own brothers?

He begins to drag himself slowly towards the forest. Clutching at grass and weeds to push himself forward, the strength of his naked forearms and stomach pitted against the dead weight of his legs.

It is slow moving. He tries to stay alert, and arms himself with a stick grasped in one fist, even as he keeps dragging himself along the path. The smell of his blood must be thick in the air; he has heard of wild hogs charging at injured men.

The jungle path is easier, the stones and pebbles scrape away at the skin of his arms and chest, but the slippery bed of rotting leaves help him to slither along.

He realises it is the same road he has walked that afternoon with the girl.

In his delirium, he imagines her cycling by. With the first light creeping in, he sees her, in the rhythm of the crooked bamboo stalk against the wind, by the shadow of the decaying giant sal, in the call of wild, unseen birds. But she is not here; she will be far away, at home, preparing to board the tracker that will take her away from here, this forest with its fevers and death, the death of his friends, his own. The afternoon seems so distant, like a memory from another lifetime. This makes him unbearably melancholic. He has to fight away this crushing despair.

Then suddenly, the light in his eyes changes.

He sees something he had not been able to see before. *The letter.* The girl was carrying a letter from her friend in the village to a lover.

V

22 September
4.30 p.m.
Dabrubil village

Reima glances up anxiously at the sky, from where drops of water fall with needle-like precision on her scalp and eyebrows. But the clouds are gone. It is only the breeze shaking down the rain caught in the leaves. The air, the foliage, the body of the forest she rides through, everything carries the weight of the rain that has beaten down all day, but it has stopped now, there is a respite.

Then, quite unexpectedly, the afternoon light bursts through the sky, a stray beam lights up the purple-red leaves that litter the path, their slow rotting beings squishy under the cycle's path but momentarily tinged with gold.

She had started late. It was unusual these days for all three of them to be together, in one place, and they had talked and talked and lost all track of time. Her two friends wouldn't let her leave, until she had stood up, resolutely snatched the bag from Rina who was clutching it, giggling, and run to her cycle, waving and calling out her goodbyes, without looking back. Rina and Najwm were still laughing madly, what a pair, those two!

They had been inseparable, the three of them, having grown up together in the village. But a year ago, she had moved to the town to continue her studies, then, Rina ran off with a boy and settled with him in Gossaigaon, leaving only the youngest of the trio, Najwm, in the village. Najwm was appearing for her class ten examinations this year. Despite the excitement of lodging in the town and attending college, Reima ached for these meetings, their conversations and laughter, and it had been terribly hard pulling away to leave. Their time together was precious, rare afternoons stolen from their new lives.

In another hour, she would reach the highway. There, she would spend the night at her aunt's house, and take the tracker early the next morning to reach the town and attend college.

She is lost in her thoughts, lulled by the rain-drenched late autumn sun and the hum of the forest, when a shriek tears through the path ahead of her, above her head …

It unsettles her, and she almost falls off, cursing under her breath as the cycle veers into the wet moss. She manages to steady herself in time. The culprit is eyeing her warily from one of the higher branches. A peacock! What an infernal cry, it doesn't sound like a bird, that thing – more like a demented spirit.

Still cursing, she is catching her breath when she spots him, the young man among the trees. She is a little surprised, but he smiles, raises a hand, calls out her name.

'Is everything alright?'

She recognises him, though it takes her a moment to fetch his name. He was from her village. They had been in school together in the early years.

'A peacock in the bush! It startled me.'

'Where are you off to?'

'Main road – to my aunt's. I am catching a tracker tomorrow morning for college.'

She smiles, and waits for him to join her. She doesn't

ask him what he is doing there or where he is going. He is in uniform, a khaki shirt and black pants, a cloth tied around his head, and though she cannot see a weapon, she is sure he is carrying one. He had joined the group after high school, she'd heard from someone.

By the time, he has walked up to her, the dark cloth from his head is gone, and she notices that he has grown his hair out. It makes him look different. Back then, all the boys had the same close-cropped hair, and he had not been one of the showy ones. Now, he has to brush it out of his eyes and tuck it behind his ears; it gives him a boyish guitar-playing charm. She realises he is looking at her too, smiling, a little nervous. He is perhaps surprised to see her as a woman now, in her dokhona and lipstick.

He has absently wrapped the cloth from his head around his arm, and walks slowly with her. Doesn't say much, but he smiles easily, takes an obvious interest in what she has to say.

It is an odd mixture of the old and the new. They had known a lot of the same people growing up in the forest village and going to school in the highway settlement. It makes her bolder, more reckless, and she chatters on. The giddy happiness of her afternoon with Rina and Najwm hasn't left her. She continues to chatter, her excitement encompassing this boy, and their chance walk together, drawing him into the forceful constellation of her childhood friendships.

And so she talks of the afternoon, her friends, the gossip she has caught up with. '… and my mobile battery – how long will it last without charging? And they don't have electricity in the village, so nobody uses mobiles. Now Najwm comes this morning and she's trying my phone, then she says something is wrong, it's switching off all the time! And I say, yes, no charge, so what important call do you have to make? And she's distraught, almost crying. She wants to make a call to this boy she's in love with. And what's so important, I ask her, that you have to cry! It's like that in love. They think just to say hello or some rubbish like that is the most important thing in the world. Like she'll die if she doesn't hear his voice. I laugh, and that makes her only angrier, she's just crazy – crazy in love.'

She rolls her eyes. He laughs.

'You know this boy, Nelson? He used to be in your group—'

Then she stops. She has confused the militant groups; Nelson was in a ceasefire group, one of the surrendered ones, not this boy's.

He doesn't mind, he's nodding; not too concerned by the content of their conversation, he seems to be happy to walk along, listen to her chattering.

She continues.

'So Najwm is in love with this Nelson, but she's too young – and she has exams – she is going to go to college next year. Rina – she's mad – she was telling her, come, let's plan an elopement. Just like that! I couldn't stop laughing. But Najwm is so heartbroken that she can't make this call to him, so I tell her, write him a letter.' She slips a hand into the folds of her dokhona at the waist and flicks out the piece of folded paper with Nelson's name on it.

'I tell her, fine, his house is not far from my aunt's,

I'll go give him the letter, he'll get your message. Then she calms down, writes the letter, and soon she's back to normal. I have to give that boy this letter now! Love, I tell you …'

She is shaking her head in mock disbelief. And they both laugh, in a shared conspiracy, at the folly of lovers.

He has overcome his shyness a little, and haltingly, tells her of a wild elephant he spotted last week along this very road.

'It was a big one, a rogue, by himself.'

'Here?'

'Around the corner. He was standing behind the trees, not making a sound, not moving, just watching us. I could tell he was there, looking at us right till we'd crossed the stretch.'

They have walked through the densest part of the forest. And now near a Santhali forest settlement. From where they stand, at a slight elevation, they can see huts, a fence made of crooked bits of wood, hear a dog barking.

He stops. 'I'll go back from here.'

They stand there for a while, neither wanting to be the first to pull away. And then she does.

Gets back on to her cycle, turning back once to wave. He watches her for a while, till the gold and orange of her dokhona is a flicker in the dusk, and she has disappeared into the horizon.

A Night in Dadgiri

'THE PROBLEM IS we put too much value on human life. That man out there – did you see his eyes? It was over for him. You think he will survive that?'

Poltu Rai stops for a moment, groping blindly for his glass. The touch of liquor on his tongue jerks him awake and he looks up, blinking rapidly. His fingers slide to the edge of the table, and he straightens his back somewhat, but his upper body continues to sway lightly, rhythmically. Then he begins speaking again, the slur almost clearing from his voice.

'We each carry our death in a kernel lodged deep inside our soul. It stays right here' – with a finger tapping his chest – 'and all through our days and nights, it is ripening, ripening, till one day it comes to fruit and bursts … and death enters our body, takes us away. Till then, boss, you're safe. You can catch a bullet or lose a hand or an eye, but no, your life will not go!'

Poltu Rai speaks while the journalist writes.

He must have been writing for a few hours at the least, the journalist surmises, from the pain in his writing hand, the cramps spreading from his wrist to the shoulder, stiff from long years of disuse. His handwriting, though, still retains the slanting elegance of his Jesuit school education; he is almost surprised by its fluency, the miracle of the words trailing from page to page.

It is late. The sound of vehicles and people on the road outside ceased a while ago. What was initially the hum of a single cicada has become a forest of arrhythmic cries circling over them in that sparse two-room shed. A naked bulb hangs from a corner of the ceiling, and on the ground is strewn the detritus of the evening, empty bottles and soiled newspaper covers of spiced gram and fish fry. The boys from Gogamukh or Goalpara, he forgets where, who had come to find work through Poltu Rai, have crawled away at some point in the evening to sleep in the room in front.

Only the three of them remain: Poltu Rai, the journalist and another man, who has been drinking steadily with them all evening in silence, not uttering a word.

Poltu Rai talks, while the journalist writes; it was this way all evening.

★

The journalist was playing a game of ludo in the party office in town when news of the accident came in. The game was hastily abandoned as the taxi driver prepared to leave for the border. Having nothing much to do for the rest of the morning, he took up the driver's offer of a ride to the accident site. Initially, they had heard that the man trapped in the machinery was working for this contractor friend of theirs. (As it turns out, the man wasn't.)

As the crow flies, or the path traversed on foot, it was a mere thirty-five or forty kilometres. But the roads were bad, dredged up by the rains and the traffic of trucks and elephants. In any case, they had not expected to find the man living, if indeed what they had heard of his injuries was true.

They reached in time enough to see the man alive, but barely so. By then, he had been trapped in the machine for a good three hours, legs eaten up to over the knees. His face was twisted out, facing the crowd, the eyes glazed. But the lips on his ashen, bloodless face still moved, mouthing some silent, terrible entreaty to those around him.

There was some murmur about an ambulance being on its way, but it never came. The men eventually pried him – or what was left of him – loose with their bare hands, too fearful of his groans and splintered flesh and bone, to use the drill or saw. The machine kept the man alive for as long as he was in its grip. Cut loose, he was just dismembered flesh and blood.

The journalist should have reached for his camera. A photograph of this man half eaten by a machine on a border site in Bhutan would have made it to the front page. He could've sold it to a national paper; who knows, he may have been able to win a prize. Instead, at the sight of the accident, he had been violently sick by the side of the road, bringing up his breakfast, the cups of tea he had had along the way and then just bile. By the time the hotel woman gave him water and he had managed to wipe the vomit off his shoes, they had extracted the man from the stone crusher. Then, he was just another labourer under a white sheet. Without the photograph, there wasn't much to the story.

Though this town on the Bhutanese side was not far from the border, it still carried about it a sense of foreignness: the buildings and houses in regulation architecture with their trademark Buddhist symbols and colours, the wide expanse of its tree-lined roads, unhurried traffic and men in the knee-length gho with socks pulled up to the knees. It was as if, by the mere crossing of the border check post, the topography straightened itself from the ramshackle tin-and-wood of the Indian border town Dadgiri to transform into a faraway foreign land of dragon spirits and Chinese consumer goods.

The heat dulled some of the charm though. Despite the low-hanging clouds, there was no breeze, nothing. And the hills that seemed to be but an arm's length from where he stood, receding into the horizon in pale ink and mist, served only as illusory, scenic props. It was the searing heat of the plains that tore through the foothill town.

The lady who had given him water settled down by the side of the road with her kettle and a stash of plastic cups. People slowly gathered around. She handed him a cup, grinning. 'Here. It will settle the head, if not the stomach.'

A thin, sharp-featured lady, she was dressed in the mandatory Bhutanese kira made of a cheap, synthetic cloth. But what stood out were the marks of her Nepali identity, an extravagant smear of red on her forehead and an assortment of jewellery, particularly the ring worn in the front of the nose.

'I always say, the devil walks this town, heh!'

A dark-skinned man, also speaking in Nepali, took a cup of tea: 'I wouldn't speak out loud so, if I were you, sister. Whoever was behind this must be a cold-blooded motherfucker.'

He was with a group of Santhali women from the Indian side who had stopped by on their way to the daily market, their produce-filled bags lined up on the road.

The shopkeepers from the town centre who had gathered there were Bengali or Bihari (ones who had acquired licences before the interdiction) and the workers and contractors too were a 'mixed' lot. This did not surprise him. By mid-day this town was swarming with people from the Indian side. Not just traders, daily-wage labourers and market people but also hordes of journeymen who came looking for work in the infrastructure and hydroelectric projects all over Bhutan.

When building highways through hills where dirt tracks had been, hydroelectric dams and airports, setting up telephone towers and electricity poles, Bhutan looked towards India: first for the corporate builders and companies, then for the worker ants, hundreds and thousands of them, increasing the quota for foreign workers every year. In Dadgiri, the Indian town on the other side of the border, workers arrived from all over: Santhali, Nepali, Garo, Rabha, Bodo, Muslim, men from north Indian towns and villages, Uttar Pradesh and Bihar. They all arrived here through their respective contractors, looking to cross the border for a few months of work.

This network of labour had now thrown up a dead man, which was not unusual in the least, but something in it had sent a chill through the crowd, captivated people in a way that, in this region, a death rarely did. Perhaps it was the spectacle of it. Even after the body had been taken away, the crusher remained. He saw a woman kiss her rosary and take a step back at the sight of the machine. But she did not move away. Like the journalist, a large part of the crowd seemed inclined to linger, even when there was nothing more to see.

The shopkeepers huddled around, wearing sombre expressions, shaking their heads. The general consensus was that there was some sinister design behind the accident. *There had to be.* A man speaking in Hindi added –

'Arre, this fellow came in without a contractor – no papers, payments – nothing. Just walked in through the gate with a market bag and took a construction job. Too many of them have been up to such tricks, someone decided to teach this one a lesson.'

'Hai, but such barbarity … no mercy till the end.'

'I heard there is to be no money for this, not a paisa in compensation.'

No one mentioned it, but the man in all likelihood was from one of the disbanded relief camps on the Indian side. Some thought he looked Adivasi or, perhaps, Muslim. Most lives were cheap here, and some were cheaper than others. There was a chance for some money if a student group decided to do politics over it but you could never tell how that would turn out.

Basically, the dead man did not have a worker's permit

or insurance – one of those interlopers who walked in and found work, evading the circuitous route of papers and payments to middlemen and contractors.

The Bhutanese malik he was working for had already fled, fearing the large indemnity he would have to pay for employing workers without papers. The rest of the building crew melted away, only the two or three with papers were still there, complaining about unpaid wages.

No family had been traced as yet for the dead man. One would appear in time, no doubt. But the compensation would be paltry. A worker without papers, Bhutanese law would give his family very little. Something could have been arranged through pity or a bribe, with some back-dated papers organised by a friendly contractor, but word was out that they were going to make an example of him. This was the final sheen to the spectacle of his death. The crowd hanging around meanwhile sipped tea and talked quietly, enjoying this respite from the harshness of the summer, the routine of shops and bazaar stalls, the everyday trials of love and loyalty, sickness and rising prices.

'The lord has forsaken us in life, we have no complaints about that. But spare us – spare us in death – from an end such as this …'

The lady had finished her kettle of tea, and took her leave with these words.

After years of covering dead bodies in paddy fields and burnt villages, the journalist could see that there wasn't much to it as a story. He did some quick calculations in his head: none of this amounted to a piece that would get him more than a hundred words in an inside page.

His friends had already left by then. He considered his options, then decided to make a quick foray into the Gelephu market. He had his notebook in hand. Whatever for, he asked himself. Was the old newsman's instinct suddenly resurfacing? He smiled at the thought.

He usually carried his notepad around to sketch down a few desultory points that he would or would not use in the brief reports he strung up for the newspapers in the capital. (He deemed his laptop too precious and cumbersome to haul around.) But over the years, he was writing less and less. Lately, he had made something of a name for himself as a translator and local source. TV people and photo journalists, newspaper and magazine writers had become fairly regular arrivals. They came to file stories every time some catastrophic, inexplicable violence ripped up this otherwise placid landscape of rice fields and foothill forests. These journalists, even the ones from Guwahati, usually knew nothing, and it was his job to take them around to the right places, get people to talk, translate for them – as he saw it, give them the right push in the direction of the stories.

He didn't mind. They would travel to relief camps, meet people, and at the end of the day, drink beer in a hotel room. Especially after ethnic clashes, when there were as many as eight to ten journalists in the town, all staying at the same hotel. It was like being back in his college hostel days.

But the stories they filed, of which they sometimes sent him a copy, were generally a disappointment. Devoid of insight or understanding, the dramatised prose embarrassed him. They were unable to move beyond the stereotypes of bloodthirsty tribals cutting each other's throats, or communal riots, or ethnic bloodlust. Killings within the same community, of course, generated less interest. The TV people were much worse. When the story of the girl's shooting broke, he had taken a news channel crew to the forest villages – the no man's land that stretched for miles through 'encroached' reserve forest without a clinic or school in sight – to give them an idea of why the insurgents could range with such impunity in these areas. He didn't expect much, but even he was stunned by what they eventually produced. He had caught the programme on prime-time news. The story had been framed under a larger theme of 'global terrorism'. The 'Indian ISIS!', the newscaster screamed, interspersing the footage of the girl's body and of militants marching with gruesome images of ISIS beheadings in the Middle East. It was accompanied by an artist's rendition of the shooting in comic book format. They even had a musical score with a narrative voice over. He had watched mesmerised by the images on screen. It was very very effective, he had to admit, but not remotely connected to the event they covered.

He sometimes wondered if his cynicism was simply envy of the big boys. He knew he wouldn't have survived the demands of television news. With his laziness and singular lack of ambition, he would have landed up as one of the guys doing the animation flames that flicker on the screen over an announcement of a 'burning issue'.

Not that he had any sympathy for the other lot, the ones who brought you the 'real' news, the ones who'd go to the village with their cameras at the insurgents' bidding, for instance. He couldn't think of a bigger set of idiots. Who did they think they were, some kind of media James Bond getting hold of original footage from the frontlines? The story came back to bite them in the ass! Both the cameramen were cooling off in jail with NSA clamped on them, and the half-hearted dharnas for press freedom weren't helping much.

He was back on the highway, with two bottles placed carefully in the cloth bag that hung by his side. Like everything else, the alcohol they produced here was cheaper and far superior than the stuff you got on the Indian side. He spat, watched the spit curl up in the dusty side walk. He was in Bhutan; for all you know, the king didn't allow spitting or coughing in his kingdom. There was not a scrap of garbage to be seen anywhere, and dustbins were placed conspicuously all over the market town.

What a messy way to die in such an ordered and disciplined kingdom.

It was odd, but he found himself going back again and again to the accident, more specifically, the image. The sight of the man stuck in the machine, eyes open, still breathing, the others heaving around him trying to unfix it. He had managed only a glimpse before rushing off to busy himself by the side of the road. But like with a fish bone embedded in a molar, he found himself teasing the image out every few minutes, going over the details. As if to compensate for the loss of the photograph, he would now be condemned to carry this with him forever.

He tried to shrug away these thoughts, it never helped

to get sentimental in these parts. He was done with this story and there was nothing more to it. He began to walk faster, away from the accident site. He had no more business in this town, better to get back. As it is, he was beginning to feel lightheaded.

He had walked along the road for a few minutes, heading back towards the Indian side when his luck turned and a beat-up Bolero stopped for him. He had raised his hand asking for a lift but didn't expect the vehicle to stop. The man in the front seat with close-cropped hair and tinted sunglasses waved him in.

'Going to Dadgiri?'

The Bolero looked like it had been on the road for a while, with dents on the side and scraped-away paint that nobody had bothered to repair. It was the kind of vehicle that would stop for a journeyman.

But he gladly accepted the offer and the four people in the back, laughing and wheezing, made space for him. 'Come brother, it's a twenty-minute ride, you can hold your breath and squeeze in here!'

A few years ago, when the peace treaty was first signed and money began to come in to the area, the Bolero had emerged as a symbol of power. Those who owned the shiny new vehicles could boast of a proximity to the emerging leaders and a coveted place in the new zeitgeist that was arriving. With time, however, its value had diminished. Now these vehicles looked old and shabby in the face of the gleaming Fortuners and Audis that the ministers used. These days, Boleros were handed out as consolation prizes to party workers who would not be given an election ticket.

'You look like an NGO officer. Are you working in some project here?'

The man in the front seat who addressed him looked oddly familiar, and the journalist was able to place him after a moment. He had spotted the man in the crowd earlier; the sunglasses with their purple-pink reflectors, he remembered them. Like him, these people were returning from the accident site.

'No, I'm from the press. My friend had some work in the town, so I accompanied him here.'

He immediately regretted letting on about his work. It would lead to many questions.

'Oh, you are here to report on the labourer's death? You have good ears. You get your news superfast!' The man laughed.

'No, no, I am not here to do any reporting. I was here just by chance – I went to take a look, that's all. Not much of a story …'

He stopped speaking, sensing that his denials were excessive. What would this lot care anyway about his reporting of this or that? The morning had tired him out and he wanted nothing more to do with the accident.

The driver piped up, 'Axomiya channel?'

'No, not TV – newspaper.'

'Oh.'

They were less interested after that.

The man in front initially spoke to him in Bodo but they moved to the Bangla of these parts once the rest joined in. A 'mixed' lot, he figured.

Poltu Rai, the man introduced himself as. A labour

contractor, in all likelihood, but the journalist could not tell if he was a Lhotshampa from Bhutan or a Gorkha, or even Assamese who had been here for long. The extra weight that settled on his face and belly betrayed a degree of current prosperity, whatever his past had been. Then there was the easy laugh, the sunglasses and flash of gold and astrologer's stones on the fingers. Poltu Rai looked to him like somebody used to giving orders and eating well, perhaps a contractor or small-time political fellow. He was the leader or employer of the rest, someone higher up in the hierarchy.

'We aren't going to stop for lunch, are we?' one of his fellow passengers asked in Assamese.

The journalist realised he was hungry. He should've picked up a plate of momos when he went in to buy alcohol.

'No point eating here today. It is the month of Buddha Purnima, you won't find a piece of meat anywhere. The king has forbidden it. Most Indian waiters and cooks have gone home on leave. All you'll get is rice and dal.'

The driver chuckled. 'Hear that – Barman Saar can't do without his cow and pork meat these days! Till yesterday, these fellows wouldn't let us drink from their wells. They had become Hindu then, ha! And now they're back to eating pigs to become tribal.'

There was laughter. The rest warmed up to the topic and more retorts followed.

The man speaking in Assamese added, 'The government is not giving away tribal status anymore. These politicians only speak about it at election time. These movements will come to nothing, only lead to a rise in pig prices.'

Barman, the man they were mocking, pitched back into the conversation. 'These leaders and elections, all nonsense, nothing good has come of it. What we need is a king.'

The journalist shook his head, smiled to himself. No conversation on politics was possible here on the Bhutanese border without somebody clamouring for monarchy. You'd think they'd rush back to Assam and crown the first man they came across, they got so fired up by the clean roads and rules.

'A king? Where would you find a king? You people never had any kings worth their salt.' It was the Assamese-speaking man. 'All you lot do is fight one another. It must have been like that in the past also. That's why you had no kings, only leaders of marauding hordes and wild brigands, a few crafty mauzadars, that's all. And which king would have your wastelands, ha? Our swargadeo didn't think this land was good enough for him, all wild people and jungle, even the tribute he took was worth nothing. For instance, from Burma we would get white elephants and rubies ...'

An upper Assam type, though going by his pale skin and puny physique, not quite a worthy descendant of his swargadeos.

The man in the front with the sunglasses finally spoke. 'Aie, it's getting crowded in this vehicle, ha! Let's take a turn and drop off this guy in the jungle. You can find some lower Assam boys, or even better a Kamatapuri tiger, to lecture about your Ahom kings.' Laughter.

But he did not give up, sniggered. 'Well, if you must, then drop me off by a river near one of their whisky distilleries. I'll safely swim up to my kingdom.'

A voice from the back seat addressed the boss. 'Saar, this was all a part of Roja Chilarai's kingdom, wasn't it?'

'Was? Is! *Is* a part of Chilarai's kingdom! The problem is no one here knows any history. Is he from this community or that? Fools! In the old days, we were all one people – Rabha, Bodo, Rajbongshi – it is only the British who said, here, you fellows are one community and you fellows, here, are another. There are so many things in the old books about this, but the Assamese suppress it. How else will they crow on about their kings. Look at this chap here. We only had zamindars he says.'

The roads on the Bhutanese side were very good and they soon reached the border check post. They passed Bhutanese vehicles waiting in queue to drive through Assam to reach other parts of their country. All imported models with ruddy-faced children standing on the back of pick-ups. The journalist felt sorry for them. They had no choice but to brave it through Chilarai's kingdom, where a dozen groups held sway over different parts of the highway, calling for bandhs at will.

The massive doorway of the check post, in Bhutanese traditional architecture, marked the official border entry. The monsoons had dulled its blue-and-red swirling clouds and lotuses somewhat, but it never ceased to impress him. This was not a militarised crossing. The Bhutanese policemen in their dark blue uniforms did not carry the heavy-duty weapons of their Indian counterparts; they politely stopped cars, checking their numbers off a register, like attendants at a petrol depot. This would be the last moment of foreignness before the dust and bustle of the Indian town hit them. On the Indian side, they would be greeted by the tall, robust CRP and SSB men in camouflage uniforms, boots and assault weapons, moving about menacingly in the Dadgiri market.

At dusk, the checkpoint was busy with daily-wage workers returning from Bhutan before the evening deadline set in. Unlike those who travelled there for long-term projects, these people from villages along the border went in to work as domestic help or to clear forest and sell produce in the market; they did not need papers, but had to return to the Indian side by nightfall. The two groups were easy to tell apart by their clothing and comportment. The groups of young men hoping to travel to Bhutan for long-term work were usually dressed in their travelling clothes, trousers and shirts, with cheap air bags and suitcases by their side, clutching at their papers. They could be seen waiting nervously in groups of two or three or more by the bus stand or the gateway, or by a contractor's office. While the other set, their work clothes and bodies sun-cursed and bleached, were in perpetual motion, always walking.

As they waited for their vehicle to be allowed through, they spotted a group of men arguing with a Bhutanese official. Speaking in a mix of English and Nepali, with a few words of Hindi thrown in, the official was holding up their identity papers from the Tribal Sangha and indicating something. They could hear the word 'illegal illegal'. Poltu Rai quickly stepped out to join them. By the time their vehicle was allowed to pass through, Poltu Rai was in business, studying the papers, barking commands into his two phones, one with a Bhutanese SIM card and the other with an Indian one.

The journalist smiled to himself, everything would be arranged for those workers now, their ration cards and identity papers, in a week at the most, for a percentage of their final pay. The worse the state of their papers, the higher the labour contractor's cut, the better for Poltu Rai.

He looked around. Where were the trackers going back to the city?

There was a stillness in the air, diffused in the day's movement towards dusk, in the gradual emptying out of the town. Most of the shops selling Thai- and Chinese-made goods had lowered their shutters, while the tea shops began fixing their oil lamps and retreating into the dark, preparing for the evening's business. The last bus left a while ago, and the people who remained were beginning their long trek back to the relief camp areas or the Nepalese and Bodo villages. The half-machine man kept intruding into his head, like a song, the workers in their discoloured shirts and sunburnt skin taking on flashes of that bloated face. The lips moving, eyes stretched open—

It must be the hunger and exhaustion driving him crazy.

He gave up and, leaning against a shop front, took a long sip from one of the two quarter bottles in his bag. A sharp incision of pain ripped through his stomach and chest as the liquor made contact. Gasping, he slid into a sitting position on the ground, his back resting against the wood of the shop's shutter. His notebook lay open on his lap and he was patting his jeans pocket for a pen, when he felt a hand on his shoulder.

Poltu Rai. The man still had his sunglasses on, and he was peeping over them, looking down at the journalist squatting in the dust. 'Brother! You're still around? Come in and have some tea, we are opening our office.'

The journalist took Poltu Rai's extended hand and heaved himself up.

*

'You people … you think I'm a killer, heh? You're thinking like that, I can tell—' Poltu Rai is grinning as he speaks, shaking his head. The light bulb sways in the breeze above their heads. The quiet man sits as if he had all night: eyes shut, back hunched, his glass half filled. The journalist keeps writing. There are moments when the exuberance of writing this story, the story that will be, wears off and the panic returns. The paan he has been chewing has killed his hunger, but his stomach hisses and rumbles, his head throbs. Then it passes, and he picks up where he had left off, and continues to write.

'I stopped the ambulance. I gave the orders. It was not the malik; these are things too small to bother the malik with. He is running a big business, doing politics, going here and there. You saw that man in the crusher – what was left of him? He was going to die, but … but this was a good time to send a message to these workers, to let them know that if they don't go through a contractor, they can't come crying to us when there is a problem. And they will come, tomorrow or the next day, for compensation, for hospital fees, something or the other, grovelling at our feet. Let them see death and, if it teaches them something, what is wrong with that? There are rules. If you break them, there has to be a price to pay. Ambulance, ha! Have you seen the roads?

'See, see …' He shakes his head in a conciliatory gesture, calming an imaginary interlocutor, even though neither the journalist nor the other drinker has expressed disagreement. Poltu Rai nods off, his head rocking.

The journalist looks around for water. His eyes burn, it is as if he is immersed in a fog. What is he doing here? Then it comes to him, yes, the story. Poltu Rai's brief silence has disoriented him, and he is relieved when the speaking begins.

'That man was still alive, they said? What do they know? Perhaps, he still had some life, but he was not of this world. He was already half machine, half air. Like the gods. We could have worshipped him in his changed form, but we could not have saved him.

'When someone is already gripped by death, pressed hard between its fingers, waiting for the final pinch, there is nothing wrong if this situation is put to some use.

'And funny they are, to speak so of me. Here, right here, they shot down those boys that year. And how many died in those camps, not just from the shooting and burning, but later, not letting them go, turning them into animals. Everybody has blood in their hands, all of them. So, what are we then, a land of killers—

'You ever watched ants? No? Then you haven't been in a lock up, never been moneyless, with nothing to do but stare at the ground.' Rai looks up, grimaces. His head, lurching unsteadily on his neck, finds a moment of equilibrium. He continues to speak in the old rhythm.

'The black household ants, without much of a bite, those ones – they carry off the corpses of their dead. They do it respectfully, with discipline, marching them off in straight lines to the storage corner somewhere, to turn into food. There too,' he holds up a finger in the air for emphasis, 'sometimes you can spot the corpses struggling, moving, fighting feebly. But the ones carrying them know it is their time. They smell it. The near-dead are carried away.

'Like news people! When you see smoke rising from villages, what do you do? You rush there with your cameras. You can't stop the fire, it is not in your hands. You don't try to. You make something out of it. You understand, it is not very different – what I did, what you do. I stopped the ambulance, yes …

'These news people, they're worse, heh! Where has that man gone, the news reporter?'

Rai turns left and right, looking around him.

Sitting across the table, the journalist wonders if Poltu Rai recognises him. It has only been a few hours since they gave him a lift in to the town. Or had it been longer? Poltu Rai will not stop, he will continue his story, speaking to the great empty beyond. And who knows how long that will take? Days? Weeks?

Looking for Mongru

In the distance, plastic sheets fluttered raggedly by a bamboo thicket. That would be the camp. We quickened our steps.

Dusk descended abruptly in these parts. The days still carried the brevity of the winter months, afternoons of pale light made way for darkness with little fanfare, no blazing sunsets or luminescent twilight. There was a dreariness in the very elements. Nothing remained of the cold either, the steady gold of the fields had been replaced by the dry, relentless winds of March carrying dust into the air and coating the trees and vegetation by the road in sallow tints. We were closer to the river and you could feel the sand on your lips, in strands of hair and folds of clothes. But despite everything, the world looked calmer, more at ease in the evening light.

I half dragged the scooter and kept my eyes ahead, looking out for small roadside shacks or cycle-repair shops selling petrol in bottles. The road was deserted, we had

come across nothing but a few stray goats. We would have to reach the camp.

The plan had been different. Sangita and Horen would go to the Muslim relief camp, while I waited out on the road. But we had not noticed the leak in the tank. Without their inhabitants around, the villages were difficult to tell one from the other. Where did the Rai villages end and the Muslim ones begin? In any case, I could not have stood by myself, on one side of the road, while they went ahead. Fatigue had clouded our minds, and we did not argue and debate as much as we had at the beginning of our day.

I was surprised to find that I still hoped for news of Mongru.

The camp was flanked by vast agricultural fields that stretched endlessly; the houses of the villagers tucked away in the horizon, away from the road. A landowner must have given them this strip of land by the river. The local authorities had not yet granted land for the camps.

This one had been set up recently. From the road, we could see the huts put together from odds and ends of material – tarpaulin sheets, polio-campaign banners, bits of tin, wood and cloth. With the rice fields on one side and the river on the other, the ragged, makeshift character of the camp broke the panorama of the tree-lined horizon, the rural idyll of homesteads and ponds surrounded by betelnut and bamboo groves. The two narrow rows of shacks packed together housed the families. Women sat by the stoves outside their huts and prepared the evening meal.

Smoke from wood fires and cooking drifted in the air; somewhere, a child cried.

A little ahead stood a more open 'public' shed, without walls. That is where the men lingered playing cards and smoking and sitting around. Horen and Sangita walked in, while I stood outside, examining the scooter's tank.

'Something wrong, brother?' A man was peering over my shoulder.

That was the problem with camps: too many people with nowhere to go and nothing much to do. It was only a matter of time before a crowd materialised around me.

I tried to keep him away: 'Ah, no, nothing much the problem. There was a leak and we ran out of petrol. My friends have gone to see if we can get some from the camp.' I kept my head lowered and looked up briefly to smile, if it could be called a smile this, a grimace tightening over my lips and stretching them out.

But the man did not seem to find anything amiss. Rather, he got down on his haunches and began looking at the engine with me. 'I'm Abdul. I used to run a garage by the Ambari road. You been that side? A workshop by the side of the road in the square, near IloveYou market.'

I asked him about the camp, if we would get petrol there.

'Petrol? Here? No, you won't find any. There are only two stalls, one sells tea and the other soap, hair oil, sweets for the children. You'll have to ask in the main village, across the fields.'

More people walked up to us. He continued speaking.

'And that's not very safe, given the way things are – even our own people in the villages around don't want us here. Where will you look for petrol now? Once night falls, we don't move out of our camp. They'll see a shadow and imagine we are robbing their chickens and potatoes.'

'We can buy from someone's bike. We have to get back. In case someone has a full tank, we'll pay ...'

'The camp leaders are away. They might have been able to arrange something,' someone said.

'And the rest of us,' Abdul smiled and said, 'as you can see – we have nothing.'

A policeman on duty joined us. Sangita and Horen returned empty-handed, with a few people following them. There was nothing to be done. One voice piped up, 'But where were you all going at a time like this?'

I swallowed. There would be no problem with Sangita and Horen, they could give their story. In a camp, what was there to do but gather outside the shacks and talk. We provided a diversion, but I sensed that one or two of the voices were hardening. The less I spoke, the better.

'Has anyone sent you here to ask for petrol? Why do you think we'll have petrol here?'

Most of these men would have plied a trade in the village they came from or worked as daily-wage agricultural labourers; you could tell from the state of the camp. They would not find work here, and it would be too risky to go looking beyond their own community. Some of them would have been doing adi in our peoples' land. Now, here they were sitting on their backsides the whole day, gossiping and shoring up all this anger at their fate. We should be out of here soon, before a troublemaker worked up the crowd. Giving us a few slaps and kicks as 'agents' would add to the diversion of the evening. Of course, if they were to find out anything else, it would not be a matter of only a few slaps. I would be rolled around in the dust and kicked to death, with my eyes gouged out and ears snipped off, hung up to dry from one of the poles.

The crowd was making me nervous. Was it my imagination, or were they pushing closer around us, tightening the circle?

'Let's take a look at the scooter, aie!'

'What other information do you want? The number of guns here?'

Sangita stepped up. 'Please, I have something to say.' The crowd cleared to face her. 'We have come here to ask for your help.'

There was silence. She continued.

'We have been on the road though there is curfew and trouble all over. You see, my brother – he is missing since the violence began. There is something wrong with his head. Since childhood, he cannot think much or talk, just walks around. We don't know what happened. Maybe he wandered away from the village and got lost. But we haven't seen him for a week. Our community has no part in this violence, but my brother, he cannot speak or give his address. In this mayhem, who will stop to bring him home? So, my husband and …' and turning to me, '… our Rai brother from the village, we set out to find him. The whole day we went here and there, asking and looking. Then, first one bike broke down, after that, the leak on the scooter happened, we have no petrol now …'

Sangita looked tired, her thin face almost gaunt, the lines around her nose and mouth more marked, but her sari was neatly in place, her eyes shining. She still retained the air of a diligent school teacher. It was hard to doubt her. And the bit about Mongru being her brother was a wise addition.

Something in the crowd changed. People discussed among themselves: which village, where, how many days. They clucked their tongue when we mentioned where he was seen last. There had been talk of bodies burnt, floating in rivers … how far will we search … he's mad then, totally mad … so, yes, there is a chance he's hiding somewhere, how far will we look? But everyone agreed we had to keep looking. How can you stop looking for a brother? That too one who can't take care of himself.

Cups of tea materialised. There was nothing to do; we would have to wait out the night.

Sangita went in with the women for the night, not before whispering instructions to us: *Don't ask any questions. Let that be, let us pass the night first. We'll see about Mongru by day, tomorrow. There will be time, let the night pass …*

Around then, the skies opened up to a sudden, unexpected downpour. The winds swooped down, raging wildly as we tried to hold down what we could of the public shed, afraid the wind would rip out the poles or the roof and hurl it away. The bamboo matting of the roof flapped on its hinges, letting in sheets of rain. People scurried about, taking in utensils and clothes from where they hung outside. Then, just as suddenly, the fury of the storm died down, leaving only a cool breeze in its place. There was no real damage to the frail structures around us, and people retrieved the plastic sheets that had blown away or house walls that had fallen apart.

The brief storm deflected attention away from us.

With the wind blowing in from the river, most of the inhabitants had retreated to their dwellings. I shivered in my shirt. Horen and I, unable to find a dry spot in the rain-drenched shed, were walking up and down, trying to warm ourselves when we spotted people sitting around a fire.

They comprised the night watch. We settled down with them. I sat quietly and tried to avoid opening my mouth. Horen spoke more, recalling his own time in a relief camp, years ago. It was the polite, measured talk of strangers. I was surprised to hear people speak of 'politics' and 'misunderstandings' that caused the trouble, a refrain someone or the other would bring up at the end of their narratives. I suppose they did not trust us. Horen and I decided to take turns to stay up. After some time, he went in to lie down in the shed for a while; the others slowly left.

I sat, nodding off by the fire. Only the policeman and Abdul remained.

The policeman looked like the kind of man who enjoyed his rice and meat, and didn't give thieves much of a chase. He jabbed at the fire with a stick, staring intently. Occasionally, he brought out a quarter bottle from his shirt, took a slow long sip, and put it back in. My throat was dry and ached for a drop.

Then, something changed in the air. The policeman adjusted his buttocks, one side and then the other on the murha, and without looking up from the fire, quietly addressed me: 'Son, you'd be in a lot of trouble if we ask you for your ID.'

There was no point in arguing or pretending otherwise.

I hung my head, and pleaded in a small voice. 'Saar, please don't misunderstand. It's not like that—'

'What is this story about a mad brother? You're here to create trouble, aren't you?'

I did not dare raise my voice beyond a whisper, my palms pressed together in supplication. 'Please ... please listen. The story is true. We're looking for this mad man. He disappeared and we have been looking for him all over—'

'How is that? How would you reach this camp by accident?'

This time Abdul spoke up. His voice had a tremor, as if he was suppressing a great anger in his body. 'You didn't recognise me from the cycle shop in the market? Me or any of my people? Ha, it's that easy, to throw people out and make them go away! Me, I remember faces. I knew as soon as you turned the corner that you were Bodo.' He turned his face and spat in the sand. 'So, what is it – it wasn't enough what you did to us? Oh yes, some of us are still alive, you have to finish what you began. When will the others come, ha?'

'Wait, wait—' The policeman was beginning when Abdul leapt up from his seat and wrestled me to the ground, slapping wildly at my face. I fell back in surprise but had managed in the struggle to land a right hook connecting somewhere on his jaw, when the policeman edged in and separated us, pushing Abdul away. Despite his bulk, the policeman moved fast, and had strength in his arms. Abdul backed off.

'Stop, you animals, motherfuckers with no brains ...' He was panting, tapping at Abdul's chest pushing him back to a sitting position. All three of us were breathing heavily and covered with sand. My face burnt where his blows were able to make contact but he did not do much by way of damage. I wanted to smirk, ah, there's a reason why you fuckers are here, living like animals.

But I held myself back. This man I could deal with, not a crowd of them in the dead of night, no. My hands itched for his throat but I had to be practical, *not now, not now*. I didn't stand a chance.

'You fool!' the policeman said, addressing Abdul. 'You'll beat this guy up. Your hoodlum friends will join in … and make a football out of him, ha … it will give you a good night's sleep, no doubt. But tomorrow, eh, what will it be? Thought of that? You'll all be dragged off to jail, or maybe you won't make it there, maybe we'll simply drop you off at one of *their* villages? Sit there, now—'

And then he turned towards me, one fat hand still resting on Abdul's shoulder.

'And you – tell us, who are you all? Why did you come here? Tell us the truth, son.

'Look around you, at this darkness, not a sound, even the spirits have been chased away. If these people even catch a scent of who you are, I can't stop them. This is not the time for lies …'

And then to Abdul, 'If he had to bring people, he would have by now. Or they are on their way. Everybody knows where the relief camps are. Let's hear him out.'

Abdul hissed, 'Get his mobile.'

I took out my mobile and placed it on the ground near the policeman.

They were both looking at me, foreheads creased, bodies bent forward. Abdul was back to rocking on his haunches. Rolling around in the dust had settled something in him, because now there seemed to be curiosity more than anger on his face.

Despite the cold night wind blowing in from the river, I was perspiring. The palms of my hands, my forehead were damp with fear mixed with soil.

I had no choice but to tell them something of Mongru. But it was such a mixed-up tale, such a strange story, that, at best, they would take me for another deranged member of the family.

At worst, I would not survive the night.

*

The bridge near Hatiputha village, you know it? It's a little past the bend where the river emerges out of the foliage and flows through to the rice fields on the other side. I was crossing the bridge, taking care to keep away from the parts where the bamboo slats had worn out, when I spotted him. He was a little further away, walking haltingly by the side of the stream, as if to see if fish or fern would leap out for his dinner.

I didn't know his name then but I knew it was him.

Though it was only when I got off the cycle, went closer to the edge of the bridge and peered, that I saw his flute. He was not holding it out or playing it like the last time. He had slung it on his shoulder with bits of thread, as one would a rifle, or as one would if it were only a rifle. He walked along the edge for a while, then stepped into the water and floated away, the 'rifle' bobbing up and down, even as his body disappeared into a tangle of hyacinths. I thought I had called out to him, but later I realised that perhaps I had not. As I stood there on the bridge, my fingers went clammy with sweat, my mouth dry, I struggled to breathe. Seeing him had brought back the old fear that held me, momentarily, in its fierce, firm grip. The gun-flute man, I had seen him again.

For the next few days, I tried not to think about it. It was so long ago in the past, so much had happened since then that I sometimes wondered if any of it had taken place at all. There was no point in talking about it to people who had not been there, a drop of jou and the hot sun they would be thinking, even if their faces bore the signs of attentive listening. But I could not shake off this vague uneasiness. So, the following Sunday, I found myself on the road again, making my way back to the bridge.

It was a still, cool morning, the horizon a stroke of gold against the sky, undisturbed, except for the occasional cycle or cart on its way to the Sunday market. Under the bridge, there were a few women with their jekhais wading through the water. I stood there for a while, watching their figures bend and straighten in the rhythm of their hunt. The concentrated tension of their bodies as they lowered their nets into the dark water and held it there, almost unbreathing, and then the rupture as the nets emerged into air, their bodies straightened, hands rifling through the catch, sorting the odds and ends of snail and shrimp. Nothing big yet, I could tell from their glum, attentive expressions. Slowly, the women drifted away from the bridge, their movement flowing into the ripples of light crisscrossing the water. The cormorants replaced them, swooping into the water and out. They seemed to have better luck with the fish. Soon the birds retreated to the higher banks, their bodies upright, wings outstretched skywards, waiting for the water to dry from their feathers like penitent bird saints.

Who did I expect to find there? I am not sure. I walked across the bridge, pushing the cycle alongside.

Then I remembered that one of my Santhali co-workers lived in a village around here. Perhaps I could speak to her about it.

I was familiar with the area. My work with the Health Mission required me to visit villages across communities and, as a part of the polio-campaign team, I had often come here. But as I turned the corner to my colleague's village and spotted the shimmer of the tin roofs, I felt a slight hesitation. It was all a long time ago and relations had mended, but the thought of bringing up these things from the past made me uneasy. It was almost fifteen years since the area had been laid to waste. In the years after that, people had returned and houses had been rebuilt. But the tin of their roofs still glittered in the sunlight, looked new. The village itself was very old, settled they say when these roads were being built by the Santhal people in British times. (One of our drivers in the office who had done twelve years in Médecins Sans Frontières before this job says that seeing a village with new tin roofs on every house makes him sick to the stomach, even if he sees them from the passing window of a train.)

My colleague Sangita was in the courtyard, clearing the

dry leaves of a coconut frond. I was surprised to see her in the green-blue check lungi pansi. At work, she was always attired in a sari; this must be her Sunday at-home dress. She was pleased to see me, and called out with laughter in her voice, 'Ah, we have a guest! Come in, come in!'

I examined her bundle. 'It will make a strong broom. Good thing to put to some use the dry leaves of this season.'

The seasonal winds build up into the occasional storm of great ferocity in this season, and the squall last night had left the coconut tree in their yard bereft of most of its leaves.

'Yes, and the price of brooms in the market! A whole thirty rupees in Bongaigaon they are asking for ...'

Her husband appeared, carrying plastic chairs. 'Come, it is cooler outside, under the trees. We apologise, but the electricity will not be back for a few more hours and it is hot inside.'

I smiled, took a chair from him and placed it in the shade of the bamboo grove. 'It is the same in our village. I don't know where they are sending the electricity from Bhutan. Our people working their dams should bring back electricity instead of those shrunken oranges.'

This amused her husband and he laughed out loud.

Horen, you know how he looks: a giant of a man, with his broad bearing and the scar that runs across his left cheek, but he has this boisterous laugh, a relaxed posture and it gives him a pleasant, easy countenance. He is a good man, a teacher in the local primary school.

Soon, we were talking about the usual things: work, corruption in the road construction, the weather and, again, the power cuts which seem to get longer and longer as we move towards summer. Sangita and I discussed a new Health Mission project that would start after the polio drive.

We had finished drinking our lemon water and the conversation was dragging a little when I approached the subject that had been on my mind. 'A strange thing happened the other day,' I began, 'while I was by the bridge I saw a man I had last seen a long time ago …'

They looked up in anticipation, though I don't think they expected it to be this. 'This was during '97 when' – I was speaking slowly, gauging their reactions, trying to find the neutral words of the newspapers – 'things were bad and people from different communities were fighting—'

I broke off with a cough. My words were a little absurd, as if these 'people' were somehow unconnected to us.

Sangita put the glasses back on the tray and moved towards the kitchen. There was no outward appearance of hurry or irritation but I suddenly remembered that Sangita was not from here; she had come from the villages in the south where the violence had been very bad. There was some story about a brother of hers who had been separated from the family during an attack on a camp, and gone missing. I hesitated. Had I insulted Sangita's hospitality by coming to her house and talking about 1997? It was quite natural for a woman to leave the men to talk politics but Sangita did not abide by these conventions. Her husband, however, looked interested and nodded, urging me to continue.

This was the story I told him: that day, in 1997, I was in Athiabari, near the border, and both communities had gathered there, facing each other with weapons. But it was a fight that never happened. That day we saw the gun-flute man. This man from the Santhali community, with a rifle that looked like a flute. He came out of the river, or the jungles, or some said, their army, and walked right across the path, the middle ground that separated the two groups. It provoked a great fright in our Bodo men, in all of us. Later, they say, the Santhalis saw him too – that he wasn't one of them. There were many rumours, but all I can recall is that he was there, walking with his gun-flute on his shoulder in the battle that never was.

My narration was an approximation of what had happened, what I could recall of it. I ironed out a few details to keep the story simple and coherent.

Horen frowned. 'Wait, I think I had heard something like that. I forget the exact event. This man, I don't know … but the day in Athiabari, when your Bodo people went away without as much as a gunshot, after waiting all day to attack, it surprised everyone. I remember hearing of that—' He looked at me. 'So, who did you see again?'

I replied, 'That man, the one with the flute-gun. He was the man I saw again, by the bridge, a few days ago.'

'Oh …' He frowned. 'But he must be much older now, it's been almost, what, fifteen, twenty years since then?'

I was beginning to say, 'No, no, he looked the same', only to realise that that couldn't be. 1997 was the year I appeared for the higher secondary exams. It had been fifteen years, he couldn't look the same but he did!

Sangita had reappeared. 'Wait, tell me what he looked like, this man.'

I told them what I could of his appearance, describing the gun-flute that he wore on his shoulder in some detail.

Sangita turned to her husband and said something in their language. Then they both smiled.

'Oh, you had me worried for a while with all this talk of the past. Brother, no ghost from your past is chasing you,' the husband exclaimed.

'We know who you are talking of – this man, Mongru I think his name is. He is from Krishnapur village, not far from that bridge. He's slow in the head, and walks around with this gun of his, slung on his shoulder. An old rifle he found somewhere; I haven't taken a close look, maybe it is a flute too, who knows! You see him around, some days he works for a meal at someone's house, then other days, he is sleeping in the fields. Not all there,' he said tapping the side of his head, 'but quite harmless, poor fellow.'

I was relieved. So that was it.

Sangita added, 'If you pass through Krishnapur on some work, or you are going by the bridge road, you will find him there, sitting under a tree with his gun, or walking around. You can take a look, maybe the gun is a flute! But yes, it is Mongru you saw the other day.'

They looked relieved too, smiling broadly. It was as if we had been hovering at the very edge of a crevice, only to realise suddenly that a mere leap would take us to the other side of that gaping maw.

As I said goodbye and wheeled my cycle out of their gate, Sangita came up and handed me a small packet. 'Here, this is the long-limbed black joha I had told you about. We got some from the field.'

I felt a little embarrassed. Perhaps she regretted her earlier moment of anger, though it was my fault, having brought up this topic at all. I accepted the gift and thanked them. They were probably glad to see me cycle away.

And sure enough, I would spot Mongru now and then, on my way home from work. Sitting by a tea shop, fiddling with his gun or twisting a piece of bamboo, or by the rivulet, looking for fish. Sometimes, he would play the flute.

That should have put my anxieties to rest. But the mind is a strange, troublesome thing and, invariably, my thoughts would worm their way back to the old troubles. I tried to let it be. Dredging up the past is a mischievous thing to do, who knows what else may come back to the surface?

*

There was so much happening that year but I remember that uncle.

One day, this fellow showed up at our house. He was my father's cousin from a village close to the border, and had come to apply for bail for his son who had been picked up by the security forces in a raid. The poor man had sold some land to try and get the boy out in time for the exams. His son and I were of the same age, and I was preparing to take the school-leaving exams that year too. It was 1997 or '98, the year the peace treaty collapsed and the violence began in earnest. The sound of gunfire was getting so common, the uncle said, that when they heard shooting the night before, they made little of it. It happened every other day. Some of the other families in the neighbourhood sent their boys away, but his son had refused to go, would not even hide in the cowshed when the police arrived with the CRP. The boy was stubborn, and look how they were paying for it. It had been three months already. We stood around while the uncle spoke. My father sat by his side at the dining table while my mother stood by the kitchen door silently wiping her eyes, my sister and I hanging around near her. None of us knew what to do or say, but then father started.

He looked up at me and barked: 'You! What are you standing around for? Go, go inside and study, anything to keep from his books – out! Let me show you.'

He had stood up and was moving menacingly towards me. I didn't understand. Maybe he was trying to console the uncle, or stop him from going on with this unbearable story, or he had lost his mind, but my father continued in that vein, berating me: 'These sons of ours, nothing … nothing in their heads … no thought for their parents and the future.' All the while, he was moving towards me, his hand raised, his face mottled red with violence, voice shaking.

He did not frighten me. But I felt such a rage, such acute embarrassment at this spectacle that I could not move. It was my sister who gently prodded me into leaving the room. My anger towards him built up over the next few days with every innocuous remark he made, every time I caught sight of his face. I did not forget that incident for a long time. I still wonder – whatever had gotten into my father that day?

There was chaos all around us, you couldn't help but

feel it in the very air – news of kidnappings and bomb blasts, of villages razed, encounters and killings. The Bodo groups were divided and the two main insurgent wings had started fighting each other. Then there were the Army operations.

It was also about then that we heard of the Bodo–Santhali violence erupting in places, the tension brimming over into skirmishes and fighting. For years, these people – the Assamese newspapers and intellectuals and what-have-yous – had denounced the dream of a greater Bodoland that would stretch across the north bank of the Brahmaputra. Our people were too dispersed, our towns and villages too 'mixed', they said. Now, finally, we were pushing out the outsiders from the region, so our people could have a homeland. Maybe it was wrong, maybe right, who knows? How can one say now, so many years later, when so much has changed? The times were different then. The Bodo parties themselves had splintered. Do you remember the violence, the fear, everybody at each other's throats?

This time, though, where the violence came from, nobody could tell. All we hear is that the Muslims are rising, they began this by killing those four of our Bodo boys, hacked them to pieces ... But let's not get into politics now. I will say something, you will have a different opinion, and what's the point of that? To go back to my story ...

I was telling you about the summer of 1997. The two people who seemed oblivious to this great churning were my parents. My mother woke me up at four in the morning to study, and father read the newspaper silently, not commenting on the screaming headlines or what was happening in the neighbourhood. Then they both went off to work in their government jobs, as if there was nothing at all wrong with the world. But events were crowding in closer and closer, moving an inch at a time, encircling them, calling out as if to see if they would twitch these two people in my home.

It was especially tense in our 'mixed' town, which had people from many communities. Then the news came in of the three Bodo women killed in the forest. Things got steadily worse after that. Battle lines were drawn and the entire town was segments and lanes that owed allegiance to one or the other community; you could not risk taking a wrong step.

A camp for displaced Santhalis had come up in the fields beyond the hospital, and with it the whispers got louder. They had made their homes in and around an old club house; the green-blue of their plastic sheets could be seen from the road. Close to it was a CRP camp with security personnel and sandbags lining the gate. We avoided the area but we still heard the stories. Our Bihari neighbour, who had lost his way after having had too many drinks at the bazaar, found himself by the camp one evening. He reported to us that when you pass by the relief camp at night, you don't hear the normal sounds of habitation – the crying babies or drunken voices, dogs and cats in heat, nothing. What you hear is the swishing sounds of hundreds of arrows being sharpened, punctuated by the clank of iron being beaten, because now they were making guns too at these camps. And we saw them: the women and children divided up into groups by day. They left the camp and walked around bamboo groves or jungle, collecting hundreds, thousands of bamboo stalks. For arrows, what else? In preparation for an attack on the town. We lived in fear.

(The sharpening of the arrows came to nothing though. In a few days' time, one of our armed groups arrived by night, attacking and killing thirteen people. The relief camp was soon moved away.)

It was around then that Leimwn brought us the news.

We were at the town centre, a few of us boys smoking and idling away the evening before we returned to the routine of our books, when Leimwn came by. He had just returned from a visit to his village and a cousin had let him in on a plan. An attack was being planned near the border. They needed volunteers; if we wished, we could be part of it. The initial excitement dulled a little when he told us that it was for the next day. We had to decide quickly. 'No weapons training?' someone had asked, only to get shouted down by the rest: can we not do one thing at a time? The next day was Tuesday. That was a problem too because we had maths tuitions in the evening, and that teacher would inform your family if you missed a single class. Nobody mentioned it but a Thursday or Friday would have been more convenient when we had English and Science. There would be less explaining to do when we returned. But this was a chance we could not miss, we all agreed. A plan was made, Leimwn who knew the area would take us there.

I walked back with another friend, Guna; our houses were close. He was silent all through. I wasn't quite sure how he felt about this. I suspected he would not be there the next morning, an upset stomach or having overslept, something like that would be the matter.

Taking the decision to go the next morning made everything bearable. For once, I did not have to grit my teeth through dinner with my father complaining about the curry and mother about the prices. I felt oddly elated, sitting in my room and cleaning the khukri we used for cutting bamboo while my parents sat watching the news on television.

I imagined that the next morning I would be up much before the alarm, but I opened my eyes to see the hand of the clock veer towards a quarter past four. I should have been at the bus stop! I jumped up and tried to get ready in a hurry, afraid that they would leave me and go. There was just about enough time to pick up the knife and rush out. The bag was not big enough and the sharp end jutted out; I would have to see to it later. I clutched a book in my other hand and was about to open the gate, when I heard my mother calling out. She was sweeping the courtyard.

'Where do you think you—'

I turned and waved, mumbled something about it getting late, going off to cut bamboo or some such implausibility, and ran. I did not turn to look because I knew she would be standing there, with her lips pursed, forehead crinkled, wondering what had taken hold of me. It must have been a strange sight, her son rushing out at daybreak with a book in one hand and a barely concealed khukri in a bazaar bag, without a cycle, without so much as a cup of tea.

I was relieved to see a group of boys by the main road. So they were there. Guna was there too. He smiled a little awkwardly when I reached. They must have thought I was going to go the upset stomach way. We joked about my bazaar bag. They had come better prepared, and I managed to find a place for my khukri in a shoulder bag. But there was a problem: Leimwn, the friend who had made the plan, hadn't arrived yet. We could not risk going back to the neighbourhood to look for him and, when the bus arrived at five, we decided to leave without him. Clutching our school bags, we looked like a regular set of passengers.

The ticket conductor, who knew Guna, was surprised when we asked for tickets to Athiabari. 'Are you sure? We were thinking of not taking the bus there today, the situation is very tense. There is some talk of the Army reaching there, curfew—'

A middle-aged passenger in the seat ahead of mine, distinct in his coloured Gorkha cap, butted in, 'Oh, it is only a matter of time before something happens there. It is entirely lawless with all the government and Forest Department people having run off. Both these people, Santhali and Bodo, have been building armies, everybody knows that. Real armies, I tell you! After they kill each other, together they will loot and burn our houses, since they won't have much of their own anyway! And will we get protection? Who will come for us?' He spoke bitterly, and showed no sign of stopping – and wouldn't have but for his daughter, who quietened him, who cut him short in the middle of his diatribe, speaking softly, swiftly in Nepali.

She then gave the conductor a sharp look. 'Brother, there are passengers in front waiting for you.'

He was about to open his mouth to respond but thought the better of it and left. We were relieved to have gotten rid of the ticket collector. He looked like the persistent type.

The girl had, meanwhile, turned back to smile at me and Guna. 'These people, they want to know everything, why, who is going where. Drives me crazy! It's much better in the city...'

I agreed with her and we talked a little. Soon, every innocuous comment was beginning to terrify me. She was now complaining about the Army checkpoints. '... and those lechers in uniform, what did they think I was carrying, grenades? They wanted to check my purse. What could I have inside here?' she asked, holding up her dainty Chinese-silk purse.

Guna looked at me. I knew what he was thinking. We hadn't bothered to find out if there were any Army checkpoints along the way. I had no idea what else the boys carried in their bags other than the khukris, how would we explain them? Guna and the girl were now talking of some film she had watched. I joined in, trying to take my mind away from the many things we had not thought of.

When we got off the bus, the girl waved at us cheerily. But the sharp edges of the bag on my shoulder made me nervous. I was sure she would shout abuses at us publicly if she knew what we carried in our bags. She looked like that kind of girl.

The Athiabari bus stop was deserted, with rows of shuttered shops on either side. It was eight o'clock on a weekday. By now, it should have been full of people making their way to the bigger markets in the towns, tracker-hands crowding people into their vehicles and groups of older boys in uniform and girls in makeup and dokhonas waiting for the bus to college. But there was nothing, not a soul. We had to get to Adabari but there was no one whom we could ask for directions. We walked the length of the market and back. Even on a bandh, there is usually a paan shop with its shutters opened a crack, or a tea shack cooking up something at the back kitchen, but we couldn't find anything that day. My stomach growled, calling out for the customary steamed rice cakes or plate of chana the tea-shop women should have had ready by now. There wasn't as much as a wisp of smoke emanating from the boarded-up shacks; it was as if the people had disappeared, the market abandoned.

We waited, munching on biscuits and cursing Leimwn.

Finally, a group of people appeared on the road, making their way towards the bus stop. As they came closer, we could see that it was a group of women and children, with a few men at the back. They seemed to be a mixed group, some Nepali, judging by their nose rings, sindoor and sarees, and others in the patanis worn by Rajbongshis. Trailing the women were three men, carrying bags and beddings.

We boys made way for the women on the bus-stop bench, helping them settle their things. They were waiting for a bus to take them towards our area, and were relieved to hear that the buses were still running on this road.

I got talking to the men accompanying them, who

stood by smoking bidis. Two of them were Nepali and the other was a Sutradhar. They came from villages close to the reserve forest but they knew of Adabari. The oldest of the three took an interest in our questions and, stubbing his bidi, agreed to accompany us a part of the way.

He was an odd fellow, his back curved somewhat, and he had a bad leg that gave him a spring in his step; he didn't so much walk as hop about. It was hard to tell if it was old age or nature that had shaped his body thus. The other two men were to stay back with the women till they caught a bus. Perhaps he was glad of the company for the walk back, because we soon had an enthusiastic guide leading us out of the market.

I was initially relieved that this man had bought our story of a sick relative in Adabari, but he had read another meaning into it.

'A good thing your folks sent you. We have been hearing things too. Take your people away. You don't know how it is going to go. It is between you all, it has nothing to do with us, but we still feel the fear.' And his nose twitched as if he could indeed smell something in the air.

'That's why we are sending our young and old away. The rest of us, we have to be here. With us, it's our cattle and homes. No point living to see another day if they take your cows.'

Then his voice dropped to a whisper, 'Look, boys, I'll tell you something. You're not from here. You'll get into trouble for no fault of yours. Now, you go to Adabari and get your relatives out, but don't take the route through the fields and, even if you do, go carefully. A boy of ours came running back from where he was herding his buffaloes along the Adabari forests. At first light, they were already reaching there – bands of men surrounding the Santhali villages. What will happen I don't know but it cannot be good. Now, when I was walking to the market, I heard that the Santhalis had banded together with their weapons too. Both groups are there. It is only a matter of time before something happens. It is better you don't meet any Santhalis on the way or else' – he made a clicking noise at the back of his throat and a chopping gesture with his hand.

'Fine day you boys chose to come to Adabari!' He intercepted his advice with low, soft laughter, as if relishing his own joke.

Then he stopped abruptly at a crossroad and bid us goodbye. To reach Adabari, we would have to continue on our own. The route he laid out for us was simple – keep to the path we were on, avoid the fields and the jungle on either side.

We stood there for a while and watched his limping figure disappear into the foliage. We could either continue or retrace our steps back to the bus station.

As we walked along the path, towards what we hoped was Adabari, one of the boys spoke out our collective fear, 'What if that old goat is sending us to our deaths? To some kind of massacre?'

There was something about him, he did not look right, we all agreed. But we continued walking down the road.

Ahead of us were fields that stretched flat for miles, bordered by shrub jungle and a few tall trees that appeared occasionally. This was forest land from where the trees had gone, leaving shrub jungle and fields that have never known the plough. We met no people. The few houses we passed by the side of the road were empty – or, perhaps, the inhabitants stayed inside, we could not tell. The dogs, however, ran around in packs, unconcerned, busy with their everyday lives. They were the only animals we spotted, and this was somewhat more worrying than the missing people. Where had the farm animals, the chickens and the goats and the pigs gone?

Someone wondered aloud, should we take out our weapons? But if there is nothing happening, people will take us to be thieves sneaking round with daos and khukris.

Then we spotted them – a group of people on elevated ground, with their back to the jungle, facing a clearing. Even from a distance, we could tell it was our people.

Initially, there was some confusion. They seemed overjoyed to see us – a few of them running up to us, grabbing our hands, thanking us for coming. That took me a little by surprise. We had not quite imagined a reception such as this, that anybody would be expecting us. But it so happened that most of the men gathered there were locals, armed like us with daos, knives, khukris and other agricultural implements. They were awaiting the promised reinforcements of trained young men with guns that would turn the tide in their favour. They had mistaken us for underground rebels!

Once the group had reconciled themselves to our status as amateurs, we settled in. A burly man with a big stomach took us aside and helped us with the grips and motions of the weapons: how to chop, cut, skewer, drive into the heart. We tried to imitate him, swishing this way and that, testing our grip, our strength. There was a strong smell of jou about him.

After the tension of the morning, I found myself relaxing a little. Like you sometimes do before a volleyball game that you think will go well, when your body is not too tightly strung and your focus is level, allowing you to savour the moment.

My friends from the village were settling down too. I heard Guna addressing the big man in a low voice, almost a growl, 'When is it, when do we go in to attack the bastards?'

That surprised me – Guna's fierce concentration, the way he held his shoulders, he had transformed himself into the role of an action hero. Unlike the rest of us who looked a little silly, awkwardly clutching our daos, mouths agape, ill-balanced limbs, like overgrown children playing at war. But Guna – he looked like a warrior. This made me vaguely irritated, impatient. *Enough, what stupidity was this, were we to stand here all day?*

When do we get at them, the others were soon muttering, mirroring Guna's sentiments pathetically. He had become our leader.

The men smiled at Guna's question, they seemed to be enjoying their role too. I wondered what they did in their real lives, these men: shopkeepers or clerks in an office, I would say. The fat man, I later found out, used to be a cook in the Army.

He didn't speak, instead he steered Guna with an arm

on his shoulder. 'Out there, can you see?' He was pointing at the horizon, and sure enough, if you peered hard, you could see the outline of a group of people among the trees. Our two groups were separated by a field, land recently cleared of jungle. It was not to be an attack but a battle.

That was it then – the enemy, already there, lying in wait. No one in our group spoke for a while. We were transfixed by the idea of the men who stood opposite us, even though we could barely see them. Then Guna must have uttered some appropriate platitude for the occasion. He was beginning to get on my nerves, but I was not brave enough to abandon my village group. Not now, having faced the enemy, looked them in the eye. I quietly took my place by his side.

An hour, then another, we stood there; so did the other group. It was a fine day for May, though I had feared there would be rain when we started out. Where we stood a few sal trees gave us shade. They must have been a part of the older forest, with their long limbs and leafy, speckled foliage. But what were they waiting for? What were we waiting for?

After some time, our group began to slacken, we eased our posture of attack, turning here and there to talk softly or look around. Though we still stood facing them, weapons in hand, the mood had changed somewhat; people relaxed, stretched their limbs, cracked jokes. I felt a pang of hunger. Finally, after we had stood for a good three or four hours, this other friend Dino and I decided to go take a leak. We excused ourselves and walked a little out into the shrub, maybe a little further than the limit the leaders warned us about. This was after all their territory, the Santhalis knew it better, and we didn't know how many men they had or what surprises they could swing. Better to stay close by. My initial excitement had all but worn out. I needed to stretch my legs and get away from those people for some time.

That's when I – we – saw him. First of all, there was the shock of seeing a Santhali man at this proximity (and despite what others had to say later – the distance he was at, the excitable state we were in – I distinctly remember identifying him as Santhali).

My legs froze under me. He was slowly, calmly walking by the field. If it were not for the jungle shrubs, he would be a plain few metres away from our men. And then what – would we have to kill him? I looked down at the khukri in my hand, and recalled the swishing, swooshing actions we had been taught. I should do something, shout out, alert him to the necessity of having to kill him. But what if my cry of warning were to draw the attention of the others in my group? My thoughts were coming too fast, too muddled.

Then I heard Dino's whisper, he sounded terrified. 'Look, he has a gun.'

Gun? And then I saw it. His 'gun' frightened me more than the prospect of killing him. It was a strange gun, a rifle, the kind the police had in the old days, an old-style Enfield rifle. You rarely saw it these days, with everybody carrying AKs and automatics. What was he doing with this strange gun? But it could fire bullets, surely, and kill us, like the arrows the rest of their people carried.

He did not, however, seem in the least interested in shooting anybody, and continued to walk calmly, with the easy pace of one herding cows on a cloudless summer day (as it indeed was). His hands, in that same unhurried movement now went to his gun. Dino clutched my arm, but neither of us raised an alarm or tried to charge him, as we should have. But what he did next terrified us more even than that prospect: he held the rifle with both his hands, lightly, tenderly, parallel to the ground and sky, and then stretching his hands away from his body, returned the gun to his mouth as if to plant a kiss. We heard a tune; he was playing the rifle like a flute! We stood immobile, Dino and I, watching this strange spectacle – for five or ten minutes, or maybe a half hour, a few seconds, I could not tell – and then he was gone. Not disappeared suddenly like an apparition, he had simply moved away, turning the corner into the neck-high jungle. Dino and I were shaking. We barely made it back to our spot.

It was a portent, but what its import was I could not tell. What is the point of a sign, if you are not able to read it? It will only drive you crazy.

I don't remember much else. We had waited all day, as had the other group. Somebody brought provisions from a nearby village, cooked lunch. The Santhalis had plenty of chances to attack. From where we were, it was difficult to tell, but it seemed that their group never moved, never loosened their grip on the weapons, nor their eyes from us. And we must have known then that they would not attack, because we had gone about eating and drinking, some took a nap, while the day dragged out. We did not attack. At the end of the day, our party took the same bus back home.

Later, I heard that the captain of the militant group that was to support us had seen the gun-flute man too when their vehicle stopped to repair a flat tyre on the way there. It had scared the captain, though he had been years in the jungle. He took it to be a sign and turned back, chose to wait. He is a politician now and wears rows and rows of rings on his fingers, amulets around his neck; they say it was after this incident.

The gun-flute man's protection, however, did not extend to Adabari the next day. Or to the camp, where these people were attacked again.

When I returned late that evening, my parents were both sitting outside waiting for me. They were worried, but my mother tut-tutted and pushed my father in, saying something about the mosquitoes and wanting to get him a cup of tea. (Which was unusual as he did not drink tea after his afternoon cup, and my mother did not make it, one of my sisters did.) Mother spoke to me cheerily, her lips bared back in a forced smile. She spoke through dinner, about relatives and her work and all sorts of things. No one else did. But she did not ask me where I had been. I don't know what they had heard, but everyone in the family seemed a little wary of me after that. And they left me alone. I welcomed it.

I did not have a chance to speak to Dino about the gun-flute man. Others from our group had seen him too. One or two of the boys from that day, I meet them here and there, they all remember the man differently.

I let it be. In the end, what matters is the story I hold. No point trying to get people to agree on anything in this land of ours.

*

Abdul brought out a kettle and put it on the fire. I continued my story with a cup of salt tea in my hands.

A week ago, the riots began. To go from my village to the office, I had to cross the highway, and so once the violence was on TV and the curfew began, I could not step out.

Then yesterday morning, I had visitors.

The knock was very gentle: one tap, then a pause, followed by two hurried taps, this time a little louder. I knotted my lungi with one hand, and groped in the darkness for the watch. It was barely daybreak. Who could it be?

The person outside must have heard me kick the chair, upsetting it in my hurry to get to the door. The knocking stopped. As I fumbled with the latch, I could hear voices. Who was it?

And who would it be but Sangita and her husband, standing in the courtyard, silhouetted by the early light that barely touched the edge of the trees outside. They were smiling, a little awkward. 'You must think us mad, but this was the only way—'

'What? Has something happened to your village?' I had shaken off my sleep and remembered the troubles.

'No, no, there was no emergency as such, but in some time, the curfew will begin and we would not be able to cross the highway to come here. We first thought we'd wait by the river till you were up. But in these times, they'd take us to be—'

Sangita would have continued to speak in her unhurried manner but I interrupted her. 'Has something happened? Why are you here?'

'It – it's Mongru ...' Horen said quietly. 'He hasn't been seen since the troubles began. We—'

I held up a hand. 'Wait, let me put on a shirt and wash my face. Here, please sit here till then.' I washed, and then made some tea for all three of us.

No one had seen Mongru for the past ten days since the troubles began. In this area, the violence had been sporadic, but the killings in ILoveYou market had created panic, boundary lines had been drawn. Despite the curfew, isolated killings and lootings were being reported by the television channels.

'Should we try the police station?' Even as I spoke, I saw the foolishness of this suggestion. We would probably get a few on our backsides for our troubles, walking into the police station to ask for Mongru when there wasn't enough police to keep people from cutting each other's throats and burning villages. We sat quietly for a few minutes.

Then Horen spoke up, 'He may have strayed into another village. The area has Bodo villages to the north, a few Rajbongshi–Muslim mixed villages, and more Muslim villages to the east. He may have wandered off, and now with this curfew, it is possible that he is not able to make his way back to the village ...'

He did not have to complete his sentence. Or else, they cut him up. Since he would not be able to say anything in his defence, if someone thought him to be of either of the two warring groups … he could easily pass for a Bodo or a Muslim peasant, with his sun-burnished skin and indistinct features.

But did they come all this way to share this thought with me?

I nodded. 'Mongru, whatever he is, god made him this way – he gives no one any trouble. That's more than can be said for all the fools roaming this land with a brain working. Is there anything I – we – can do?'

'We thought about it all night. My old man was not so keen. He said you'll take us to be crazy. But I said no, he'll understand. He came looking for Mongru one time too …'

This woman was certainly mad. I could hardly believe she was saying all this. What were we going to do, drive through shoot-at-sight orders with people hacking each other up, asking for Mongru?

But I got pulled into the plan anyway. They had assumed that I would accompany them, and I could not bring myself to refuse. Initially, we planned to take a quick look around a few villages and return home by late morning or noon. It seemed foolhardy but not altogether foolish. And in all likelihood, the violence was abating.

So we drove off, just as morning broke clear into the sky, looking for Mongru. Horen and Sangita on their scooter, and me following them on my brother's bike.

My reconciliation with this plan wore out in ten minutes. We were driving over the bridge where I had seen Mongru, taking him to be the man from my past.

Maybe I still hoped to spot him by the river looking for fish, and though I drove slowly, my eyes were not on the bridge, skirting instead the banks and the river hyacinths at its edge. That moment of inattention cost me, a nail tore through the back tyre of the bike and punctured it. I had always feared this. Strips of bamboo have been placed over the old decaying wood of the bridge. But nothing has been done about the odd nail here and there that has loosened itself from the wood and lies hidden like a jungle trap beneath the bamboo, waiting to spring. And it had to happen then. I pushed the bike down to a relative's house close by and left it there. We would have to continue the journey on the scooter with all three of us riding together.

I would be sitting in front driving it, with Sangita and Horen, the couple, at the back. It was an odd sight to say the least. I was much shorter than her husband. Sangita – you saw – is reed thin and around my height. While Horen is this broad-shouldered giant. No one could take us to be mischief-makers. We looked too desperate a party: a curfew-day circus.

We were driving through the east of Krishnapur. No burning or shooting had happened here but people kept off the roads. The markets were abandoned except for a few women who sat with small bundles of firewood or a handful of dried fish by the side of the road. I had heard of some killings, of auto-drivers and market-going villagers who had landed up crossing the wrong road and into the other's territory. Now and then, bodies washed up in the river, and it was difficult to ascertain whether it was a casualty of the conflict or a case of robbery. Where we saw people, by half-opened shops or sitting by the road, we inquired about Mongru, leaving our mobile numbers in case they heard something. A few relief camps had come up but it was a precautionary measure. People hoped to stay for a few days until the tension cleared, and then move back to their villages, or they took shelter at night, going back to their villages by day. Sangita and Horen inquired in one or two of the camps as well.

On account of us being three on the scooter, we moved slowly. It was almost noon by the time we stopped for tea. Sangita had gone behind the shop to use the toilet, Horen was smoking a bidi by the door and I was asking for another masala egg when a loud clamour broke outside.

I could smell it in the wind by then, the faint stench of burning. Outside, people pointed at the horizon, at the angry black clouds billowing out into the sky. It was a village across the river, not too far from us. Then the cries, we could hear that too, maybe gunshots.

It had come. It had reached us, or we had reached it.

The tea-shop woman pulled down the wooden shutters of her shop, and the three of us rushed in with her, dragging the scooter and her cycle into the back. Inside, we sat and peered at the road through the slivers of light where the wood-frames of the walls were joined unevenly. We spoke quietly, not knowing what to expect. For a long time, there was nothing, then the sound of hurried footsteps, close to us. The woman opened the window a fraction, pushing up the wooden board supported by a piece of bamboo. All four of us huddled under it to try and see what was happening.

There were people on the road, lots of them, wailing and shouting; they were heading somewhere. The woman had told us that this village consisted mostly of Rajbongshis who were not aligned to either side and had no part in the conflict. But in the heat of battle, who was to say? Across the river, there were many mixed villages. Some of the Muslims from those villages had taken shelter in a camp not far from here. Our view through the window crack was restricted to a few inches of the road. We could see people running but could not follow them further. Then Horen, who is a tall man, stood up on a bench, and peered through the opening where the wall and the roof met. The bamboo sheaves of the wall did not reach the roof. People were running off the road and towards the river. Somewhere on the other side, a village burned. We had seen the smoke spiralling into the sky earlier. But these people, what were they doing by the river side? I clambered onto a table to get a better view. The people, yes, they were by the river, some of the men jumped into the water, first one, then another, trying to get across to the other side. We waited in silence. After some time, smoke appeared in the sky again, surging out from a different origin, somewhere along the direction in which the swimmers were headed.

The tea-shop woman's reading was that people from the relief camp first watched their own village burn from the other side of the river, then losing their mind over it, crossed the river to set fire to the houses of the other group.

We sat in silence while the wind blew with it the ashes of village after village. It was too dangerous to risk being out on the road. We stayed at the shop till darkness fell, and then left with the tea-shop lady to take shelter in her house. The village we were in was untouched by arson or injury, but not a leaf stirred, even the dogs seemed to have gone quiet. An obstinate rooster had begun calling for light but its cry was abruptly throttled and the silence remained undisturbed for the rest of the night.

Then something else happened. That night, we heard a story, the story that was to eventually bring us here to this camp.

The tea-shop lady's husband had gone for some work to the town and was expected back by the afternoon, but that had, of course, not been possible. There were no tempos or autos on the roads and he was lucky to have found a bus that brought him halfway. After that, he walked through the fields to reach the village. He came home accompanied by two others whose villages were even further afield. The sudden violence took everybody by surprise. Despite the curfews and setting up of camps, everyone thought their area would be spared.

We sat around sharing stories and talking after the night meal. We told them of Mongru and his gun, and his mental state, and our fears for him. (We had left out the details of the context in which I had seen him, emphasising instead his inability to communicate. We also added that he was a relative of Sangita's to keep things simple.)

One of the men who had accompanied the husband home, a Bihari fellow, took an interest in our questions. In fact, he declared that he had heard of just such a gun. He had a spot in the market where he sold onion and potatoes, and was friendly with the Muslim traders there. The rice trader whose stall was next to his had brought along a relative the other day. The relative came from the Narayanpur area near the forests where the violence had begun a fortnight ago. His village had been burnt and he was taking shelter with the rice dealer. The refugee had regaled the market people with stories of the riots. Some of them were rather far-fetched, said the Bihari, including one where two men on watch nodded off in the dead of the night and woke up in fright to see what they took to be a ghost – a man playing a gun like a flute, walking by the bamboo grove!

We were astonished at this story. Could Mongru have wandered off and got mixed up with the violence in the Narayanpur area? It would be half a day's walk from his village. It seemed too incredible, and there was always a possibility that this man had simply told us the story for a laugh. But it was the only piece of concrete evidence we had gathered that day, so what harm would it do to check with the people who had fled Narayanpur? They would be in the camps now.

The next morning, we set out for the camp that housed people from Narayanpur. The incident of the day before had put some fear into our souls, and we resolved to return home by mid-day. Driving around the area was not so simple either; villages were aligned one way one side of the road, and another way on the other.

As we were crossing the highway, Sangita had another idea. 'Stop – stop the scooter!' Then she made me get off and commandeered her husband to the front. 'We cannot have him drive from here on. His people have burnt their villages. We'll never come out of there alive with him in front …'

So I slid off and sat at the back. But within a few minutes we'd reach another village where it may be safer to have me in front. What were we to do then? This was too tedious. 'Wait, we'll think of something. I'll tell them I'm Rajbongshi or Assamese. Fine? After this one, we'll pass through a Bodo village, what if they take your husband to be Muslim, then what? This was a stupid idea to begin with—'

Sangita had no time for my opinions. She looked straight at me: 'If you want to be Assamese when it suits you, you should have learnt to make your 'pa' and 'ka' sounds …'

I was about to open my mouth and give her evidence of my ability to voice them, but she continued, exasperated, 'Oh, please, don't argue. Believe me, I have seen that happen. I know what it's like to watch your house burn, lose everything. It makes you … go mad. These people, they will not be in their senses.'

So, that's what we did. Every few kilometres, Horen and I changed places, took turns to drive the scooter. It took us the whole morning to go from village to village, to carefully steer though the curfew along back roads to arrive at the camp in Santipur, only to be told that it had been disbanded a few days back and the inhabitants moved to smaller camps. Till then, things were on course. I had waited at a market while they went to the camp.

But on the way here, the scooter developed a leak – and …

*

The mosquitoes woke me up. My feet, sticking out from under the sheet, were aflame with bites. Daylight was streaming through the frayed bamboo strips of the wall. I didn't feel rested, my shoulders hurt. Shedding the layers of sleep, I struggled to make sense of the aftertaste in the mouth, the stiffness in the jaw. Then I remembered.

Outside, people were already milling around, cries of babies and chatter, animal sounds from the village surrounding the camp. I might have been asleep for two or three hours at most.

Sangita was sitting on a plastic chair under a tree, surrounded by women and children. She was giving medical advice for skin infections and children's coughs and colds, women's problems, making vague promises about sending medicines. Horen appeared. He had made a foray into the village and returned with some petrol.

We were filling the tank and preparing to leave when Sangita walked up to us.

'They say the gun is here – Mongru's gun!'

Mongru is here?

'Not Mongru, his gun. They say a gun like Mongru's has been seen. It's in the camp.'

And Mongru?

'I don't know.'

We should leave. Get on the scooter and go. Now.

'They will take us there. Come.'

The bamboo grove behind the camp marked the edge of the fields. A narrow path slipped through the dark edge of the vegetation to lead to the river bank. In the rains, the water reached up to the patch of earth on which the camp nested, but this was the dry season, and the river had receded to its core, leaving behind the sand and rocks of its underbelly. The sand shifted restlessly under my feet as I tripped and slid down the steep descent from the grove to the river's lower banks. A dense fog rose from the water and made its way inland. We lost the sunlight of the upper reaches and I could barely see the groups of people who had followed us down. Some coursed ahead and I followed.

The mist blurs the borders of the elements – air water sand. Only the children are unaffected, able to make these sand banks their playground. This is where they are chased away when they get underfoot, as they often do in the narrow confines of the camps. You could see them in small groups all along the river. One group was burning something, a rubber tyre, and its stench filled the air.

The children in the mist were scraps of sound and movement, and we followed them. A few ran around kicking a battered, patched-up football. Watching by the side were more children, mostly toddlers in the keeping of older siblings. A young girl was running with a baby strapped to her back. The children stopped their game and looked at us expectantly. One of the men asked a boy something. He turned and pointed further away.

We turned in that direction, some of the children trailed us while the others continued kicking the ball around.

Sangita's sandals sank into the sand. Horen slowed his pace to support her. I left them behind, moving with another group.

Then I spotted it. Mongru's gun, with its distinctive

barrel and the holes along the flute side. I moved closer. The thread Mongru used to sling the gun-flute over his shoulder had been replaced by some coloured rags knotted together to make a rope. A girl was holding it. She looked ten or eleven – though I could not be sure, she could be older. She was wearing an odd mix of garments: a too-big men's checked shirt over a long skirt, a torn cloth clasped around her waist and across her shirt like a sador. She had one green eye, the other seemed half shut.

She stood there, facing us for a moment. Then sprang up, jerked the rifle off her shoulder in an abrupt movement and, clinging to it with both hands, fled.

I broke into a run, tried to follow her.

But it was not easy.

She had drifted away effortlessly into the grey mass of river and mist but, for me, it was a struggle. The sand sank beneath my feet and pulled me down to my knees. I had to scramble with my hands and elbows to keep moving.

I could hear the flute, is that what it sounded like?

I could see glimpses of the girl as she ran deeper and deeper into the sand and mist.

Saŋgita and Horen were far behind. Sangita was trying to say something to me.

But I could not wait for them.

I shouted back, *No, it will not be today, I have seen the gun-flute! Not today …*

Meanwhile, the men around me were edging closer. The sand did not seem to disturb them.

Sultana Walks Home

IF THERE WAS anything, people agreed on, it was that the new government had built their roads.

Sultana felt a thrill each time she took the turn from the highway into Chapaguri, leaving behind the ragged traffic of scooters, trackers and the boisterous local autos of Bongaigaon to sail through the quiet rice fields along the newly paved road. With the exception of the occasional car, there were only a few cyclists and pedestrians on the road, loitering goats and market-goers peacefully sleeping off their extra drink by the roadside. She would ride down this road till the Bismuri market, then past villages with broad-shouldered trees lining the sides, to finally arrive at the immense open skies of the newly built bridge over the river Aie. Her husband's village was across the river, while her mother's fell a little short of the bridge.

Sultana has become so used to doing this route on her battered, faithful Kinetic, the walk feels truly endless. Then comes the ache of regret at having to leave her bike behind in office. It is the only thing of value she possesses. So perhaps it has been wise, it will be safer in the office shed.

She had largely ignored the developments of the last few weeks. It was like keeping score in a children's game: one killed this side, followed by four on the other side, then three here, a whole family there. Sultana had no idea who had started it, what the original wound was, on whom it was made and by who. She had had other things to keep her busy.

Breathe, take your time to breathe. She has tucked the last of the tamul into her mouth and carefully spits into the grass, closes the gate behind her and walks. Then it comes back: a sharp pricking in the eyes as they well up. *Oh lord*, she pleads, *not now, not here*. (The tears are not of sadness or fear; it is anger she feels. But she is ashamed of them and, under these circumstances, they are bound to be misinterpreted.) It is dusk, though, and if she gives it some thought, she will know that no one can see the marks they leave on her face. Not that her companion notices, he is too busy grimacing, and trying to demonstrate his contempt and disapproval of her decision.

She registers with a slight shock that his manner is familiar; it reminds her of the other men in her life. The men she knows with far greater intimacy than she ever will the man by her side, the chance companion of this walk back home. It is his bearing, this sense of disapproval that his entire being exudes and an entitlement to this disapproval: *what gives you the right*, she wants to shout at him, *just what, can you tell me, please*. Her own anger at his behaviour completes the circle of intimacy; connects her to him, this man, and him to all the other men, the husband and father and brothers.

But her husband would have handled this situation better, if anything, and thank god for that, he was not a coward. And then, she cannot bear to think of her husband either, so she goes back to this man by her side. He opens his mouth again to say something, and she wonders if it is indeed better to have him talk than to listen to her own thoughts.

She lets him speak.

'You people try to save your money by not charging your phones or what? Your mother has a phone you say, and you can't call her – you have to walk ten kilometres to reach her. All so unnecessary. This is not the first time. I have seen this often with your people. They come to the tea shop and ask, can we put the phone to charge while we drink tea? And then, of course, five people will come and one will drink tea, and the rest will charge their phones, so this way, they save money …'

She gives him a look, rolls her eyes. But the voice in her head has adopted his tone: *Oh yes, we save our money, we save and save, sell our mothers so we can buy your tribal land cheap, and drive your people out, isn't that it?* If she says it aloud, he will probably agree.

She was the only woman from her community who worked there, that's true. She had never thought about it before. After finishing school, she had joined this organisation and learnt everything from the older women here. A large part of the community work she did was in Bodo villages. She spoke their languages, had stayed in their houses. Today, there was a training programme in the neighbouring district, and all her colleagues were there.

She had skipped the event, choosing to come in to office to settle her accounts instead. That's how they came to be the two people in office. The other accounts lady had left early but this man had stayed, waiting out the office hours dutifully till it was time to leave.

They were both old employees, but their interactions had never gone beyond the usual pleasantries and the monthly settling of accounts. Sultana didn't have much work at the office today. She stepped out for a leisurely cup of tea at the market, then came back to her desk to look at photos from the training. She had to leave for the train station early next morning for a workshop in Nalbari, and thought it better to spend the night in office instead of going home. Somebody or the other was always there.

But the afternoon changed things. First, the phone calls. She had suddenly been inundated by phone calls, they came in wave after wave; she could barely finish a call, and there was another, and another. She should have hurled it into a pond – the mobile had served to ruin her day, and nothing else. The whole world had called her, the first calls were from her Bodo colleagues and friends inquiring about the violence, if it was true that her community had called for war that hundreds of people were arriving with weapons from Bangladesh, preparing to finish them all off.

She had no idea. Then she called her contacts in various organisations to inquire, only to be told that it was the Bodos who were out to massacre them. People from her community were shocked to hear that she sat phoning them from a Bodo village. They were going to cut her up, surely?

She wasn't too bothered initially. The first few phone calls served to mildly irritate her, that she should have to spend her time talking to these hysterical people instead of finishing her report and watching a film on the computer with another cup of tea. Every day, people died, killed others. In this land, has it ever stopped? If it reaches the news and TV, people panic, otherwise they carry on. What did this have to do with her?

But the information from the phone calls was more specific now, reports coming in from here and there that the violence had spilled over into their district: villages were being burned, people killed, the Army had been called, that there would be curfew from tomorrow. People took the trouble to spell it out for her: if the Army was coming in tomorrow, there was a window of time, between now and dawn, when the violence would be at its fiercest. It would be advisable to not find yourself in the wrong place.

Sultana had worked in this area for years; she had a fine network of auto drivers and a bike to get her past bandhs and curfews. How else would she have gotten anything done at all? She sat with the bills spread out on the table. Her mother's phone was unreachable. She waited for news from the village, a call from a neighbour's phone, but there was nothing. And then it was too late – the decision was thrust upon her.

She smiles to herself at the thought of her mother saving money by not charging the phone battery. That woman, money went through her hands like water through a sieve. It was either the neighbour's grandson who fell sick or some young man who needed a loan. The phone was another matter, though. It was Sultana who charged it each time she went home, so her mother could speak to her two sons who lived in the town. Other times, it lay on top of the TV with a crocheted doily protecting it.

Had they not heard anything in their village? Surely, her mother would have thought to bring out the mobile from the net cover, go to a neighbour and have them call someone, Sultana or one of her brothers. But none of them had heard from her.

And though she didn't want to admit it, there was the niggling fear. What if this were to be the real thing, what the older people spoke of when they recalled the violence of the 1990s, if this was the moment when it tipped over and they capsized into a full-scale riot? That's when she had stopped looking at the bills and decided to act.

She glances at the man pushing his cycle and walking with her. The narrative so far pitched each side evenly, and for a situation to be poised so delicately, precariously on the edge, is a frightening thing. Especially because she knows the guns, the power is on the other side. It will be easier to force her people to leave than convince them to stay. She cannot for a moment imagine a home elsewhere. They had tried; her husband had rented a place in the city, only to return a few months later. Neither spoke of it but it had been a lesson to them all, this was home, there was nowhere else to go.

But what if they did not descend into hell and the violence clung on in this current scoring format. Did that mean that, for a Bodo woman killed somewhere, she, her walk through these villages, would serve as a counterpoint?

This man, walking with her, she appraises his physique: the narrow wrists, the strength of his hands pushing the cycle, his balding head, the way his shoulders stooped, he was only about as tall as she was, maybe even a little shorter. No, she reckons he does not have the strength to pin her down in a struggle. But what if there are others? What if he is driving her to an agreed-upon point, giving her over to a gang? This is how it is sometimes done, she knows that.

The man … is it possible that all this while he has continued speaking? She has been so caught up in her own thoughts that she cannot tell. She decides a conversation may be the only way to escape her rising panic and softens her previous sharp demeanour. 'Dada, do you have a family at home?'

'No, no, with this salary, how is it possible to bring home a wife? I'm giving these exams, even a clerical job in the government is better or a sepoy in the Army – anything! In the villages and towns, everywhere nowadays, it is all about the money,' he says. 'You are a very smart lady. You are lucky your husband allows you to move about so much. In your community, it is rare.'

She sighs. No longer angry, she lets him speak.

'They talk about it in the market – look, look at Sultana, she has wisely caught her man. Anyone else and his love would have run dry the way she rides about on a bike, staying away from home so long!' He laughs, as if recounting an amusing anecdote. 'But you have no children, it has been a few years, no? From what we see, mostly in your community …'

She lets him talk on. No wonder he can't find himself a wife. Who will give their daughter to a balding man sniffing about in other people's marriages?

She is slowly recovering her spirit and about to set him straight when she spots it. He must have too, because he stops talking. In the distance, from the blue-black smudge of vegetation, an angry plume of smoke is rising into the sky. She strains her ears. Was there any sound, of people, gun shots? She tries to discern the distance; it couldn't be very far from where they are. So, the reports were right.

It should have propelled them into some kind of urgency: they could have turned back, or walked faster to their destination. But they do none of that; they simply walk on in silence, pace unchanged. The man stops chattering for some time, then whispers:

'I've heard the Muslims have guns now, that they can shoot from a distance, from behind a grove of trees or the top of a house.'

She feels contempt, this time at his profession. These accountants carrying on their trade from the comforts of an office, with a fan over their heads and lunch in a tiffin box, they don't notice the life that surrounds them. All they see is money and figures, not people. This one couldn't even tell a Bodo village from a Muslim one.

'These are all Bodo villages,' she says quietly, adding, 'on both sides of the road. For as far as the eye can see …'

She says this with some arrogance: she should know, she had spent the last five years walking through these villages every day. But why did she add the bit about how far they stretched. That isn't true. It is probably a

Muslim village from where the smoke rises. What if he interprets it as a threat, as an inference she is making about the ethnicity of the burning village? But her companion does not think so far, or hear so much. When she turns to him, wondering if she should clarify her statement, he is looking his cheerful self again, put at ease by the information that he was surrounded by Bodo villages on both sides of the road.

On her bike, she would have reached her mother's village by now. But it was safer to walk. She did not spell out the logic of her decision, it was quite simple: she was certain that when the people in these villages saw who she was, they would not do anything. *They will know it is Sultana.* Being Sultana is her only safeguard today. On a bike, they will notice the markers of her community: her salwar and dupatta, maybe a flash of her nose pin, her curly, unkempt hair tied up in a bun. There may be a mistake, they may not recognise her. But if they see her clearly, walking down the road, *if they know it is Sultana*, no harm will come to her. Of that she is certain.

They are nearing Bismuri. News must have reached; the shops will be shut and people making their way home.

They have to cross this market with care, Sultana thinks. Often in these situations, it is a throwaway remark, an abuse hurled by a crazy drunk or a young boy looking for some mischief that ignites the trouble. From where they stand, they can see the bridge over the small stream, before the turn towards the market. And they can see the people on the bridge.

It is a favoured spot for young boys going home on

their cycles, to catch a quick smoke, hang around and talk. On another day, she would not have given them a thought, but today, she hesitates.

Her companion notices them too. He stands still and peers at the figures. She is surprised to see him look nervous. Oh, she reassures him, in case he thought she was lying: 'They're not Muslim, I can tell. Come, let's keep walking.'

She can sense despite the distance that the men on the bridge have stopped doing whatever they were doing and turned to look at them, trying to figure out who these two people are, and where they are heading at dusk in such troubled times. Now, if Sultana and the man continue to stand there, they will look suspect, be taken for troublemakers planning some mischief. But her colleague won't move. She is tempted to prod him in the back.

'Keep walking. What are you worried about? They're from your community!' Her voice is terse.

'Yes, they look Bodo, but – how will we explain this – you walking to your village at this hour? They won't believe us! The villagers this side, I don't know anyone here. This will be trouble—'

She finally grips one handlebar of his cycle and forces it ahead. This fool, whatever will happen, does he not know that there is no turning back? What does he intend to do, get her to run through the rice fields, perhaps on his cycle, while he carries on, pretending to have nothing to do with her? He allows her to steer the cycle ahead. It would not do to be standing in the middle of this road, tugging at a cycle and squabbling.

They are moving closer to the bridge when she spots him. It couldn't be! All this fuss over nothing, because there standing on the bridge, armed with lathis and machetes, is a group of men and right in front stands Shambu! He was a friend of Sultana's, the auto driver who drove her around even on a bandh day, picked her team up from the railway station in the middle of Rajbongshi bandhs when cars were being burnt in the next alley. (In return, she would give him advice on his love life.)

She calls out to him, 'Aie, Shambu!'

Shambu spots her too, and is grinning and waving his stick at her.

Her companion goes pale and stares at her as if she has suddenly gone mad, turned into a dancing monkey or grown horns on her head.

She knows most of the men. They are from the village. They exchange pleasantries, the awkwardness dissipates a little with Sultana teasing the auto driver, 'Aie, I couldn't believe my eyes when I saw you! Total hero you look, standing with that bamboo in your hand, the river behind you. Take a photo on your mobile, he!'

They all laugh. You see, someone says, we have nothing against the villages around, or your people. It's the troublemakers one has to watch out for, the rumour mongers – those who will seize this chance to make mischief.

It is all politics, everybody, including her companion, agrees: misunderstandings between communities must be avoided, it is better to be alert, make sure no troublemaker enters the village, all precautions should be taken. Sultana nods, yes, you are doing a good thing, she assures them. This is going to be their night stake-out, from where they will keep watch, stand guard over their villages. The mosquitoes are already thick in the air, and Sultana wonders if she should ask them to get nets, one ought to be careful in this season of sickness. But she decides against it. It is better to leave quickly instead of standing around talking.

She can tell that one or two in the group are uncomfortable with the ease of their interactions, suspicious of her identity: is she an informant, will she let on about their defences? One man in particular has very pointedly turned away from their laughter, and now stands with his back to them, his hands on the bridge railing, looking towards the water. But within earshot, Sultana notes. She does not blame him; if he has doubts, it is only natural. And as the night stretches and the shadows get longer, the wild cries of the insects and the swaying bamboo, the mosquito bites and the fatigue will bring back these thoughts to their minds, *what if what if* … The nightly vigils will begin in every village along this road, for both communities. After a week, they will become like animals, living their nights out in the open, clutching at their weapons. Meanwhile, her co-traveller who was initially a little bewildered by this interaction is warming up.

'You see,' he lectures them, 'in times like these, if something were to happen to Sultana going through our villages, it would bring a bad name to our people. Of course, these women don't think of all this but …' and so on.

Sultana and Shambu exchange a glance, and she tries not to laugh out aloud.

Two of the men walk with them for some time, and then return to their posts. Sultana's village is not far now. The last of the light is dying away in the sky and the early fireflies hover between the road and the fields. All around them, the twilight chorus of insects is rising. She spots the old peepal tree by the roadside, its branches weaving over the road. From here, the Muslim villages begin. She has been so caught up in this and that, through the walk, that she has not asked the man where he was going, the name of his village.

So she turns to him, 'You are heading towards Amteka or Koila Moila?' These were villages further down the Ai river; some of the office people came from them.

He looks surprised. 'Amteka? Why would I go to Amteka?'

'So, which village are you from?'

'I live near the town, near Haorabari. You have to take a left turn from the main road.'

Sultana stops in her tracks and stares at him. 'Haorabari is far behind, on the opposite side. You came all this way?'

He looks puzzled. 'Yes, that's fine. I have my cycle. It will be much faster than walking. It won't take me long to reach home.'

'Yes, yes, but it's the other way, why did you come – here?' she stumbles, even though she knows the answer.

'I came to drop you. Why else?' He sounds a little irritated at having to explain this.

Sultana takes a deep breath. She had assumed his home was in this direction, which was why she had agreed to walk back with him.

She had accepted his company as one of those coincidences, chance companions of a walk home, and one she couldn't wait to get rid of. But she understands now what he has tried to do. She struggles to find a way to thank him for this gesture. Words get in their way, and god forbid, her gratitude should launch him into another tirade on the protection of women and their virtues.

Instead, she asks him to stop. 'From that tree, the Muslim villages start, you have to turn back.'

'It's fine. You'll protect me.' He laughs. 'It's getting dark. I'll go till your village.'

'Ha!' She joins in his laughter. 'But I will have to walk you back to this point again from my home, and we will be walking each other up and down this road all night.'

He likes the joke, and laughs delightedly. 'Yes, yes.'

'Okay, you should be safe now.' As he says this, he seems to puff himself up a little, stand a little straighter. He turns his cycle, settles himself on it and turns to her, 'How will you come to office tomorrow? Should I come to this point and get you?'

Sultana smiles, tries to think of something to say. 'I'll phone the office and inform you if I need help.'

Then he goes on, bobbing his head righteously, 'Lots of employees will use this violence to get a holiday from office, of course. And you didn't settle the bills today. I don't know why women work so slowly, thinking of other things, easily distracted, I always say ...'

She doesn't feel the usual rancour flooding through

her veins. Instead, there is a sudden urge to run alongside him, holding his cycle and letting it sail, like they would as children teaching each other to ride. It seems like a fitting goodbye.

Later, passing the long empty hours in the relief camp, Sultana would think about this silly man in her office; it made her smile.

The Stranger

When the thread snapped the second time, Urmila knew it was time to stop. The frantic rhythm of the loom gradually ebbed away, and though she finished the rest of the row with care, the harm had been done. She disentangled a dry leaf from her hair; was it the weather? Where was her mind today?

The dry winds of March had been relentless. All month, they had swept through the land, raising up dust and leaves and pollen till the trees stood skeletal, bare limbs glinting, leaves burnt gold and brown. The loom was set up

towards the back of the house, and though a small thatched roof protected it from the sun, there was no escape from the wind, which travelled from the river over the bare fields. This river would never leave them in peace, not when it was full during the rains, and not now. In the dry season, the Hel river transformed into a series of strangled streams, baring its miles and miles of sand and stone. The mining trucks had made it worse, dredging up the sand and scattering it, giving the wind its sharpened edge; she could taste it in the air. No respite, not a drop of rain in sight, the wind chasing away any stray cloud, leaving them in this season of emptiness. And Urmila's mind wouldn't stay on course, on the work of the moment.

It was not new to her, this restlessness – it came now and then. Especially during the rains, in the months and months of being inside, cooped up, boarded in, and the endlessness of it, drop after drop of rain till there was no night or day. It used to drive her crazy. To calm the beast, she had started inscribing her designs on paper. And through those long months too wet to set up a loom, she would sit with a sharpened pencil and fill the pages of her notebooks with designs. These books of hers took on a life of their own. They travelled from village to village, and were much coveted by the young women who sat at the loom not as a chore but with the yearning for a cloth that would make people gasp with its workmanship.

All her life, she has woven the cloth of her tribe, following the three-part division of colour for the kemlets, and the accepted pattern of the kambangs with the intricate centrepiece and supporting borders. But her inspirations came from everywhere: she could take a pahar agor, a hill motif, from an old scrap of dokhona and twist it with a double thread till even the Bodos would not be able to see it was their pattern, or disguise a horseman of the Karbis with cowrie shell designs, or adopt a stray parrot from mill cloth into the borders of her weaving. She would make them all her own, no one could tell that she had not been given these patterns by Rani Galo herself at the beginning of time.

When she worked with the traditional patterns, she favoured the intricate ones that demanded time and patience – the tiger's eye, the fish tail entwined with brinjal flowers, deer and fern, the elephant hunt; designs that were rare these days. Of late, though, her work was becoming simpler. The frightful, many-layered ornamentation and invention of her younger years turning on itself, recovering its core, revelling in negative space, in the simpler geometric forms of the old designs. She sometimes wondered if it was the gradual dimming of her eyesight that brought these newer patterns to her, like the sparse pickings of the late spring. In her younger days, spiteful neighbours would sometimes snigger at her elaborate weaves (even as they devoured the books and fingered her cloth, counting the threads to steal the patterns to make their own), and she would know what they were saying, what they were thinking, how they saw in them her life's excesses. But there was no undoing the past and her life's journey was what it was. And so, she sat on the loom and, gradually, with its rhythm beating into her body, the darkness and the oppression in her breast would leave her.

She had always wondered, at such moments, what did these others do after they gave up the loom, stopped their weaving? Was it having a family and children that dispelled this darkness in one's being? But when the husband goes drunk and the children turn out bad or die, how do they live then if they no longer weave? She thought back to the weavers from her youth, the younger ones she had taught in the villages of the east, some very talented ones; of all those girls, very few still made cloth. Does it dissipate your strength, all the childbearing and rearing, the nightly duties by your husband, keep you less able to sit at the loom?

From the corner of her eye, she could see the other two looms standing in her courtyard, each with the thread carefully set on the frame, waiting in mid-design for the weaver to return. They were a reminder of her tardiness, her neglect. Maybe it was time for her to stop. Her mind went back to the cloth she was working on. She peered closer, ran her hand through the taut wall of string, then to where the cloth was beginning to come to life, thinking with her fingers. The slight, small knot of thread that she encountered midway made her flinch. The knot was so minute you would not be able to tell when the cloth was unfurled all done, less so when it was worn. But this was not a consolation to her; the knot was a blemish, an error. And in the loom, an error could not be easily undone.

That was yesterday's knot and, today, she had broken another thread. It must be old age, she thought (though her hair was still dark, her face unlined, she knew that with women who do not marry or bear children, old age often comes unexpectedly). She imagined this was how an old woman would think – *so many broken threads, a spirit must be in the loom, bad news must be travelling* – and the thought of this made her smile. She would see to it tomorrow. But there she was again, peering at the thread, she could not leave it alone. Unable to keep from tugging at this and that, and causing further ruin, she resolutely stood up.

She would go to her brother's house. Her sister-in-law and the niece at home, none of them were interested in weaving. The loom in their house gathered mud and was sinking into the earth after the older daughter's marriage. There was no danger of her accidentally spotting a half-done weave somewhere and fussing over it. A cup of tea would be nice.

Indeed, she was not to be disappointed. The events at her brother's house quite took her mind away from her bad day at the loom.

They were all there, standing outside the kitchen talking, when she arrived. Not a regular conversation; possibly a disagreement or a minor quarrel – their faces still bearing the strain of their engagement when they looked towards her. Her brother called out, his voice cheerful, 'Look, Eli, your ati is here. Make us all a cup of tea, won't you? We'll ask her what she thinks of this.'

He sounded relieved for the interlude, she thought. He must be the culprit then, and he must have made up his mind already to do what the women were trying to dissuade him from. Urmila was right because the sister-in-law's frown stayed where it was, arched high into the lines of her forehead and drooping into the corners of her mouth. She moved away to the bench under the coconut trees and sat down: she had given up. The niece smiled, called out a greeting and went into the kitchen to make tea.

'It was the usual,' the sister-in-law said, 'grown up children and all, his teeth shaking—' they didn't look like they were to Urmila '—and so few hairs on his head, but once something comes into his mind, there is no stopping him. He is like a dog that cannot give up its taste for shit. Whiff of something and he'll be off to see what it is, poke his nose into matters that he should leave alone. And his family? His family will have to put up with whatever the new plan demands.'

Urmila listened to her patiently. She has been her sister now, for what, twenty-eight, thirty years? Yes, they could be sisters having lived in this village so long, sharing this and that. So, she waits till her sister-in-law is ready to tell her what the matter is. Her niece Eli serves tea. She is trying to hide her smile. The brother has meanwhile vanished into the house. Urmila meets Eli's eyes – what's the matter, she signals with a slight jerk of the chin. Despite the quarrel, there is an air of suppressed laughter about the situation, some merriment. Another of her brother's idiotic schemes. She knew that already, but what, what was it this time?

Eli sat close to her mother, patted her knee. 'Amai, baba has not had anything to do with this, it just came to him. He's curious. So am I. What's the harm in going to the town to see what it is all about? And he doesn't get excited about that many things these days. What does he do all day but work? He doesn't have many people to talk to here – it's not like the way it used to be earlier. Let him go.'

Her mother didn't say anything, sighed and looked at the ground. It was kind of Eli to give her mother this means of averting defeat, an honourable retreat. Urmila's brother adored his wife and would spar with her endlessly in his attempts to win her over. But win her over he would. Her sister-in-law did not have the conviction or stamina to match his passion for argument; they would be doing this day after day until she gave up. Eli was wise to save them all more trouble. The brother emerged from the house. He was wearing trousers now with a shirt, and a cloth bag flung over his shoulder. He was grinning as he pulled his cycle along. The sister-in-law in one last attempt to heft her side, called out to him to stop. *Wait, if you're going to go twenty kilometres to the town, you may as well get us some things we need*, and she rattled off, *salt biscuits, torch batteries and incense*. Her brother looked alarmed, said his goodbyes quickly and was off before the list got longer.

Urmila soon found out what it was about. She was not angered or amused by it like the mother and daughter but it was certainly very curious. The neighbour's boy came back from the town in the afternoon, stopped by their house looking for her brother, Eli's father, Someswor. He was cutting up some bamboo to fix the wall of the store room and he came out to talk to this fellow. The boy said he had been at the Serphanguri bus station when something strange happened. Having travelled back from Kokrajhar by bus, he had stopped by one of the shops when he saw this crowd outside Madonna Hair Saloon. They were gathered around this man who was sitting on the ground. Dark-skinned, thin, in trousers and shirt;

nobody knew how this man had got there, possibly on a bus. He didn't look like a mad man or a beggar, but he couldn't understand anything people were saying to him. He tried to say something, the others tried to say something back to him, nothing worked. They could not understand each other. Then the man took out a slip of paper from his pocket in which was written in English letters 'Someswor Rabha'. And below it was the name of their village, Soraidaka. Some people knew Someswor and they asked the boy to inform him. The boy was surprised to hear that not only was Someswor not expecting any guests, he also could not recall an acquaintance that fit the description of this man in the bus station. The boy left but the seed was sown in her brother's head. He had walked here and there, shared the story with his daughter and wife. Next thing you knew, he was making preparations to go to the Serphanguri bus stop to see this man, or at least the piece of paper with his name on it.

The wife added, 'I shouted at him, what will you make of that piece of paper? It was written in English letters, the boy said. You can't even read it. And he had the gall to ask if perhaps Eli could go with him then. Willing to drag his daughter to Serphanguri in the evening over this nonsense!'

She broke off but Urmila could tell that she had more to say.

'You know, he recalls the old days as good stories, a laugh sitting around the fire. He does not remember the fear, the sickness of it, the trouble he put us through. That day, I see him by the shops, sitting with Samsan and four, five other people. He is telling the story of when the boys came here during the Movement. And he's laughing, showing all his teeth, changing his voice, doing the sounds of boots, the guns, telling a good story. It made me so angry, I had to bite the edge of my kambang between my teeth, clutch my hands by my sides and walk away. It has become a story for the public now?'

She turned to Urmila. 'You remember those days. How these children grew up with all that going on around them? I sometimes think it was a good thing they were small, because it would have been much harder if they were older …'

Eli says softly, 'When was it – when the boys came for the evening meal?'

Urmila was not in the village those years, has her sister-in-law forgotten that? But she has heard the story before, Eli must have too. These long evenings with the same people; they all repeated stories, especially the stories of the Movement years. Urmila didn't mind hearing them again. But her sister-in-law must be upset if she was telling this one story. Her telling was in the same bitter vein.

'With the river in spate, the Army and the police did not come here very often, all of this,' she gestures with her hand, 'was shrubs and trees. The jungle stretched till the edge of the village. So the boys from the Movement, they came to our village, asked for a meal, a place to sleep. They weren't like the underground people you see now. They were fighting men then, decent men from good families …'

Yes, Urmila thought, that was like her sister-in-law. She

had a kind word for everyone; she could see good, that's why Urmila liked her. But this benevolence did not extend to her husband's faults. She caught herself and smiled, she was thinking like a sister now.

'They said their prayers, remembered Jesus before their meals. And after eating, they stayed a while and then disappeared, either into the village or the jungle, we did not know. We thought it better not to know. Because these men, they were not bad but their fight, it was not ours and they had guns – it could only mean trouble. But your father, he entreated them each time to come again; brought the best fish from the pond, killed a chicken, this and that, as if they were relatives of his come down from the moon. He spent hours talking to them, looking at their guns, listening to their stories. So, they came to our house more often because of your father, it became known … You don't know what it was like, that time … the Army would shoot villagers, drag them to jail, the police was worse, like beasts. They could take away anyone, and there was nothing we would have been able to do. I worried so much; running around with the children, the cooking and cleaning, then the worrying, all the worrying I had to do, what if what if … Without your father, with two small children, what would I do?'

Eli sighed. 'Oh, I wasn't there?'

'No. And your brothers were very small, one still at the breast, the other saying his first few words …'

These stories were not exact with facts, Urmila knew that, even though it had not been that long. But Eli, she could kill a story sometimes, this girl. She persevered,

'Michael was small, yes, but Rosong must have been nine, ten years old then?'

Her mother frowned. 'No, he was small. This one – oh,' she broke off, 'Urmila, did I tell you that Michael may come home soon?'

Oh, Urmila smiled. That boy, their younger son who went off to work in the South after causing so much trouble here. He was coming back?

'Will he be here for some time?'

'Oh, we don't know anything yet. The message came, a letter through this friend. Since then, we haven't been able to get through to his phone – network or battery, there is always some problem. The last three days, no one has taken the phone to charge in the town so …'

And she was off again, complaining about the electricity. 'All these fools, even the Bodos here, what have they gained from the agitation? The biggest fools in the land are in our area, cutting down their own electricity, and see now, to talk to my son I have to …'

It has been twenty years since the electricity went, Urmila thought. Listening to her sister-in-law, you would think it was yesterday they destroyed the transformers, carried them away. Eli has never seen electricity in her own village, and she is a young woman now, but the complaints continued, as if it was something new that they were becoming accustomed to.

Her sister-in-law did not finish the story.

Rosong, the eldest, was here, carrying vegetables and an armload of wild yam leaves for the pigs. Despite having moved to a new house, he stopped by often, did chores for them. Nobody had expected him to leave. He was always their ordinary son, not very quick with the thinking but reliable, good to have around the house. Their younger son, the one in the South, he had been their child of promise, the one they thought would help the family rise out of its precarious farm life. Life had, of course, not gone that way. Urmila would sometimes feel pity, perhaps a little shame too, when she saw Rosong toiling around the house, building this or that, hauling off a log or shearing the bamboo stalks. He was capable of such hard work. A feeling made worse by her knowledge that despite everything, like his father, she too, the aunt, loved the younger boy better.

Urmila mused, watching Rosong carefully sort out for his mother the fragrant limes, ferns and yam he had bought, that it was finally the wrong woman he had embraced out of compassion who helped him break away. People were surprised when he moved out of his parental home a few months after his marriage, but everyone accepted that it was for the better.

Rosong spoke to them for some time but did not inquire about his father. As he was leaving with a chicken trussed up, his mother mentioned the man in the bus stop and his father's going to the town. Rosong was not amused. He shared his mother's irritation. But now she played it down, laughed a little; it won't be anything, you go home now. Rosong, frowning, said he would come to see her tomorrow.

It was getting dark, so they started shelling the peas, cleaning the ferns for dinner. Most days, if Urmila came by in the afternoon, she stayed on to gossip till it was dark and often ate her meal with them. There was nobody else in her house today. Some days, a niece stayed with her, but she'd gone to visit family. Many of the younger people with jobs had rented accommodation in the town or, like her school-teacher nephew, were building their own houses there. Nobody wanted to live like this now. The ones who remained moved from house to house, visiting and gossiping through long evenings; there wasn't much else to do. It was the same in this house, one daughter and son married off, both living away, and one son working outside, just Eli at home until she married someone.

Dinner was almost cooked when Someswor returned. The man from the bus stop was with him. Urmila did not get a good look when they entered the courtyard; a frail, small man shuffling along with his eyes to the ground. The sister-in-law's mouth opened and shut like a big fish outside water. She was struggling to say or not say something. Urmila looked to leave their house as soon as she could. The men had their dinner in the front room in the light of an oil lamp. After they had finished, Urmila and the other two women ate in the kitchen in silence, the sister-in-law's anger was palpable and Urmila hurried off to wash the utensils. She would not wait for Eli to walk back with her today. As she turned the gate, she could hear her sister-in-law's voice rise, 'That man, if his head was not full of all this rubbish, he would have remembered to take the phone to the town and charge it. My son, what must he think, his mother and father do not want to hear his voice, even though he toils in such a faraway city? What if he is already on his way home …'

Urmila followed the sliver of moonlight on the road to make her way back home. The night sounds soon swallowed up the voices from her brother's house. But that Eli, why was she laughing?

*

Urmila had not had the time to think of the strange man in her brother's house for the next two days, there were a few pieces she had to have ready for a handloom exhibition in Goalpara. Only after finishing the last weave, washing her clothes and taking a long afternoon nap did she make her way to her brother's house. The man was there, and daylight confirmed her first impression of him as a slight, frail man with a downcast shape to his person. They were all sitting by the shade of the coconut trees at the back of the house, where the breeze was cool for this time of the day. The man, he sat on the grassy knoll that slid down into the rice fields behind the house. The rest of them – her brother, one neighbour and his handicapped son, another nephew – they sat on the bench, speaking in Kocha.

Seeing Urmila, her sister-in-law stepped out. Her mood seemed to have changed for the better, as Urmila had known it would. She was smiling, eager to relate the anecdotes of the last two days.

One or the other of the men on the bench would break off from their conversation and say something to the man in broken Hindi, and they would laugh. The man would look up to listen with some attention, but either he did not understand the language, or could not follow the villager's version of it. Urmila could have tried, she spoke Hindi well, having spent five years outside, but she was too shy.

Her sister-in-law gestured towards the men. 'These people – they have found something to keep themselves from work, so they're happy. He doesn't understand anything, so we have to make the signs with our hands, eat, sleep—' She made the gestures with her hand as she spoke and laughed. 'Funny man, we still don't know where he has come from and why, must be wrong in the head, I say.'

Their older son Rosong had come the next morning (as he had told his mother he would) and tried to speak to the stranger. He spoke some Hindi, but mostly made gestures and signs with his hands. The stranger responded in kind, muttering in some language and illustrating the sounds he made with the gestures of his hand. They learnt that he was on a train, and someone had robbed him of his bag and money, leaving him with nothing but the small polythene bag he carried with him. More than that, they did not know. It took a good while for them to learn even that. But Rosong was less suspicious of him after that, and promised to come back and talk to him again.

Everybody was mystified by the scrap of paper, with Someswor's name and village, in his possession. Was there someone on the train who knew Someswor and thought he could help this man? It seemed improbable but you never know with relatives, where they take your name, or who they cast around your neck.

Urmila went in to the kitchen where her sister-in-law was making another pot of tea. After they became

Christian, they no longer prepared the customary jokot in the house, though her brother got himself a drink now and then at the bazaar. Some extra milk had been kept aside for the day to accommodate the guests who were bound to stop by for a look at the stranger, but it had run out already. They brought out wooden stools and joined the men outside who had occupied the bench, sitting down to sip the red salty tea.

For the next few days, Urmila felt herself drawn to her brother's house after the morning chores were over. She tried to sit at the loom but with her mind wandering and restless, her hands lethargic, she became fearful of more mistakes and gave up. She would hurriedly leave the house, avoiding the three looms that stood around like neglected sentinels. Sometimes she thought it was the thread: she didn't like the thread in the market these days, the bright synthetic yarns that were available cheaply. Perhaps if her nephew Michael was coming from the South, she could ask him to get some cotton thread from Salem. A lot of the weavers from the cooperatives were using that now. It was a strong thread, stayed well on the loom, but did not weigh down the cloth. She had some experience of the different types of threads used outside in the time she had been away from the village, but for a long time she had put these thoughts aside. There was a comfort in the large reaches of the Hel river that kept their village away from the world.

Perhaps it has been long enough, her penitence. She had started to think of those bazaars in the city, the varieties of thread that had so thrilled her then. Michael, her younger nephew, the troublesome one, left because he could not be here anymore. His entanglements had become too dense for the family to keep protecting him. His older brother married the girl Michael had ruined and then refused to marry, but in doing so, Rosong had laid down a condition: the younger brother must leave home till he could show some good sense.

Michael was doing well in the city, sent home some money every other month, maybe some good would come of it and he would serve as a bridge to that outside world. If not for anything else, at least some new varieties of cotton thread for Urmila.

The stranger had been at Eli's home for a few days now. He drank every cup of tea they offered him and ate what was served, took a paan leaf sometimes. While the family performed their chores and went about their day, he would sit at his spot under the coconut trees, gazing at the fields. On this side, the forest was almost gone, except for an odd sal tree that rose into the sky. The stretches of land were mostly shrub vegetation or rough clumps of ahu grass that harboured small animals, rabbits and foxes. The vegetation then gave way to the banks of the Hel. During the rains, its waters would traverse the jungle at will. But in this season, the river was reduced to a tepid stream, revealing a vast underbelly of sand and rock. It still served as a barrier to the outside world, though; there was no bridge, no road for bigger vehicles. You had to walk or ride on a cycle or a bike through the miles of sand and shrub, cross several small streams to reach the highway that connected their village to the block centre.

Meanwhile, people continued to come to see the stranger. In the afternoon, sometimes in the mornings too, they would come in ones and twos, sometimes a bigger group, sit on the bench or the ground, to look at the stranger or 'speak' to him. Men, women, the younger people (mostly Eli's friends), everyone came to marvel at the stranger and his appearance at their house, partake of tamul if not tea, and then gossip about the usual things, quite forgetting the reason for their visit, the original object of their interest.

Was it possible, Urmila wondered as she washed the betelnut leaves for the visitors, that this season of the udang botor, the bare climate, was as unsettling for these other people as it was for her. The winter was long gone, the trees bare, their dry leaves caught in your hair and clothes, covering the roads, the fields, the yard. The long wait for the farming cycle has begun – for the rain to start and for it to stop, for the sowing and the ploughing, the sickness and the overflowing rivers, then the clear skies of the harvest. Nobody knows what will come. The dry, dusty wind holding these restless days together, this is when the young people will make their plans to leave. They will look around and see these fields under the sun, see a year of labour stretching ahead with uncertain gains, and they will decide to get on to a train moving westwards, or run off with an unworthy girl or boy. Is it this season of uncertainty and waiting that pulls these villagers to her brother's home to see the stranger? What auguries do they await, what hope do they cling to for this year to be different, perhaps an unexpected plenitude or a chance to undo the mistakes of the past, avoid the vagaries of the future? Or then, sitting in the shade, with the wind broken by the bulk of a tree, meeting someone or the other from the village, it is simply a way of passing another afternoon.

It may have carried on this way, if it wasn't for the incident. The evening before, Urmila had already sensed a shifting of the mood, a nervous tension in the air. Passing by the house, just before dusk, she had seen her sister-in-law by the gate with the phone to her ear. She looked distressed, near tears. When Urmila asked her what the matter was, she said that Eli had finally charged the phone on her way to college but she could not get through to her son's number. She had tried all over, walking up and down, in the places they usually got reception, where the phone caught the waves, but it wouldn't go through. Urmila made her look at the number again, both the women peering into the screen. Yes, that was right. They tried to call and got the voice that spoke in some language, then in English, but it wouldn't ring. Urmila suggested gently, try a little later, but her sister-in-law clutched the phone with tears in her eyes, her body shaking and ran back into the house. *This weather*, Urmila thought, *unhinging us all*. Her sister-in-law's reaction alarmed her; she hoped this distress would not set off the pains that periodically wracked her body.

The next morning, it broke. Urmila was by the jackfruit trees trying to dislodge one with a bamboo stick for a curry, when she heard the raised voices coming from her brother's house, then the wailing. As she neared the house, though, she slowed down her steps. It was hard to tell when to interrupt a fight and step in for calm and when not to. But her feet had carried her there, so she went in. If they didn't want interference, they shouldn't shout so. (Later Eli would tell her how grateful she was that Urmila arrived when she did.)

Her brother stood in one corner of the courtyard, bare chested, his face bathed in sweat or tears she couldn't tell; he was pleading with his wife to stop. The sister-in-law was by the well, where they washed the dishes, beating a wet twisted sheet of cloth on the stone. She looked quite mad. Her hair was undone, she had no blouse, just the kemlet tied high across her breasts. She was shrieking wildly, the force of her exertions throwing her against the wall of the well, and the wet cloth flying back, twisting around her body. What on earth had possessed this woman? Eli stood at an arm's length, trying to speak to her with a commanding air, *Amai, stop, stop this madness*, then again in a softer, calm, low voice. But the woman seemed to not hear a word. Finally, Urmila sent her brother away from the courtyard, *go, go, we'll look after her*, and her sister-in-law, exhausted, collapsed. She and Eli took her in, changed her wet clothes and let her sleep.

In the quiet after, Urmila prepared some tea and handed Eli a cup. They were making their way to the bench outside when Eli gripped her wrist and directed her away from there. *The man.* Urmila had not noticed him but he was still sitting by the grass under the coconut trees. They went into a room instead.

Eli's hands were shaking, Urmila was puzzled too. 'Was

it a big fight? Did he hit her? God, what was your mother trying to do, pounding the cloth like a washerwoman from hell?'

Eli told her what had taken place that morning. Her mother had been upset because she couldn't get through to her younger son on the phone. Seeing anyone pick up the phone would make her angry, she needed to keep the battery till the evening, she said. Her anger then found a target – the stranger and her husband's decision to keep him there. She started to needle him with it, *Your guest, look at the amount of rice he eats, he is dirty, does not bathe, look at his hair*, and so on. She didn't mind the people dropping by during the day on his account; on the contrary, she had started to enjoy this festive air around the house. But now she wanted him to leave. Her husband did not pay it much attention. He hoped she would be able to speak to her son in the city soon, it would settle her. Then her mother discovered that the stranger had urinated in his sleep, soiling the mat and sheets. Eli and her father were sitting in the courtyard; Eli was trying to read, while he fiddled with the radio. Her mother came out and stood there dragging the sheets behind her, berating her father, *Throw him out, what a dirty man*, and so on. They tried to reason with her, throw away the sheet, put the mat in the sun, let him sleep on it or clean it if he wants, you let it be. This made her mother angrier, her voice growing louder, till she was screaming, *Throw him out now, not a son in the house. He chased them both away but invites strangers – this filthy man – in.* This is when Eli became unsure of what happened next.

She was already alarmed and exasperated with both the father and the mother. Her father was mostly quiet but surely, she thought, he could have told her mother, fine, we'll send him away, and wait for things to settle down. Then something his wife said touched him, maybe her saying he drove away his own sons, he said something that seemed inexplicable to Eli. He laughed and said, with a sneer, why this care for his body being bathed, the stink of his bed clothes, do you think you have to share the bed of your guests?

Eli's cheeks were red as she narrated this to her aunt. Something like this, she wasn't sure what the exact words were; this was it more or less. With that, her mother had started screaming uncontrollably (that is what Urmila had heard) and rushed to the well. Her husband must have thought she would jump in, so he ran after her. But she stopped and instead swung the sheet first at him, then at the well and the water – and then Urmila had arrived.

Urmila was looking down at her hands, frowning. Her niece expected her to say something, explain the madness of this morning. It made her nervous. Just then, they heard her sister-in-law calling out from the other room. Urmila was relieved. 'Oh, she must be thirsty, your mother, after all the excitement.' But she had made up her mind on another matter, she would have to speak to her brother today.

They fetched some water for the mother. Eli sat on the bed, gently running her hands over her mother's forehead; a headache was coming on.

She wouldn't get up for the next two days, the pains once they came, made their home in her body for days.

After a few sips of water, the sister-in-law turned to Urmila. 'Don't tell Rosong about what happened. I want the boy to have some peace, live his life. I don't want to bring back the old anger ...'

Urmila nodded in understanding. 'Don't worry about these things. You get some rest. We're not telling anyone anything.'

When they stepped out of the room, Eli looked at her aunt expectantly. 'What did she mean the old anger? Why shouldn't we tell Rosong? He should know.'

Urmila tossed aside her question, smiling. 'Oh, you know how things are. As it is, Rosong and your father are not on the best terms, what good will it do, talking about it all over the place, better to keep it quiet.'

Eli gave her aunt a look. But Urmila had had enough of all of them. She was not going to let herself be caught up in any more trouble this morning. What is with people? Why can't they let the past be? And the two old fools, bringing these things up now. 'Call me when your baba comes back home, I have to talk to him.'

Eli didn't reply.

When Urmila's brother did come back, late in the evening, having spent the day drinking in the bazaar, Urmila knew that it was not the best time to speak to him. But she decided to do so. He was smiling, having transcended the morning's ugliness with the brew in his veins. She told him that it was time to let this stranger go: send him to Guwahati or put him on a train, it was not their business looking after him. She feared it would create trouble for the family, as it did today, what with the sister-in-law being so frail these days.

The smile did not go, his good cheer remained. He nodded, acknowledging her concern. 'Yes, yes, we will send him away soon, why are you all worried? But there is one thing,' he whispered, 'I need to know ... I need to know what brought him here to my home. How did that piece of paper with my name on it come into his hand? You saw it – it was there, my name ...'

*

The next morning, Urmila's sleep broke early. It was not yet day, the air filled with the clamour of birds impatient for light, the shadows still grey, indistinct. She swept the courtyard, prepared something to eat. By then, the light was in the sky and the stray sounds of the morning had fallen into a familiar routine: cows being taken out to the field, the clanking metal sound of a bucket being let down into a well somewhere in the distance, children's cries. Urmila sat at the loom and let the sound of her labour enter into a rhythm with the morning. She suddenly missed the old days, her sisters, the time when the three looms would echo in the courtyard and, rising above the sounds, would be their laughter, snatches of song and gossip. Her mother herself had never moved to the taat, weaving on her back loom, the kontong, her whole life. Urmila wondered where her mother's kontong was these days. Somewhere in the cowshed?

Seeing her sister-in-law lying in bed yesterday, her voice rasping, face blanched and strained by pain, the impression of her thin body under the sheet like that of a child's, it reminded Urmila of when she saw her sister-in-law after her return to the village. When she had left home, she had told no one, only writing a letter after she reached Guwahati. But she had passed her brother's house on her way to the bus stand. (They had planned it well. She had already passed on a small bag with her belongings to her lover, the cloth trader from Ludhiana, earlier in the week.) She had walked through the village as if it was any other day, and passing by her brother's house, stopped to speak to her sister-in-law who was carrying the second boy in her belly then. She stood there radiant, her body filled up, laughing.

And look at her sister-in-law now; she seemed to have forgotten Urmila's missing years. How could it be? But that morning of her departure, Urmila remembered the image clearly, her sister-in-law leaning against the gate, her first son running around, the second already making her heavy, exhibiting her fullness to the world (also because it was an image that would haunt her the next few years till her return, this image of plenitude against her own inability to conceive, but Urmila swiftly put those thoughts away).

But no, she is getting them mixed up, because seeing her sister-in-law yesterday, it was the other figure, the one that greeted her on her return five years later, that came to mind. Heavy with child again (this time it was Eli), she looked very different, a hollowed-out impression of the woman she had been. Her stomach stuck out, but her cheeks and eyes were dug in like shadows, her thin legs and hands helpless appendages to her swollen belly. They couldn't bear to see her dragging herself around. Her husband was relieved when she took to her bed. Urmila would go and sit by her, having nothing much else to do. She wouldn't go back to the loom for a whole year. The five years, of which neither spoke much, and different as they were in their individual experiences, had turned them into sisters. That was also when her brother had built the bench under the coconut tree, so that his wife even on a still day could catch whatever invisible breeze shook the leaves.

Urmila's thoughts broke; someone was calling out to her.

'Ati, you're weaving?' Eli called out, as she pulled aside the bamboo pole of the gate to step in.

'You're here early. Good, it was time for me to have a cup too.' Urmila smiled, the girl seemed to have walked straight out of the swollen belly of her thoughts and into life. She felt a sudden joy, looking at Eli walking in, pulling up a plastic chair and making herself at home. They had done quite well by her, this young woman. Urmila finished the row, carefully replaced the stick, and stood up.

Eli had come to talk. 'My home is a mad house sometimes! I'm going to come and live with you here, ati. They can bring their daughter-in-law to help them. It's quieter today but yesterday, I was so—'

'How is your amai feeling?'

'Fine. She slept well. She washed in the morning, took her tea. The pain is less. She's sitting out. I thought I would go to college today but, with all this, I felt exhausted. I wanted to ask you something.'

'Eli, wait – I've been at the loom for a long time, let me stretch my limbs and make a cup of tea. After that you tell me.'

'What tea, I think we should get some jokot! After sister married, she never comes to see us, find out how things are, and I don't like to involve Rosong. He seems to have some peace now, so there's only you …'

With a cup of tea, Eli was smiling again. (But the jokot was a good idea, she thought, must get some from the neighbour, maybe this evening.) Urmila tried to talk of this and that, get Eli's mind away from whatever she had come to ask.

But her niece was not one to let go so easily. 'Ati, tell me what happened when the Army came. Mother's stories are always so muddled these days. I have never heard the whole story. And last evening, when the pain was making her head spin, mother kept mumbling about the Army, the underground boys, her two sons. Then it was something about some Sibu's mother, she was suffering for what they did to Sibu's mother. She said it so many times. I wrote down the name so I wouldn't forget. Who is Sibu – Sibu's mother? I don't know anybody in the village called Sibu …'

Ah, Sibu, Urmila tried to put it off. 'I wasn't around then. You know that.' She wondered if Eli was as curious about her story. Eli knew about it, everybody did. But would she come to ask her one day? Perhaps not. Other people tell your stories better.

Eli had expected some resistance on her aunt's part, and come prepared. 'Yes, but you know what happened even if you weren't there. If you don't tell me, it's fine. I'll go ask someone else – Baran's mother or the tea-shop woman. I would rather hear it from you, though.'

'Enough. Wait. Let me try and recall …'

'And I'm not a child, please tell me what you know … mother would have told you.'

No, Urmila thought, you have the right to hear the story, but the story that everyone else knows, not the one your mother told me.

Beginning at the beginning, from before things went bad, Urmila smiled.

'Sibu. I haven't heard his name in so long. He was, what, twelve-thirteen years old when he first came here. I remember him from then. He was from the Santhali villages. I forget, Rehabari or Siyalmari, one of those. After his father died, he started to go from village to village to find work for the day. Soon, he was a familiar face, and with every year, he was growing stronger, and he could work, that boy – cutting jungle, chopping wood, driving the cart full of grain, toiling on the potato fields. He was like Rosong, the kind of youngster who could do two people's work. He was fluent in Kocha and Bodo, and had started working regularly in our village. When your mother was with child for the second time, your father moved the house from the other end of the village to where it is now. He decided he needed some help; he was digging a pond to fill with fish, planting betelnut trees for the market, and there was the work in the fields and putting up a roof in the new house. He was full of energy then, your father, and he wanted to do so many things. Our people would laugh. Your father saw Sibu's strength; he was a good worker and had helped Someswar often, so he promised Sibu grain from the fields, fish from the pond, bananas and betelnut – a portion of whatever the earth would yield to your father's hand, in return for Sibu's labour. And Sibu was still a boy, maybe fourteen or fifteen then, so he would also look after your older brother, play with him, sometimes cook a meal if your mother was sick. He became a part of the family.

'It was a big help to your mother. You could see them coming back together from the market, your mother walking slowly, with Rosong in Sibu's arms. It had been six years since your older brother was born; there had been one or two problems in the middle, so your father wanted her to be careful, not work too much. They were good with each other then, all this bitterness came with time. We, unmarried ones, would be jealous of them!' Urmila laughed. 'Men here, they didn't care so much about their wives. As it is, it had been so many years since the first child.

'Then, I was gone. Maybe I have brightened the colours a little, because that is what I took away with me. I thought I would never see this village, my family again—'

Eli interrupted, 'That was when you left, ati? How long did you go away for? You didn't tell anyone when you left?'

'You know all that. Your mother must have told you. In every house with a young daughter, they narrate my story! No, listen, I'll tell you that one later.

'By the time I returned, the world had changed. So much had happened: the Santhali villages were gone, the electricity had been cut off, the roads dug up, bridges broken.

'I was in despair, in shame. I had imagined the fields ripened, the trees, the river – everything that I had hungered for – all green and beautiful the way I had left it, and I thought I would stand out in my sin against this perfect world. But when I returned, there was nobody to mourn or ridicule me and my fate. Everybody was trying hard to cope, to get by: fleeing their house to take shelter by the riverside, in the jungle; keeping the men hidden under straw in the cow shed; standing guard all night with villages on fire in the horizon. We were like animals, terrified of everything. Nobody gave my elopement a second thought.

'When I left, the Army had not yet moved into this area. Even though we knew about the Movement and we had heard of things being bad, our village had not been affected. But on my return, things had changed. Beyond our village was the jungle. Not like what you see now. Then, the animals came right till … but you know all that—'

Eli laughed. 'Yes, the jungle!'

'The boys would come out of the forest at night, visit the nearby villages, eat a meal, sometimes leave money. They would be somebody's relative, a man who was married to a woman from your husoong, an acquaintance, often they were more like guests. Our boys had joined in some places, or married their women.

'Also, they had guns, they were powerful. You could not say no, so you prepared a meal, maybe they slept in the courtyard, then they were gone. And then it would be the Army's turn, they would come into the village. They did not care that the Rabhas were not part of the Movement – we looked the same to them, we were all suspects. People were scared, but you could not turn away the guests from the jungle. That is when things turned bad. And that's what happened to your family. One evening, after dark, the CRP surrounded the house. Inside, they could hear the sound of boots, of people moving around, commands in the darkness. The door was kicked in and these big men, tall, with guns, entered. Your mother locked herself in a room with your two brothers. Michael was a baby. She had pushed cloth into his mouth to stop his screaming, all three of them crouched under the bed, hiding. They came into the house, went from room to room, turning things upside down, beating up your father. They were looking for the militants but there was no one. Then they stood outside the room your mother was in, their guns ready. Your father later told me he had to beg them to let him speak to his wife, ask her to come out. He was so scared they would shoot. If there are children in the room, why weren't they crying, the men asked him. Because they were too scared to cry, he begged and begged. Finally, they let him speak to her, pushed him in front of the door with their guns prodding his back when the door opened slowly, and your mother and the children crawled out from under the bed. They beat your father, and then took him away. They didn't find anybody, but in the kitchen fish was being cooked. Two big rohus from the river, vegetables and potatoes, chicken smoked over a fire, freshly brewed jokot; enough for a feast. How much fish do you cook for a meal? How much does your wife eat? They took him away.

'You see, the CRP had got the right information. The boys, they were to come that evening. Because of their friendship with your father, they had sent word so he could get some fish from the river. Two of them had fled through the window of the room your mother was in. The others had not arrived. It was a fortunate thing the CRP took your father away. Or else, he would be a suspect too. Two of the militants had been caught outside the village; there would be a price to pay. Someone had told the police, given details, right down to the day and time, and identified the house.

'Around that time, the Bodos and the Santhalis had started to fight. It was beginning here and there. Nothing had happened in our area yet. We were in the middle, with the Bodo villages to the east, the Sathalis to the west. Sibu came from one of these villages. After this incident, everybody in the village started to say it was Sibu who informed the police. The people were angry; the police had taken away five young men from our community in the raid that night. The rumours began: that Army and police jeeps had been seen around the Santhali villages, hiring informers, giving money, *it had to be Sibu.* Your mother was so worried about getting her husband out, she did not think of Sibu, did not send out a warning to him. Maybe she suspected him too, I don't know. They say he tried to come home once, to speak to your mother, but someone noticed him and chased him off. He did not return to our village but he should have run away, gone further.

A day before the attacks on the Santhali villages, Sibu's body was found on the crossroads, between the villages. It was a warning, everyone agreed, but nobody could say for certain who killed him – if it was the militants who suspected him of being an informer or his own people, for his contact with the Rabha and Bodo villagers. But he was dead, and the next day, the violence began, the Bodos attacked the Santhali villages. Attacks and counter-attacks followed. The Santhali villages were torched and they left for the camps in Patgaon; our village people fled to the camps in Serphanguri. Your father joined the family there after a week. It was years later, after my return, that your mother started to think of Sibu's mother. Sibu's mother was blind, he supported her. Once or twice, your mother tried to get people to look for Sibu's mother but she didn't get very far. How to begin, where to go, after all these years …'

Eli spoke quietly, unravelling the story in her mind. 'Did they find out who told the police? Rosong was six or seven years old then, he must remember something. Is mother still angry about this? But I don't understand why she would be angry with father—'

Just then, there was another voice by the gate. It was the neighbour's daughter. Eli's father had sent word, asking her to come home. 'They have guests and need help in the kitchen.'

Eli looked irritated. But she had resigned herself to the duties of a daughter, she would go. Before leaving, she placed her hand on her aunt's arm and squeezed it. 'You're the only sane person here. I'm going to come live with you, you'll see!'

And they both laughed. This has been Eli's refrain to her ati for years now, whenever things were difficult at home, she tells her aunt she is coming to live with her. She never has.

Urmila suddenly remembered. 'Is your brother Michael coming home soon? Your mother had mentioned something.'

'Oh no, no news from him. You know how he is – we won't know till he takes the train and gets off at the station here. And then, from the station to the village will be another matter!' She laughed, then turned serious. 'But I'm glad he is not coming home now, we have enough on our hands as it is, and Michael is always trouble.'

With that, Eli turned by the gate and was gone.

*

Urmila had expected Eli to come by her house the next day. She sat at the loom for a good part of the morning to finish a kambang that she had promised a neighbour would be ready in a week. On good days, the work was almost mechanical, the pattern of the cloth a melody embedded in the movements of her hands and feet, it required no effort, no thought; like walking or singing. But as the day wore on, her mind flitted here and there: why did Eli not find the time to come by, were they sending away that strange man, would her brother permit it? He wouldn't be able to stand it, never knowing how that man came by his name. God, the stories he would make of it.

The afternoon saw Urmila make her way to her brother's house. But something was the matter. What were all these people doing outside the house? As she went closer, she saw there were more people inside – some around the bench by the coconut trees, others squatting on their haunches in the courtyard speaking quietly. It was like a village meeting or a house of death, except, she quickly marked, there were no expressions of grief. Then she spotted Eli with an empty tray, having left a fresh supply of paan on the table. (What a relief. The other possible event would have, of course, been an elopement, but Eli was a sensible girl, she rebuked herself.) Eli met her eyes and indicated the kitchen with her hand. Urmila followed her there. Eli giggled at her ati's puzzled expression. 'Oh, you're wondering what has happened: they're here to see if some precious redwood is growing in their back yard. And if so, the stranger will make them rich overnight!' She broke off into more laughter.

Redwood? The stranger? Who was becoming rich and why, Urmila wanted to know. Had they all lost their mind?

She pulled out a stool and sat on it. 'Stop, stop! I haven't understood anything of what you are telling me, or what is happening outside. Tell me clearly, without any jokes, please.'

This is what Eli told her: after all the trouble, her father too had come around to the opinion that perhaps it was time for this man to go. He'd give him some money, take him to the train station and let him go where he wanted to. The stranger seemed to be of sound mind. From the train station, he could continue his journey to where he had come from, or where he was going. Eli had not paid all of this much attention. But the next morning, the people – these people had started to stream into the house.

'Rosong told me that he and a few others had come back from the market with some fried eggplant wrapped in a newspaper. They were sitting there on the bench by the coconut tree, and they gave the man some, passing it to him in the newspaper wrapping. The stranger ate the food, then straightened the greasy paper and looked at it for a while, as if reading. Then he stood up, came to them and, with signs and hand signals, he told them why he was here.'

'What – just like that? What did he tell them?'

Eli nodded. 'He told them he was a businessman. He had come here to look for the wood that they write about in the paper. It was an English newspaper, and there was a photo of logs of wood that had been caught by the police. It was this wood that he had come in search of. The trees were found in these jungles and nobody knew of their value here. If they could find this tree, his company would give a lot of money, start a big business here.'

'He said all this with his hands, without any language? And your brother understood him?' Urmila was surprised. Would it be so simple in the end?

'Rosong believes it. He was the one who told me the story. The news got around, and now everyone is looking for this wood.'

'What kind of wood? From the forests?

'Yes. Wood, the bark of the tree, I think. People weren't sure, so yesterday, they came carrying with them bits and pieces of leaves, bark and saplings, seeds, twigs, wood, vines, flowers – everything, ati! The village woke up, looked around the lord's world, and any plant that they took to be suitably impressive, close to the smell or taste or texture of heaven, they struck down, wrenched from the ground, and brought it here.' Eli was clearly enjoying this new turn of events.

'Like sandalwood? For oil?'

'Oh, Rosong says it has many, many uses. Its oil can be

used for aches and pain, for cancer and for when children do not grow. Its wood is in demand for making tables and chairs in cities, and precious statues. People pay a lot of money for it. That's why those people were caught. They were trying to send the wood to Burma, then China, where the money will be big. The man saw the paper and knew that this wood, it was here. Now they are all trying to find it.'

'And he can tell, the stranger, from just looking at it, that it is the redwood?

'The man, he knows. The company taught him so he could see for himself if the wood is real. He does a test, and he does this test only when someone brings bark or wood. No more ferns or leaves or vines. He has a small fire lit there, by the coconut tree, and he puts the piece of wood in. Then he waits for it to burn and release its smell. He can tell from the colour of the smoke and the smell whether it is redwood or not.'

Eli sighed and rolled her eyes, 'The man has been busy doing this since yesterday. People are coming all the time. Couldn't that Rosong keep it to himself? If this wood is here, fine, or else all these people making the courtyard dirty and drinking our tea and chewing paan, all for nothing.'

'This wood has not been found yet?'

'No, no. But he has become somebody special. People are bringing food, fruits and vegetables for him. If he pees in his sleep again, there will be plenty of people to clean the sheets!' She laughs.

'And your mother? She knows about this?' Urmila whispered, glancing at the door, in case her sister-in-law suddenly appears.

'Yes, Rosong spoke to her. Told her something about how it will bring money to the family, asked her to have patience. He offered to have his wife come and help in the house, in case it was too much work for us.'

'He did?'

'But now it's father. He is not happy with all this. He doesn't say anything but he has that look about him. He can't object, because Rosong has spoken to mother, and you know how it is, Rosong will insist father is creating trouble just to spite him. But something is bothering baba ...'

'What about you, Eli? Do you believe this man? Do you think the redwood could be something precious, worth money? These things have happened before. A fern or a tree has properties for making medicine, and people can make money but—'

Eli frowned. 'I don't know. But he can't be telling the truth, can he? And that too just when we were going to send him away. When we were younger, Rosong was a good brother. But he never had any ideas of his own, he did what the rest of us wanted, even though he was older. Now, it's strange, he only listens to his own mind.'

Yes, Urmila understood what Eli meant. Rosong had changed so much in the last few years.

And then Eli hissed, 'You have to tell me the rest of the other story, ati. I haven't forgotten.'

'What story, Eli? I finished it.'

Urmila wonders if she should ask her sister-in-law if they have heard from Michael, if he is coming home soon, then decides against it. It will upset her sister-in-law if her son has not been in touch. And Michael was like that. He would simply show up one day, as he did the last time. She smiled, imagining Michael's reaction to what was happening here at home. He was trouble, yes, but he could make them all laugh like nobody else could. And they needed some laughter, this lot.

*

The next day, Urmila was surprised to see them at her gate, Eli and her mother. When her sister-in-law had an attack of her pains, she often stayed in bed for days. But she looked better, and they were both smiling, arms linked, coming for a visit after the morning's work. The stream of redwood-bearing visitors had dwindled, so they thought they would come out and see her.

Urmila was weaving a kambang for her sister-in-law. She had specified the colours and spent time with Urmila deciding on the design, so they talked about that first. It was stretched out on one of the three looms in the courtyard. Her sister-in-law admired the border of the central design, and this pleased Urmila. She had added a few flowers from a Mising pattern. When Urmila entwined the deer-nose motif with the Mising flowers, it was such a small thing, she wasn't certain it would be noticed. But her sister-in-law was bent over the fabric on the loom, running her hands over it, the beauty of it filling her up, making her smile.

Eli, though, was impervious to the nuances of design and colour, despite all of Urmila's attempts at instructing her since childhood. It was a good thing she studied well at school; she would never make a halfway decent weaver.

After talking about this and that for some time, her sister-in-law started on the subject of her husband. She was half laughing, but her voice had an edge of bitterness. Urmila had imagined that the troubles of a few days ago had passed; but it was as if the couple's relationship was becoming increasingly abrasive, any contact seemed to make the other bristle. Has this bitterness come to stay, Urmila wondered.

'My old man, all this while he keeps this stranger, this filthy man in our house, and there is nothing to worry. But now his son says, mother, I want to go look for this wood, it will change our lives. And my son, why does he want to do so? He thinks that with this wood, if there is any money in it, he will take me to the hospital in the city for my pains, for the sickness, so his mother may live better in her old age. That's my son—'

Eli mumbles. 'You're not old, amai …'

But her sister-in-law barely hears it, continues to talk, her bile rising. 'The old man is now looking all worried, sleepless his nights have become, he says. And why? Because he harbours a great secret. He has finally found out what his guest has come here for, to our house, to this village. No, no, not to deliver redwood and fortune to us, no. His older son thinks so, and how can he agree with anyone in his own family, particularly his older son? You see how this old man thinks, about his own children that too …'

Eli and Urmila do not speak. They let her finish.

'So he comes up with this story. Turning our lives into

stories for the tea shop, he has lost his mind. He says, his friends … they took this man away to drink one evening, to loosen his tongue, see if he could speak some language in his drunkenness, give out some secret. Because they had started to say in the village, maybe he was an informer from the police, acting mad to see what is happening here and to report back. This redwood thing he did to stay here longer when he thought he would be sent away.'

She laughs. 'So, they give him jotok and he drinks, the others drink too. I told the old man, maybe these friends of yours drank more than him, maybe they saw more stars than him. Because they say, he told them the reason he has come here, his mouth loosened by alcohol. He has come here to die.'

Urmila started in surprise. This reaction pleased her sister-in-law. 'Yes, I wanted to ask him why, after all these years, why are you behaving like a thief? Making up stories to tell your family. Who comes to a village he has never seen before, no language nothing, then eats rice like an elephant every day, and then, you say he has come to die! He's lying, my old man is, or he has lost his mind.'

Eli sighed. 'I knew baba had something on his mind the last few days.'

They sat quietly for some time. The sister-in-law's health and cheer dissipated. She looked exhausted, her shoulders beginning to droop.

Eli cleared her throat. 'There is something else. I didn't tell anyone. One evening, when that man went walking with a neighbour, I – I looked into his polythene bag … the one he came with. There was a small knife there.'

Urmila tried to stay calm. 'What kind of knife? And what else was there?'

'A packet with some paper, scissors, a comb. And a knife without a handle, but I felt the blade, it was a knife.'

Urmila thought for a while, then it struck her. 'He must be a barber! They sound like the tools of a man who shaves, cuts other people's hair, doesn't it?'

Eli frowned, then laughed. 'Yes! There were a few small bottles of scented water and oil. So he's a barber not a killer! What a relief! Better he has come to die than kill.'

Oof! Urmila swatted at Eli's hands. This girl, she was impossible sometimes.

There was more news. Rosong had gone off to the forests of Bhutan with another young man. They were certain they would find the redwood there.

On hearing this, Urmila instinctively thought, the poor boy, he doesn't have much time; he better find this redwood before the younger brother came home from the city. Because Michael would always outstrip his brother. He would either mock Rosong's falling for this lie or come up with a grander scheme, either of which would be difficult to swallow.

Once again, Urmila did not ask her sister-in-law if she had heard from Michael, if he was coming home soon. It did not seem the right time. If there had been a phone call, she would have announced it by now. When Urmila saw them at the gate today, smiling, her first thought had been of Michael, maybe they had heard from him.

After seeing them off, Urmila went back to the loom, where she hoped to retrieve the rhythm of the morning.

But looking at the mesh of thread, she felt herself drawn, instead, into the tangling and untangling of her whole world. She finally gave up, and went in to get herself a cup of jotok. Good thing she had bought some the other day. Everything seemed to be beyond her understanding.

*

While many significant and insignificant events took place in the next few days, Urmila ignored them and kept to her loom. She sat for hours, the way she had done when she was younger, before the eye strain and the neck strain, the boredom, set in. She conjured up cascading brinjal flowers looped in gold, threaded in the birds she had so liked in the Karbi cloth, except they were tiny, so minuscule, they could be the birds come for the tiny stitches of the threshed grain running across the neat borders. The kemlet for the neighbour was done, but it had been woven with so much care, she wondered if she should keep it aside for Eli's trousseau. She could make another one for the neighbour. When she got off the loom, it was a few days later. Her neck and shoulders were on fire but she felt somewhat rested, and curious once again about how the world moved. Maybe the curse had been lifted.

She found herself on the way to her brother's house.

There was still no rain but the wind had spent its force, leaving behind a lazy breeze that rustled the leaves half-heartedly. Urmila looked up at the sky: was there a storm in the air? No, not tonight – the sky was clear. A downpour would have settled the dust on the roads and the leaves, brought some respite. But the rain at this time of the year had a mind of its own. And when it comes, it will be the petty squalls that will not water the world so much as wreak havoc, throwing things around and creating a mess. It will not be the heavy, torrential rain that will fill ponds and river and bring back life. That is still a few months away.

To her surprise, there was no one in the courtyard of Eli's house. The man was not at his usual spot under the trees or squatting in a corner of the ground; nor was the usual coterie of villagers anywhere to be seen. Then it has passed, Urmila thought, the great search for redwood. People have forgotten about it, let it go. Rosong would be back from the forests of Bhutan with smoked wild boar or deer, in all likelihood, and herbs, and that would be a welcome treat too.

Seeing an open window, she called out to Eli, and after a few moments the girl appeared. Something was the matter. Eli's face was puffed up, her eyes red, the lids heavy.

No, no, Eli murmured, it's the sleeping in the afternoon, it does not agree with me. She tidied her hair and sat on the bench. The darkness of sleep had not left her, and they sat quietly. Urmila asked about Rosong, then the stranger, he was not at his spot, was he sleeping inside?

I don't know, Eli sounded tired, her eyes glazed over.

Had her niece been drinking? That may be. Urmila went in and made some strong red tea, and they sat and drank that. It was unusual for Eli to be so quiet but Urmila decided not to make too much of it. It was not unpleasant to sit under the trees and sip your tea. Urmila was still infused with the glow of her finished work.

That will last for some time before it gives way to some other desultory thought. But for the time being, it was there. So, she sipped her tea and thought of the threads she would get Michael to bring her. Maybe she could visit him in the city, see some threads herself. This was the first time, after her, that anyone from the family had travelled so far.

Time must heal, she reflected, as they say it does, if she was thinking of crossing the river Hel again to the outside world.

It was around then, a little after that, when the dusk was settling in, that a friend of Rosong's came cycling to their house. 'Hei, Eli, you people never charge your mobile or what? Rosong called and asked you to come to my house. He will call again in some time. He's calling from one of those Silmari villages, the network is very bad, I couldn't hear well, but he sounded upset. Something may be wrong, come fast!'

As the boy spoke, panic seized my heart. I started to walk towards the gate, but Eli kept sitting, still keeping to her own time. She thanked him, and said, *We'll be there, we'll be there soon.* She sounded calm, almost as if she had expected this. This strange message, Eli's calm measured words, it was all bewildering.

Then she turned to me, and said, 'Will you come with me? It may be an important call.'

'Yes, Eli. Let's go.'

'Amai!' she frowned, raising her eyes to the other room. 'Baba must be on his way back from the market. Wait …'

I stood outside, while Eli walked into the room where her mother was sleeping and woke her up. In a few moments, my sister-in-law was standing outside. She seemed to have taken ill again, but despite her frailty, despite the fact that she was holding on to Eli for support, her eyes were alert, suspicious. 'Why, Eli?'

Eli did not respond. Instead she gently moved her forward. 'It's better if you wait in ati's house. The neighbour lady is weaving there, she'll keep an eye on you. We are going to the market, we may be a while. You rest there.'

And so, under Eli's directions, they slowly moved back to Urmila's house. Eli's voice was gentle, low, but she did not say anything more, simply assuring her mother that we may be a while in the market. Sleep some more, how was the pain now, and so on, softly droning these senseless phrases.

They left Eli's mother with the neighbour watching over her but, instead of heading towards the boy's home, Eli lingered at the gate, and leaning on the bamboo, said, 'Let's wait here. Rosong has no patience these days, he'll pass on the message to the others, and we won't have to go all the way.'

Urmila couldn't bear this anymore. 'What is happening? Something has happened, hasn't it? You all know what it is. Tell your ati, Eli, what is it?'

A strange terror seized Urmila; she wanted Eli to stop this, her calm voice droning on, flat, devoid of emotion. Something terrible had happened, she could feel it.

'Wait – can you hear?' There was a low rumbling in the distance. Urmila walked to the edge of the garden, where the fields began. 'That – that's nothing.' They could see lights in the distance. 'There is a wedding somewhere out in the Santhali villages, the noise must be from there.'

Eli was by her side, 'No, the sounds will not come from there. They'll be heading to our house first.'

Then she added casually, her voice still calm. 'Michael is dead, ati. The man in our house, he killed him. He was Michael's neighbour in the city.'

She came up for air, then got out words, half strangled: 'Come, ati, I can't bear this anymore … walk with me.'

So, they walked, on the path leading away from their houses. Urmila following her niece wordlessly. It was dark now, but the road and the fields were illuminated by starlight and a crescent moon. An aunt and her niece walking together, along a moonlit path; it was such an ordinary, everyday act, she was tempted to let it be, to choose silence over everything else, unhear what had been said. So they could simply be that and no more. But now Eli would not be stopped.

She placed a condition. Eli would tell her the afternoon's story, but Urmila must finish hers from the day before. Her niece was striking a bargain; Urmila wanted to laugh out loud. Her brother was dead and she wanted a deal.

Instead her voice, when she spoke, was calm, like Eli's. 'Has Rosong found out why this man is here?'

'Yes,' she said. 'Yes. He must have. The news must have reached.

'Finish the earlier story, ati, I need to hear it.'

Urmila took a deep breath. She could hear the sound of wailing, women's voices. It was from the village, but she pushed it away from her mind. *The story, Eli wanted the story*.

'It was not Sibu who told the police about the militants

visiting your parents' house. You see, it was not so simple. One of the men from the group had courted your mother a long time ago. He was not from our community but they had expected to be married; and your mother as a young girl, she was pretty, she had had many suitors, but this man she had liked. Then something happened and they did not marry. She was given to your father and she made peace with it, built her home. Then one day, her old lover reappeared with this group from the jungle, sitting down to a meal in her courtyard. It upset your mother, she was not happy to have him there. Maybe she had been rejected by the other man, because of the community or because he chose to fight, I don't know. But she did not forget her broken heart, you know her anger, how it can be. Your father, meanwhile, became friends with these men. He had wanted to go out, see things, and these militants with their guns and tales of adventure took him into that world. He liked having them over, organised elaborate meals for them. But your mother, she suffered, and she thought your father invited them to punish her for her past. And maybe he did. It was between them. These things between a couple, what are we to make of them?

'But your brother – he was not so small then, he saw your parents fighting, your mother crying, maybe your father raised his hand at her, people gossiped. And Rosong, he built up this big anger against his father and these men. Then, after your father was taken away by the Army, Rosong fell ill. He had nightmares, wet his bed, cried all the time. Finally, he told your mother, it was him, Rosong had informed the police. They were playing by the river and these policemen came, gave the children biscuits or sweets or something, took them around in the jeep, asked them if they had seen guns, people with guns who came at night. Rosong told them. Told them about the men who came at night. Told them they were coming that night. He had seen his father building a fire to smoke the chicken, and bringing fish from the river.'

Eli was crying, her lower lip trembled, her face was wet. They held each other, the aunt and niece walking together on a moonlit night.

Eli spoke, it was her turn. 'In his polythene bag, along with the scissors and knife, there was a packet of newspaper clippings wrapped in plastic. I did not look at them the other day. Then I became curious. He carried nothing with him – not even a cloth – so what were these papers? I thought about it all the time. This morning, I didn't care that he sat by the trees looking out, I went to the room, shut the door and opened the packet he kept under the mat. My hands were shaking, ati – I knew it would be something but I didn't know it would be this.' She was sobbing now.

Urmila tried to brace herself for what would follow, and saw that there could be no preparation for this.

'The first two were newspaper clippings in some other language. The third was in English. It had Michael's photo – and this man's, the man in our house. It said Michael had been killed by this man, his neighbour in the building.

'He was in Michael's house one night. They had been drinking and there was a fight, then Michael, our Michael, was dead. This man killed him and came here – and my father let this killer into our home.

'I knew Rosong would find out soon, he was travelling and he would stop by the villages where the other boys who went to work with Michael came from. The news would have reached, someone would have heard, it was only a matter of time.'

Urmila held her hard, though it felt like they were both sinking, their figures coalesced together in the shadow falling ahead of them. They had to turn back; they were at the end of the village. The men, by now, they must be on their way across the fields.

Eli went on, 'I thought of Sibu and Rosong – I don't know why – and I let him live, that man. I held the newspaper clipping and stood in front of him, threw his bag down. He got up and ran, looking back once or twice, slowly then faster, his feet bare, he was running across the fields. I stood there watching him. He came here to die he had said; why come here to die?'

We will all die, Eli, we will all die. But there were still the others to save. You have done well, child, we must turn back. And they turn and walk back, up the road to where the men would be readying for the hunt, arming themselves with what they could find, setting out in every direction for the jungles and the fields, for the long banks of the river Hel that kept them away from the world.

Peace Has Come

A Triptych

I. The House by the Highway

As soon as Bir Bahadur heard the sounds, he knew something terrible had happened.

He stood still, his hand frozen on the gourd trellis, his bidi a point of fire in the darkness. In the silence that followed, he stubbed out his smoke and, turning to the horizon, quiet once more, he wondered what had happened, how far and whether he should be alarmed.

Several acres of rice fields lay between the highway and his house. The road stood higher than the fields on either side. Intermittent clumps of bamboo served to mark the edge of the village, shielding them from the road. But at night, sound flies like the devil, and over the years, disturbances on the highway had started to trouble him more and more. A burst tyre would keep him up for hours, the stray whistle of a truck engine worm its way into his sleep, leaving him turning this way and that – causing, he believed, his struggles with acidity and indigestion. It had been almost twenty years since he had moved here. In his moments of bitterness, he sometimes wondered if the highway had extracted too great a price from his nerves. But by the light of day, when rational thought came easier, he looked back at his decision to settle here with some amount of pride. This had been a long stretch of wilderness, extending from the southern bank of the river Hel, all along the road for miles on end. The bigger trees were already gone, but it was then still jungle; uninhabited, hostile, unyielding in its dense mass of creepers and climbers, wild ferns and tall grass. The early days had been a regular battle with nature: the snakes and scorpions, the wild cats screeching in the shadows, even the occasional leopard preying on the chicken. It is hard to imagine now, the landscape was so unlike what one sees today, the pastoral glory of serene, endless rice fields with houses tucked neatly between betelnut and rubber plantations. His own family, while happy to see him leave the homestead of six brothers and a few acres of arable land, had been dismayed at his choice. Better to find a job as a watchman somewhere than to go live like wild people in the jungle: surely the buffaloes would be dragged away by jackals and other predators, never mind human beings and so on. But his decision had been shaped by the future and the road. He had gambled on it becoming an important route once the conflict ceased, and he was proved right. After the peace accords, it had become a busy highway carrying trucks and buses, linking Bengal through a strip of Indian territory to Assam and all the other states around it.

Highway 31 cast its blessing on those closest to its dark vein. The villagers around it were able to transport produce to the bigger markets in the towns, and primary schools and health centres cropped up in the area. Their fate was in marked contrast to the villagers on the other side of the Hel, on the northern bank, or those further away. You could see them, even today, ferrying sick people and pregnant women on handcarts that rattled through riverbeds and jungle, with their young people either sent away to stay with relatives in the town or reconciled to logging wood and working in the fields. Neither Bahadur nor his wife had much schooling, but he believed that his fortitude and a touch of luck now and then would let him wrest a little more from life for his children.

But there were other things that Bahadur had not foreseen. The construction work on the road had begun a few months after the peace treaty had been signed. But years had passed, and it was still a raw burst of loose sand and pebbles, with the cranes abandoned by the side. Stretches further ahead had long since been completed with the tar road now gathering potholes, but in their part, the construction dragged. Their road, Bahadur's wife liked to joke, was like the peace: too slow to get there, too fractious and fragmented, like a garment caught on a nail, every slight movement ripping it further.

Of course, even in its incomplete, sand-blown state, the highway still linked them to the world far more effectively than they had ever been, and was the source of their relative prosperity. But it had served another purpose, had another effect, the people here were slowly discovering. The highway had also sucked them into a battlefield. Made them the unwitting pawns in a long-drawn out endgame.

It did not help that Bahadur's Bodo wife Riswgi had a brother in one of the underground groups. They had not seen him for years and took him for dead, but there was renewed interest in Dwimalu of late. For young men like him, the peace did not yield anything. The ceasefires and peace treaties did not include all the militant groups; the boys from their village, for instance, were a part of groups that had lost out on the government deals. These groups that continued to remain underground were pursued by the security forces, the government and often their old comrades, now turned collaborators of the state. They took heavy losses and splintered into factions. They stayed away from the villages close to the road and within reach of the state military forces and, in turn, the security forces avoided crossing the river Hel into the Kochugaon Reserve Forest and the villages on the other bank, where these rebel groups were known to have their strongholds. The security forces preferred to raid 'sympathiser' villages like Bahadur's, closer to the road. This is where the police, the SSB, the CRP swooped down to avenge their losses, from where the first suspects were hauled out after every attack by the rebels. They became a part of security lore, the villages that provided a fodder of suspects. And so it happened that for the villages around Bahadur's, edged between the Hel and the highway, the peace announced the beginning of a new war.

The Hel in spate during the summer months swept up all kinds of odds and ends: branches of trees, clumps of hyacinth, bamboo posts or part of a roof, sometimes dead animals, a bloated cow floating with its legs in the air, they would all appear for a few moments in the raging current. News of his errant brother-in-law was like the seasonal flotsam on the river; once in a while, something or the other would drift in. Bahadur did not take every piece of market gossip seriously. He had shrugged off the busybody at the paan shop who told him recently that his brother-in-law was next in line to be the area commander of a splinter group. The thing he dreaded, quite simply, was news of Dwimalu's body being found somewhere, but that was an anxiety that had become a part of their lives.

Then something else happened. His daughter Jonki arrived from school one day and locked herself up in her room, only stepping out once her mother had left for the river to wash clothes. Bahadur had thought it was a bad test paper or one of her usual fights with her mother when Jonki had asked him to come in. Securing the door, she brought out a crumpled piece of newspaper from her bag. It was a Bodo newspaper. Jonki pointed to a small ink-smeared, hazy photo. Below the photo was a declaration by the police of a reward of a lakh for any information on the fugitive. His daughter read it out to him. The photo may or may not have been Dwimalu's (the backdrop was too dark, and some of it had smudged the eyes, the photo seemed old) but the reward information listed a series of aliases Dwimalu was known to use, the various names he had adopted for the struggle, and Bahadur was familiar with a few. He had calmed his sobbing daughter and quickly disposed of the newspaper fragment in the kitchen fire. Father and daughter resolved to keep it from Riswgi. There was no point, really, in burdening the poor woman with something none of them had any control over. But it had made Bahadur more alert; he kept an eye out for trouble. *Dwimalu, he had been fond of that boy.*

Bahadur shook off his thoughts. It was late as it is. An argument earlier in the evening had led to their ten-year-old getting a thrashing from his mother. Though the domestic squall had blown over, the ensuing tears and reconciliation had delayed the meal. Riswgi and his daughter Jonki had washed the utensils by the well and gone in for the night, though Jonki would keep the lantern burning in her room to study for a few more hours. He was usually the last one outside, taking a few moments for a smoke, checking to see that no cow had strayed into their vegetable patch. Then he would latch the kitchen door and take the stairs to their upstairs living quarters.

Like most of the old houses built when the area was still jungle, theirs was a toongsi house. The kitchen was to the left, at ground level, but the living quarters were elevated from the ground, held up by strong teak pillars. The ground floor was used to store wood and grain, sometimes an animal. Without any walls, it served as a welcome refuge from the heat of the afternoon. The children had placed desks there to study during the daylight hours.

As he neared the wooden stairs going up, he saw his wife peering down from the bedroom door, her hair loose, tucking her dokhona wrap into her waist. He could spot Jonki behind her, holding the oil lantern in her hand. They were preparing to come down.

He indicated to them that they should stay where they were, he was coming up.

Inside, he was greeted by a barrage of questions.

'Father, did you hear that? What was the noise? Was it from the village?' With her brows creased like that, Jonki looked so much like her mother, Bahadur thought with a smile. Though his daughter had inherited the highland cream-and-rose complexion of his side of the family, there were moments when an expression on her face seemed to match her mother's perfectly. That, and the temper.

Riswgi had taken the lantern from her daughter and lowered the flame till there was only a faint glow encircling the three of them.

'Yes, I did. But it's nothing. A wedding party setting off fire crackers, somewhere down the road ...'

Bahadur put a hand on his daughter's shoulder; she was as tall as him. 'Jonki, you look tired. Better to turn off the lantern and get some sleep. I'll wake you up early, before I take out the cows.'

Jonki looked like she was going to say something, then changed her mind, nodded at her father, and went into the inside room she shared with her grandmother and brother. She was too serious for her age sometimes, but there were flashes of real beauty. Bahadur wondered when it would turn into something for him to worry about.

Bir Bahadur and Riswgi lay on their bed for some time but sleep would not come to either of them. The bamboo sheath partition that separated their room from the children's was too thin, and they did not want to awaken them with conversation. So, checking once to see that the children were asleep, they went out to sit on the wooden steps. This was a habit from the old days, when any small disturbance, a cat in the kitchen, a drunken cry outside, would awaken Riswgi and she would sit up, convinced it was her brother Dwimalu come to seek shelter.

They did not bring out the lantern, sitting by the light of the night sky on their elevated post. The slivers of moonlight, where they fell, softened the edge of the darkness, and the house and their bodies became a part of the craggy, uneven landscape of the vegetable patch and the towering betelnut trees.

'We would be better off in some forest village, with no schools or roads. At least, we'd sleep in peace,' Bahadur muttered. There was fatigue in his voice, but the rancour was ebbing away. He did not mean to be taken at his word.

Riswgi replied, keeping to the script. 'Ah yes, and I'd cross the river on your back each time a snake bit or the fever struck. Yes, yes, that would be preferable. It would save us all the money we have to pour into the children's exams and books. We could hitch up the cows at day break …'

The moon had ducked behind the clouds, there was only darkness now. The familiar sounds of their domestic world in slumber lulled them into silence. A low cooing from the hen coop in a corner, the grunts of the sleepless sow further down the yard, the murmuring, muted fluttering of the pigeons sheltering on the eaves of the roof. Riswgi sat counting the moments between the soft, hollow call of the owl that perched on the mango tree. Bahadur lit a bidi.

That's when they heard the noise of a crashing against the fence, and a low cry, something between a choke and an animal whimper. It was from the other side of the vegetable patch; they could see no disturbance from where they sat. Husband and wife waited a few seconds. Then they slid down the stairs, slowly, feeling their way in the darkness, picked up what they could find around them, a spade and a stone, and made their way towards the fence: a fox or a rabbit or one of the village drunks, in all likelihood.

They tiptoed around the house and, in the mottled darkness, spotted something like the outline of a figure along the fence. The bamboo sticks had given way under the weight of the stranger lurching towards the ground and the body was strangely fixed upon it, a part of the torso hanging, head bowed, arms tucked in, like one keeled over in the kneeling position of prayer. For a moment, Bahadur had thought it could be a woman running from a drunken husband, but on seeing the heavy shoulders, he wondered if it was a dead thing. He scrambled down on his knees, pushed the head up, and saw it was neither a woman nor dead. The eyes were half open, the breathing heavy.

'He's alive.' He whispered to Riswgi. Then he addressed the man in Nepali: 'Bhai, sanchai? Are you okay? Can you hear me?'

No answer. Just the breathing: heavy gasps, hot, guttural. Together they peered at his face. His hair, face, clothes were lined with the white dust of the construction site on the highway. They couldn't tell from his features if he was from the village or outside, Nepali, Bodo or Rabha.

'Should I get water?' Riswgi asked.

'Wait. Let's take him inside first. In the dark, I can't tell if he has an injury or what.'

Bahadur placed the man's arm over his shoulder, and slowly shifted the weight from the fence and draped it on to himself. This man looked young, with a sturdy build and, Bahadur reckoned, heavier than his appearance. 'Here, you take his other arm,' he told Riswgi and together they half-carried, half-dragged the man.

'Careful with your shoulder,' Riswgi hissed, but Bahadur tossed it aside with an irritated snort. 'Just get him into the house first.'

In this intimate grasp, Bahadur inhaled the sour rankness of sweat mixed with fear that the stranger's body and clothes gave off. He could detect the traces of other smells, the dust of the highway and damp grass and vegetation, but he could not smell liquor, not a whiff of it. *It must be the other thing then, the thing that made that noise on the highway.*

Riswgi was a head shorter than Bahadur, and despite her petite appearance, had arms and shoulders strengthened by years of labour in the fields and hauling water. But she sagged under the dead weight of this stranger, her long hair loosened out of the bun fell over her eyes, and she groped her way blindly towards the door. Arriving at the entrance to their house posed another problem. *How to haul this man up the stairs then?*

Riswgi steered them towards the kitchen; that would be

easier. She let Bahadur bear the greater share of the weight, and managed to open the latch without tripping over.

The stranger found the strength to stay upright on his legs, managed a few faltering steps, then collapsed on the kitchen floor, one flailing arm upsetting the bottles on the shelf and a pot of water with a clanking sound that promised new complications. Even his mother-in-law could not have slept through this din, Bahadur cursed.

Having deposited their burden, they sank down to the ground, gasping and out of breath.

Riswgi reached for the oil lantern, turning on the flame. They could see him clearly now, sprawled on the mud floor, his body shaking. With some effort, the man rose up on his elbows, holding his chest and began retching. She managed to put a vessel under his chin in time, and he vomited, spitting and coughing.

After, he seemed to feel better, or perhaps exhausted by his ordeal, he lay back again.

Riswgi turned up the flame of the lantern, letting the light pour over his body, illuminating it in patches. *No visible injuries, at least no blood, no bullets*; that was a relief.

The kitchen door creaked open from the outside, and Jonki and her brother Doel entered. The boy was rubbing his eyes but looked thrilled by this unexpected piece of drama. Bahadur looked up at them and commanded silence with a finger to his lips. The little boy mimed him in agreement, finger to his lips, solemn.

The family congregated around the man. His head rested on a bag of rice against the wall, and the rest of him lay on the mud floor. Riswgi had taken control: she was slowly splashing water from a bowl on the man's face, cleaning the spit and specks of vomit on his neck and face with a wet cloth, while speaking to him gently in a mix of languages, Assamese, Bodo, then Nepali, while she gave the family instructions: more light, heat some mustard oil in a pan to knead his arms and legs, a cup of milk tea for the shock, and so on. Each of them had something to do, and they worked silently, keeping an eye out for the demented grandmother in case she had stumbled down the stairs and appeared by the door, and for any signs of recovery from the man. They communicated through whispered instructions; it was unlikely their voices would carry far, but Bahadur kept a look out for suspect noises from outside, the bamboo poles of the front gate being disturbed or the crunch of twigs underfoot, anything that announced a new arrival in the scene.

Jonki knelt by her mother, lifting the stranger's head gently, while Riswgi ran the wet cloth through the back of his neck, where the spittle had flowed. In a quiet voice, she asked her mother,

'Is he a tiuria hanja, a fighter?'

Riswgi looked up from the face she was cleaning, met her daughter's eye and looked at the man again. 'I don't know. I can't even tell if he is from our community or another.'

Jonki added, 'He's not wearing shoes.'

Riswgi shrugged. The body under her care was shaking again; every few minutes, a tremor ran through it, as if a stray memory had lacerated a nerve somewhere. She continued to stroke his head with the wet cloth, reassuring him with touch.

In a while, the oil rubbed on the limbs or the warmth of the room, something worked. The shivering stopped and the stranger drifted off to a deep sleep. Riswgi put a shawl over his body to keep him warm.

'Is he dead?' The ten-year-old looked up at his sister.

'What? No, he's – he's sleeping.'

The boy wasn't convinced and tried to edge his way closer to the sleeping man. Jonki elbowed him away. 'Do you want a slap? Stay back.'

Her mother pulled up a low wooden stool, and sat down, wiping the sweat from her forehead. 'He'll be fine …'

Bahadur went through the pockets of the sleeping man's cotton shirt and polyester trousers. Nothing, except a few coins and a crumpled ticket in his trouser. His wallet must have been in another bag or he had dropped it along the way; they would have to wait for him to wake up to find out more. Bahadur stood up, flexed his shoulders and neck where the strain was beginning to creep up after his exertions; he had forgotten how heavy a knocked-out body could be. He thought of ordering his son back to bed, but didn't have the strength to begin an argument. And there were other things to think of. The children, aware of such a possibility, sat quietly without asking any questions, content to be a part of the drama.

Jonki moved to the cooking corner and was soon prodding the half-burnt logs in the stove to get the fire going for tea. They drank their tea in silence, moving away from where the man lay towards the cooking hearth.

At some point, they noticed the man move and Bahadur helped him sit up. He drank some water and looked around him. His eyes still flitted around, but he was able to focus on the shadows of the kitchen.

Bahadur decided it was time, he would try asking him some questions, his name. 'Naam, naam?' The stranger mumbled something. Mohinder? Mohan Singh? Then he began speaking. The family surrounded him, bringing the lantern close to the man. He was speaking in Hindi but not the way they spoke it here. As he spoke, Jonki who could not follow what he said, noticed faint traces of tears skirting the edge of his eyes and flowing down his cheeks, making tiny glistening tracks on his grimy skin.

He was travelling with his cousin and uncle from Siliguri to Guwahati. They woke him up when the bus stopped on the highway. He saw the armed men in uniform get in and ask the passengers to step out. Outside, the Hindi-speaking men were separated, made to stand in a line, while the rest of the passengers were sent back inside the bus and the driver was told to go. The armed men asked them to run down the highway and began firing their guns after them. There were screams all around. Stumbling, he fell over and rolled into a ditch. He waited for the gunfire to stop, then fled into the darkness, running blindly, away from the road through the vegetation until he reached their fence and collapsed.

By then, the man was incoherent and sobbing. He didn't know where his cousin and uncle were, if they were still alive. Bahadur spoke to him in Hindi, asked him to quieten, repeating again and again, *We will help you, you are safe here, brother ...*

The kitchen was now stifling, with the number of people inside, the smoke from the stove, mixed with traces of vomit and heated mustard oil. Bahadur moved towards the door and opened it a crack, letting in the cool night breeze. Inevitably, his gaze skirted the horizon. To the right, a strip of highway was visible through the dark mass of the bamboo groves. *Something was happening*. He stepped out to take a closer look. In the long stretch of darkness, one portion of the highway was illuminated, what was it, the headlights of vehicles? It was more than two hours, perhaps three or four, since he had heard the sounds of gunfire. Enough time for someone to have alerted the police or for the bus driver to have reached a police station.

Riswgi had followed him to the door. He pointed in the direction of the light on the highway.

'That's what the fellow was talking about. Can you see? That's where it happened. The police must have arrived to pick up the bodies.'

Riswgi stepped out, her eyes fixed on the illuminated patch. She had made up her mind about something; 'Fai de, come inside', she tapped his shoulder and briskly walked back.

Inside, she latched the door and gestured to him, moving towards the kitchen hearth. The two children looked tired. The boy had crouched on the ground with his head on his sister's lap. Still fighting sleep, his eyes followed his parents' stealthy movement across the room. Jonki had brought out a mat and the man was now lying down on it. His body covered by a shawl, he had drifted back to sleep. It was a strange sight, seeing this harswa from god knows where, fast asleep in their kitchen. At the same time, Bahadur realised, the figure did not seem particularly out of place, more like an unexpected guest or relative who had missed the evening bus, and was camping in their kitchen for the night.

Riswgi was speaking to him, 'This man,' pointing at the sleeping figure, 'he has to go, you understand? And he has to go soon.'

Bahadur was surprised by her vehemence, the agitation in her voice. *Of course, but—*

She continued, her voice terse, implacable, 'We cannot be involved in this. We have no part in it. Yes, he came into our house and we helped him. But look at him, this Mohan or whatever, what if he has lost his mind and cannot explain to the police how he came to be here, or says some gibberish about us trying to kidnap him. We don't know who was involved in the highway shooting, or what the police will make up. They'll think it has something to do with Dwimalu.

'Who will believe what you or I have to say?'

Bahadur nodded, she did not have to say more.

Riswgi had put her hand on his arm. She caressed it absently for a moment and then withdrew. He didn't look up at her. They had broken the bone below the elbow, of course it was nothing, he had lived and it was such a long time ago. After that, the Army had not bothered them for years, but who was to say what the future held. Jonki's exams were a month away. He could not risk the old troubles being dragged out.

Bahadur went down on his haunches to address his son. The boy had almost dozed off but sat up when he saw his father.

Bahadur touched his head lightly. 'Doel, you're not tired?'

'No, baba.'

'Good. You have to do something for me. Go by the back garden to your uncle Daimary's house and knock softly, just a few taps on his window. Not the door, the window to the left, it is close to his bed. He's a light sleeper, he'll hear you. Go slowly, don't trip over anything and make a noise. When he opens the window, you tell him I sent you to fetch him. Okay?'

'Yes, baba,' he sprang up at this chance to be a part of the action. Jonki stood up to follow him, but Bahadur raised his hand, indicating she stay there. 'No need for all of you to be running up and down in the middle of the night. Let him go.'

Riswgi called out as the boy went out of the door, 'And if someone sees you, say you're going to the toilet.'

The night was receding. The three of them sat in silence. Bahadur stretched his legs out on the floor and was rolling his shoulders to relax his neck, when he saw his wife start, sit up. Then he heard the sound too. Riswgi rose up on her knees, the lantern in one hand and a finger to the lip, sshh. They waited a moment.

Then Jonki let out a small laugh. 'That's nothing. It's grandmother snoring. You can hear it all the way here!'

Her mother didn't smile, just swatted her hand in irritation and settled back on her stool. The old lady's snores soon dissipated into the night. They were replaced by the pre-dawn chirping of an early bird, a lone voice calling on the world to hurry. Then finally, the sound by the door they waited for.

Daimary looked quite a figure, standing there bare chested in his faded green-checked gamsa, hands on his waist, glaring at the figure huddled on the floor. Then his eyes turned to where the family was sitting.

'So this is the man—'

He had begun speaking in Nepali as was their custom when he was with Bahadur. But he was surprised by Riswgi's raised hand silencing him. She tilted her head at the sleeping man, 'Bodo, speak in Bodo.'

Bahadur nodded, that was wise; everybody understood Nepali these days.

Daimary switched to Bodo: 'Doel said there was firing on the highway and then this stranger landed up here. It so happens that just yesterday I charged my battery, so I thought, let's try and put the TV on, if there's something—'

'So soon? It must've been ten–ten thirty at night when the incident happened.'

'Oh, these TV people reach everywhere nowadays, you have no idea! It was in the news already. They were talking of the killing of Hindi-speaking people by underground militants. Someone had filmed some bodies lying in the dust by the side of the road on a phone camera. It was a terrible scene, the bodies all white in construction dust, the headlights of police cars making the air blue. Some villagers had reached too. They were trying to see how many were killed and—'

'Did they say anything about him?' Bahadur gestures towards the sleeping man.

'No, no. It's too early. The police have picked up the wounded and the dead. That too only the ones they found on the road. You think they'll be out in the middle of the night, looking around? The news said that the ones missing have been kidnapped by the militants. Why did you bring him here? This is going to be trouble.'

Riswgi snorted. 'Listen to this man, why did we bring him here, indeed! What do you think, we have no brains? You think we invited him over for a cup of tea? What were we to do—'

Bahadur intervened. 'Please, softly – speak softly. Dada, we found this man hanging onto our fence, near the chicken coop, sometime after the shooting. We thought he was a dog or a drunk who lost his way. We couldn't just leave him out there. What's done is done. We have to find a way out.'

'Yes, I understand.' Daimary could see the burden of the night on the family, especially his cousin Riswgi who was picking nervously at her hands. Something had to be done.

No one suggested calling the police. Till a few years ago, every time the security forces came in here, they would find whole villages emptied of men; the men would have all fled to the forest, staying there till the police left. Even if they had come to distribute blankets. Things were better now but it was not an option.

Bahadur had an idea.

'This man is not hurt, his legs seemed to be working when we brought him in. Let's take him further up the highway, at a distance from the village, and leave him there by the side of the road. Someone will find him.' He was looking at his wife as he said this.

Riswgi nodded slowly, following him. 'Yes, but he's

still unwell. What if he dies, lying out in the sun, by the road, like that?'

'He's a young man, he'll manage for some time. People will be moving out towards the market, to the fields, in an hour's time. The early morning trackers and buses will be on the road by six – somebody will spot him.'

Daimary agreed. 'To be certain, we'll send one of the young ones, Rajen or someone, on a cycle with bananas for the market. In case your man is still there, he'll stop and inform the local people, take him to the hospital or the police station.'

'Finding him by the highway will not look suspicious. Even if the man were to talk later of a village where he spent the night, it would be impossible to tell which one.'

Riswgi was already up, moving towards the sleeping man.

'Go – go soon, before it is light. Don't go through the rice fields, you'll get more cover if you walk along the rubber plantation and then the bamboo groves. It will be a longer walk but no one will see you.'

She bent down to minister to the sleeping stranger, waking him with care, so as to not startle him. When his eyes opened, she gently helped him sit up.

Bahadur addressed him in Hindi, 'Chalo, we'll send you home now. Are you feeling better? Some water, you want some water?'

Jonki fetched some water, and the man sat up and drank. His eyes still carried panic in them. He didn't look up, but nodded in understanding. Slowly he was gathering his strength, they could tell. The sleep had done him good.

But the excitement and stress of the night made a

sudden onslaught on Bahadur, and he felt a great weariness in his bones, its sting prying into his eyes and shoulders, the acid rising in his stomach.

He gestured to his wife. 'Wait, put some water on the stove. First, let's have a round of tea.'

Crouched near the fireplace, he ate a plate of cold rice in salt and water; no tea. The rest of them had a cup along with sweet biscuits.

Doel had fallen asleep on the kitchen floor. They left him there. It was still dark outside, and a light drizzle greeted them. Something like thunder or trucks roared in the distance. But they had no time to think of that now. The stranger, a little unsteady on his feet when he stood up to his full height, was much taller than Bahadur. (The man had seemed somewhat frailer, more diminished the night before. They must have let his feet drag on the ground.) Daimary and Bahadur walked on either side, fencing him in and supporting him.

*

Riswgi and Jonki watch as the three walk into the darkness of the trees in the backyard and are lost to the eye. They have not carried the lantern out with them, and the mother and daughter stand there for a while, sensing the route the men take even though they cannot see them.

Riswgi is back on the steps where she had sat with Bahadur earlier in the night. Jonki is tired but does not leave her mother's side. Riswgi does not ask her to, though she should get some sleep, then wake up and do her exams revisions. They sit there till a breath of rose breaks out in the sky, and their world slowly takes form, comes to life: the impatient lowing of cows in the backyard shed, the squabbling chicks and roosters in their morning glory, the chorus of birds all around them.

'Do you think Dwimalu amai will come back?'

Riswgi sighs. 'You never know. He may, so many have returned.'

She gets up to rinse the tea cups and cooking pot from last night and begin her day.

On the highway, the military vehicles converge and ring out along the paddy fields surrounding the village. Jonki keeps her vigil by the steps, her eyes on the road, and the rice fields that seem to spread as far as the eye can see before the horizon intervenes. Sometimes she thinks she can see someone, but it is only a shadow or a bird.

II. The Boys on a Haystack

In the future, a long time from now, when the town has eaten its way into the heart of the countryside, and the rice fields and homesteads and betelnut plantations have given way to commercial centres, with tar on the roads, dusty shacks and fewer trees, there will still stand the sculpture, at a little distance from a newly constructed roundabout with a traffic policewoman. Like the roadside shrines under old trees, the buildings will grow around the ungainly body of the piece, and someone or the other will keep it free from the ravenous ferns and creepers of the land. The plaque with the inscription 'Peace Is Here: The Boys on a Haystack' will still be upright, though a bit worn with each passing monsoon and the increase in traffic and dust.

There has been the occasional petition to the local government for the maintenance of the sculpture but, not followed up by more urgent and persuasive appeals, it has fallen by the wayside. Now a host of unrelated people – nearby shopkeepers, road sweepers, school students – clean it occasionally. The plinth and the wirework underneath remains fairly strong, but they fear that without some touching up of the surface work, the cracks will deepen, spread like veins along the body, leading to a slow disintegration of the entire edifice. As it is, some of the finer details, the gold edge of the patina, a nostril, a fingertip, some letters in the inscriptions, have worn thin.

In another region, another country, this would have been considered something of a state treasure. The sculptor was recognised during his lifetime, and had been awarded prestigious grants and commissions. This piece was possibly his last work (there were, at best, a few minor pieces after that) – definitely the last of his 'giant people' series. For the art lover with a taste for the arcane, the twists and turns of the artistic life, this was *the real thing*, art embedded in biography and politics. The material he used for the sculpture was a cheap local option unsuited to projects of such skill and ambition. He was used to the finest – he worked with bronze and imported fibreglass (particularly Taiwanese fibreglass), and had had a small army of diligent assistants at his command. But this was a work of his twilight years; by then, his workshop and reputation had dwindled to nothing. He was almost blind when he set to work on it and the story goes that, having fallen out of favour with his patrons and political friends, he could not find anyone to finance the piece.

He went ahead and did it anyway with what little money he had. But it meant compromising on the material: he had to eschew the bronze and bell metal he had favoured for his more famous statues of Ahom generals in the capital or the one of Thengphakhri near Bijni. But the brittle economy of the material combined with the ambitious design of the piece only served to increase its strangeness, impart a frail, precious quaintness to what could have otherwise passed as another sentimental monument to the dead, or more precisely, to the dead of the Movement years and after. The land was littered with them, these monuments. And despite the fact that several studies had practically exhausted what was left to say of them, the student who showed up that day was certain that a new and important thesis would come to him, would inform his analysis of this monument by the old master.

But as he stood there with the small group of people who had slowly congregated around him, he was taken aback by the sheer joy of the piece, the nostalgia that seemed to overcome them all at the sight of this image of plenitude. The cascading mound of straw spilling to the ground and all around the haystack: it conjured up images of harvested rice, overflowing granaries and courtyards of villages, the threshing taking over roads and empty fields. A pull of nostalgia so strong it was impossible to resist. (Even if the student himself had not grown up in a village or ever been at a harvesting, it was the nostalgia of the sirens, the déjà vu of art, he sighed.) They could almost sense the fragrance of the cool December air, the shouts of villagers urging the cows at the threshing, the creaking of straw-laden carts, the songs of those still at the fields …

'Ah, but it was at night …'

And then someone noted the stillness. Of course! It was a haystack by night, the shadows, the relaxed posture of the boy at the top, illuminated by moonlight and its shadows. The student smiled. He had been fooled by the lines, the meticulous detailing and its abundance, by its aura of youth and fruitfulness, mistaking night for day. The now washed out, decaying patina of its surface was hand-painted by the sculptor and his helper. It had aged well, having now acquired the sheen of an underwater Pompeii green, the aura of the old statues buried for long in earth or water. But it was the gold, the edges trimmed by gilt that gave this piece its air of mischief, its sense of play, teasing out the elements of light and dark, and the interstices of shadow.

Then there were other theories.

One of the elderly men piped up: 'It could not have been possible, for young boys to be milling around a haystack with nothing to do in the harvest period. There was always someone calling out, something to be done, if not at home or in your father's field, it was at your neighbour's! There was no peace for an able-bodied worker no matter how young. It would have to be in the evening, some time for the stars!'

'Look at the boy, he's holding a half-eaten orange in his hand. And one fruit is caught by the sculpture in mid-roll, as it slides off the side of the haystack!'

There is delighted laughter at this charming little detail. A group of older men who were sitting by the shade had made their way here on seeing the student with his notepad and camera. The boy from the tea shop and another hanger-on passing the day at the bazaar comprised the rest of the crowd. The sculpture had been a part of their lives for years, but when a visitor stopped by, they liked to point out these details with excitement and pleasure, as if they had only just noticed the curve of a hand, the grains strewn by a careless gust of wind.

The student had his notepad out. He had a question, even though he had read of this sculpture before and knew the incident that inspired it.

'But why would these boys be out on a haystack at night?'

This question pleased the crowd; it is as if they had been waiting for it. There was a wooden plank that served as a bench, and one or two sat down on it. They were a ready group of informants.

'Ah, that was the crux of the whole problem! I believe the families didn't get any compensation. Because the Army took this position – why would three boys be out on a haystack in the middle of the night if they weren't militants? And who would explain all this to them?'

The man's face crinkled into lines as he spoke, smiling. He wore a wool cap, even though it was early March, and he clutched at a stick. To the student, he looked ancient. *Would he happen to remember the incident, perhaps from his childhood?*

'You see, this entire area was rice fields then – nothing else, just rice. The fate of the whole year depended on your harvest. Through good times and bad, this was the constant. Very few people from these villages had government jobs or shops in the town, it was mostly agricultural work. We had to toil so we could eat. That winter, the people say it was a good harvest, bountiful – everywhere you looked, there was the threshing of grain, the granaries were full. People don't mind this work, because there is Christmas for the Christians and then the harvest festival. It is not like the sowing period when you toil in the rains amidst sickness for an uncertain year, not knowing if some river will turn its course or what pestilence will visit your crops.'

One of his companions, missing hair on his head but still upright of carriage, added: 'It was also a good time for the children. The examinations were over, school was shut. You could go fishing in the creek or the jungles once the paddy had been brought in, plenty of vegetables and fruits to steal from your neighbour's garden! And some of the tension was easing off. It had been a few years since the peace had come. People were beginning to hope again—'

Another voice cut in.

'I was a small one then. And I don't remember the next few years being particularly peaceful. So, it couldn't have been all so good, the problem with the past and the storytelling of these Jambas is—'

This did not sit well with the original narrator, with the shaky knees and walking stick. 'I am a Jamba, indeed! If you remember it so well, Nabla, you tell the story.'

The student knew this part of the story. He had read accounts in the newspapers of the period, the background reports, but did not want to upset the man who was talking. 'Grandfather, please go ahead. You are telling the story well.'

This appeased the old man, he snorted and continued, 'So, these three boys, they are cousins. No … two of them are cousins, one is a friend. Something like that. They are all in school, a ten-year-old and another twelve, the third was a little older, in class ten. Now, there was a custom in those days for people to stay out in the fields through the night to guard their harvested grain. It was an important precaution, you had to watch out for thieves and other mischievous elements, stray cows and raiding elephants. So, Anthony – he was the class-ten boy – his older brother asks him and a younger cousin to spend the night on the haystack, watching over their harvest. The neighbour's boy, who was drinking tea in their house, decided to join the two boys. It was a normal thing to do during the harvest—'

Another old man chuckled. 'The boys must have been more than happy to do this. Lying under blankets munching on snacks prepared by your sister-in-law, with the stars over your head, maybe a chance to sneak a puff on a cigarette – this is what childhood is.'

The tea-shop boy laughed. 'A whole lot of childhood it left them with, their picnic by the stars!'

Despite the earlier rebuke, the one they called 'Nabla' had still hung around the edge of the crowd. He looked a little younger, or perhaps he was better preserved. He wore trousers unlike the other old men who wore informal gamsas and lungis. He stepped back into the narrative, casting a comment into the fray but with his face turned the other way. 'Yea, all the boys were innocent in those days, of course. Pah!'

The student stepped away from the squabbling old men and moved to take a closer look at the piece. It was not a benign piece of sculpture, no, despite his original impression. At first glance, coming from the road, he had been taken in by the lassitude of the figure on the top of the haystack, the boy on the blanket watching the stars with oranges in his hand, but as he took a few steps, other pieces of the sculpture came into view. Near the knee of the first figure sprang an outstretched hand, in a gesture of appeal or helplessness, clawing at air. Walking to the left, the hand led him to the rest of the body. This second boy seemed to be caught in a moment between the haystack and the ground, as if a great force had ripped him from the surface and pitched him into uncertain air. Something like the bullets of an automatic rifle. The student felt a chill, even though it is not a December night but an afternoon in spring. As he walked round the haystack, other aspects of the story unfolded. The third boy was slumped heavily, already felled by the bullets at the bottom of the haystack. He was the youngest at ten. His body was not defying gravity and force, even momentarily like the second figure, but was of the earth, had been called back, put to rest. The three boys shot down by the Army in the early hours before daybreak on suspicion of being militants; each of them captured by the sculptor, at different moments, perhaps in the few minutes before and after the shooting. He had read all the accounts and newspaper reports from that period – there weren't too many of them – and his eyes skirted the ground for the supposed 'evidence'. He was not sure if the sculptor had depicted the two grenades and an assault rifle the villagers had said were planted upon the boys after the shooting, and what the security forces had alleged the boys were carrying when shot down.

Accompanying the haystack, at a distance of about two feet, the ground still coarse with moulded straw, was the figure of a kneeling bespectacled man. Like a chastised, harried angel, the figure knelt with an open book in one hand, exhibiting it to the world. He was the head teacher at the boys' school.

The student went down on his haunches, facing the sculpture, in an unconscious mimicry of the man's supplication. He almost expected to see lice-ridden, ruined wings collapsed around the man's shoulder. He was not so much a figure as a broken thing sinking into the mud.

The tea-shop boy joined him. 'That is the class attendance register in his hand.'

The student nodded. He had read about it in the case file. The one valuable commodity that could be used in the defence of village boys in that period were their academic records: they attended classes, had done their examinations well, how could they be dreaded criminals worthy of death in an encounter if they spent their days in a classroom preparing for English examinations? The families were farming folks with no influence, so the head teacher had been the main defendant. He had gone to the press and the committee with this proof of the children's innocence. It had not worked. In those days, in cases of shooting by the security forces, the burden of proof rested on the victims, mostly dead victims.

The student took a few photographs. But it was near evening, and he worried about the texture of the light. Maybe he ought to get a professional photographer the next time. The details and the dull sheen of the sculpture might look commonplace and shabby if the photos were not taken right.

Meanwhile, the voices in the crowd were getting louder. He looked back to see that two of the old men are well into an argument. He was not sure if he should join them or simply leave. Then he went to them, but only because he saw himself coming back here again and did not wish to antagonise the locals. They did not interest him.

The old man 'Jamba' was shaking his stick at the provocateur in rage. But Nabla had the field now and could not be stopped.

'Oh yea, listen to this idiot old man, the good ol' days the good ol' days the good ol' days! When our young still felt for the community. Indeed! They were nothing more than a bunch of rogues with guns, not doing any work, cutting throats and looting people.'

Jamba faced the student. 'Yes, tell the visitor! See, there are no stories here. Why are you wasting your time? The only stories worth writing are from when this man was a cook in the Indian Army, running through the fog and pine trees of Kashmir with a pot of rice! Now, that's bravery and courage, I tell you. Cooking for a bunch of cut-throats and rapists, oh, but they're in uniform so we must stand up and salute – oie, Bahadur at your service!'

The student was momentarily taken aback. Perhaps they expected him to be the judge of this argument. Or maybe not. He realised that this must be a routine they had perfected down the years, even though the bitterness was real.

Nabla said, 'You watch it! What kind of image do we want to portray to the nation? Celebrating terrorists or looking ahead to development, to nation building?'

The student intervened, 'It's getting late. I'll take your leave then, grandfather. I'll be coming again.'

Jamba took his hand. 'They were children! The sculpture is here, so we remember what we lost. What the violence did to us. They were children on a haystack and their murderers in uniform got away, probably got promotions! What is wrong with this man?'

The student thanked him again and was about to move when he heard Nabla snigger. 'Oranges, indeed. Look closely. Your sculptor was not so innocent. Those are not oranges, bulging out of their pockets, in their fists. See the way the ridges are carved along their spheres, they are grenades, not oranges!'

And the crowd turned their heads towards the frozen boys and the objects in their hands, the spheres spilling around them. Looked at them again. The December chill returned. The student, after a moment of hesitation, scrawled on his notepad 'oranges/grenades'.

III. The Letter

'Prabin da, it doesn't look like an accident. I think there's checking ahead.'

Dwipen and Prabin waited by their motorcycle. Around them were cycles laden with assorted market produce, motorbikes, a passenger jeep, people on foot – all of them brought to a standstill, wedged between the overflowing baskets of vegetables and racks of cloth that lined the narrow passage through the Athiabari bazaar.

As ubiquitous as the piles of leafy greens and ferns, the counterfeit T-shirts and jeans hanging on poles were the soldiers in uniform walking around. They were a regular feature in this bazaar: their giant bodies oddly perched on the narrow benches of the tea shops they took over, or standing around in twos and threes, their guns hanging casually about their uniformed bodies, glowering at the crowd, picking their noses or looking into the distance.

Initially, the duo had waited patiently; it was only a scuffle, or a cycle cart carrying bamboo caught at an angle with a truck coming from the other side. But Dwipen had stepped away and, craning his head, he noticed the olive Army colours of the nets around the temporary road block. *Something was the matter.* He left the bike and pushed his way ahead through the crowd. The unruly mass narrowed into a neat queue of vehicles, cyclists, bikers and pedestrians waiting to pass through the checkpoint. The Army had taken over the forest department's checkpost cabin; people were frisked by the roadside, then sent into the cabin. On the other side of the checkpoint, he could see several military vehicles, distinct in their dark olive tints. It did not look good. The battalion camp was in the next town and the soldiers were at the market most days, patrolling or setting off on expeditions into the forest villages closer to the border. But for a checking like this, something must have happened along the highway. The non-ceasefire faction had stepped up their attacks of late. Nothing grand or spectacular like the old days, mostly isolated attacks on security establishments, hit and run in the dark, away from the city and towns, the tactics of a depleting guerrilla movement.

None of this affected the main towns much. Not like earlier. A few years ago, Prabin would not have risked travelling around in these parts. The situation was far more clear-cut now. This area was fine during daylight hours and Prabin and Dwipen had hoped to be back in the town by late afternoon. They had not anticipated the roadblock.

As his colleague wiped his forehead with a large handkerchief and looked around, Prabin felt a twinge of irritation. He was fond of Dwipen and looked forward to his trips to these districts. After the training in one block centre or another, the two would ride back to the town, pick up vegetables and meat or fish on the way, and cook themselves dinner in Dwipen's rented apartment, washing down the pork or fish cooked in yam with some of the local brew. He rarely mixed his work travel with drinking. If word got around, the ones in the Guwahati office would use this as an excuse for their own profligacy and recklessness, at office expense too. But Dwipen was something of a brother, somebody he trusted. And then he sighed, caught himself; that was the problem with family in the first place – you had to put up with their craziness. He had berated Dwipen several times about his bike papers, but it had always been this and that, someone was perpetually arranging for them, it was a matter of a few weeks and so on. It had been two years since Dwipen bought the bike second hand and the papers had yet to materialise. It didn't matter that much in the town. Dwipen cut an impressive figure. He was taller than average, with the muscle and bulk of a man of action, or an ageing man of action, which did not detract from, but rather added to, his stature in these times. His close-cropped, stiff hair, dark face, and there was something in the way he frowned, the way it reached into his eyebrows – it gave him an air of impatience, of restrained aggression. This created an impression around the town, especially with small-time ruffians and policemen. There is a story about how he was handed a bag of cash as he waited with a friend at a leader's house; somebody simply assumed he was an enforcer. In truth, Dwipen had no underground or political connections. In fact, Prabin often found that his own instincts worked better than Dwipen's even though he was a virtual stranger to the politics of these districts. The local police left Dwipen alone and he knew most of the traffic police in the town; the CRP and the Army were, however, another matter. The very qualities that kept him immune to the local policemen's attentions rendered him suspect and vulnerable at an Army checkpoint. Prabin's irritation was replaced by concern.

'Should I try to drive back to the highway?' Dwipen asked.

Another foolish question, Prabin sighed. The crush of people and wheels behind them was getting bigger. The market was breaking up and people were returning home. Manoeuvring the bike out would draw too much attention. The Army men, who had been drinking tea and lounging around, had straightened up, taken position, with hands on their guns, scanning the crowds. Whatever chance the two had of sneaking past the checkpoint without being asked for papers, being singled out now – by drawing attention to themselves, pushing and shoving to drive back – would do them in.

It was just bad luck. They could very well have been sailing through the highway instead of waiting at a checkpoint. Initially, they took NH-31; it was a straight road down to Kajigaon, from where a right turn would have taken them to the town. But after driving on it for a half hour, the sand from the construction had left them covered in white, barely able to breathe. The road construction has been going on steadily for years, but the dry season made the dust of the unpaved, sandy expanses unbearable; the workers on the side of the road were like white slow-moving spirits. They had decided to leave the highway and take the road through Serphanguri to Pathgaon, driving through the Nepali villages to come out on the portion of the highway that had already been completed.

'No point trying to get out of this. Don't panic. They'll keep your bike and we'll have to catch a ride back to the town with someone else. After that, it's your problem.' Prabin didn't want to start on the papers; there was no point to it right now. 'You have your license, no?'

'Yes, yes.'

They waited as the queue dwindled and they got closer. Some of the people, women, market folk, were allowed to pass, while some were called out to be frisked and sent into the guard house. Prabin kept his eye on Dwipen. His colleague shouldn't look too nervous. After all, riding a bike without papers was a minor offence. But fear and the perspiration around the eyes could lead to other misunderstandings and more trouble.

He was so lost in these thoughts that they had already called out to him twice, and it was only when Dwipen shook his arm, hissing at him, 'Prabin-da, they're speaking to you', that he looked up and stumbled ahead.

'Here, you – you! Step aside, come here. Can't hear?'

The crowd parted for him, people turning to see who the voice had marked. The armed men were indeed gesturing towards him, speaking in Hindi. Prabin felt his legs sag under him. *It couldn't be him they were looking for, it was too long ago, and things had changed a lot.* He had known people driven insane by fear, people who, years after leaving the organisation, would continue to see military intelligence everywhere. He had resolved to not become one of them. *But why now? What did they want with him, here of all places, and now?*

He half stumbled ahead, smiling a little excessively, he thought. Surely there was a mistake, why would they want him, the absurdity of it all, his expression tried to say. But people around looked uncomfortable, peered at him as if he was slightly unhinged. He had lost Dwipen in the crowd behind him.

One of the soldiers was looking towards the forest beat cabin and calling out something, 'Teacher hai!' They frisked him and pushed him ahead but as he moved towards the forest beat cabin, the escorts who flanked him nudged him in the other direction. There was another house, just across the dry overgrown ditch. He had not noticed it. It was an old Assam-type house, with cream-coloured walls and a tin roof, surrounded by a garden of white bark eucalyptus trees, coconut and jacaranda in bloom. Military jeeps and trucks resting in the shade. He was being marched in there.

It looked like a temporary base. Inside, it had the bare, stricken look of an empty government office, with a few chairs and tables, no files or computers. They made him sit in the room in front, where some plastic chairs were placed in a row. Whatever it is they did to get answers – and he had a fair idea of its terror and that it was always beyond one's imagining – it was not going to be here. For the real questioning they would take suspects to their camp in the next town. He tried to keep his panic in check. What did they mean by *teacher*? The way those louts had mouthed the word, it sounded sinister, almost menacing: *teacher*. He knew these stories well but found it difficult to read the signs around him: was it a good thing being asked to sit? What if it had something to do with his colleagues? He didn't know too many people here, and he could vouch for Dwipen, that man was not involved in anything. Or was he? He knew this agitated whirlwind of thoughts amounted to nothing but he would persist. Then it struck him, the truth of it and it made his stomach lurch. He had absolutely nothing to give away. Not any longer. Not here. That placed a man, at once in a secure place where they wouldn't be able to reach him and, at the same time, marked him as one already written off, with nothing to offer, no terms for a negotiation.

His two escorts, the louts, were still there. They seemed to have no interest in him. He was like a slightly unpleasant insect they watched out for, with half an eye, but with no real apprehension for its ability to strike or stage a surprise. They looked bored, almost lethargic; the slow heat in the air bogging them down, in their combat paraphernalia of heavy boots, camouflage uniforms and helmets. They would have liked a chase, some sudden disturbance, a bout of clean, quick action. Like chained dogs in light slumber, they dreamt of flight. Prabin was careful not to move, his shoulders sagging, head bowed, hands on his lap, a figure of obeisance, submission.

They called him into the inner room, where there were more of them and somebody who looked like he was higher up in the chain of command. The louts directed him to one of the chairs. He sat and waited. The officer on the other side of the table was looking through a file. He continued examining it for a while, coughed, looked up at him, as if noticing him for the first time. He spoke in Hindi.

'You are a teacher?'

'Yes, sir.'

'You are not from here. Where is your village?'

He named his village. 'In Darrang district, sir.'

'And you are teaching here?'

'Yes, sir, I give trainings. I am in the education

department, the DIET, so I come here to do trainings. My posting is in Rangiya but—'

This seemed to confuse his questioner. He was suddenly impatient, and cut in.

'Okay, okay. You're not local, that's good. The locals are all haramis. I want you to do some work for me.'

Prabin was relieved. Voice cloying in its enthusiasm, he says, 'Yes sir, anything sir.'

'Here.' The officer held out a piece of paper with some writing in ink. 'Read this and tell me what it says. And you have to be quiet about it, or else we'll find you and break your legs.' He was smiling as he said this.

Prabin can feel the louts grinning as well, the idea cheered them up.

As soon as Prabin held the paper, his heart sank. It was a formal letter of sorts, he could make out. He stared at the words with great concentration, forcing out a meaning, at least from the subject line. But it was of no use; he had a good memory for words, and he could read the Devanagri script, but this is in Bodo, a language in which he knew a half-dozen words at most. He ran the first line in his head again and again but eventually gave up. These were not words of the everyday conversations he heard on his visits to this area, and he couldn't as much as muster a guess.

In his panic, he did a seemingly mad thing. He pushes the letter back at the officer, and said, 'Sir, but this is in your language, Hindi. I don't know any Hindi, sir. You can read it, sir.'

'Hai?' The officer glared at the paper. 'This is some kind of local language here – you can't read it? Aren't you a teacher?'

'Sir, but I don't know any Hindi, sir. You will be able to read it.'

'Arre … what kind of …' The officer, looking confused, absently gestured to the louts. 'Throw this one out. Waste of my time. Let me see now …' and continued staring at the paper, slowly struggling with the letters, mouthing the words.

Prabin mumbled, 'Thank you, sorry, sir.' One of the men touched his side with the metal of his gun barrel. 'Move.'

He was escorted back to the road and left there. The two turned back towards the crowd. About a hundred metres away, under a tree, Dwipen was waiting with the bike and, seeing him, yelled out his name. Prabin waved back and indicated that he should wait there.

'Aie, Prabin-da! I was worried. What did they want with you? I almost pissed my pants when I saw them take you towards the other room. I had started calling some of my contacts.'

Prabin nodded. 'Drive, let's get away from here.'

But as they came by the river, he could not resist anymore. Prabin asked Dwipen to stop the bike; it seemed safe enough. Then he took out a notebook, wrote down some words on it and held it out to Dwipen. He had been running the words over and over in his head to preserve them, and it was a relief to write them out.

'There was a letter in Bodo. Someone told them I was a teacher but not from here. The officer wanted me to read it for them. Confidential. I couldn't understand anything. But the subject line was something like this – here, I've written it down. Can you make sense of it?'

Dwipen took the paper and looked at it. 'The Bodo writing is different from the script of Hindi in some letters. Your spellings are a little awkward but I think I can see the logic. It's an announcement, it says: *Peace has come, peace has arrived in our land!*'

Oh. Dwipen slapped him on the back and burst out laughing. 'Peace has come and those guys, they don't know it because they can't read the language!'

Prabin stared at him for a moment, and joined in his laughter. They were both laughing so hard, they had to hold each other and the bike for support, snot flowing from their noses, tears flowing from their eyes.

It took them a few minutes to get back on the bike and continue their journey.

But as they veered away from the highway towards the town, dusk fell, swiftly turning the colours of the land. The dust road ahead became a pale white river against the dark of the rice fields and the sky ahead, a deep deep red of sleep. Suddenly, a great sadness weighed down upon them and they felt the loneliness of tall trees and silent hearths.

Peace had come to this land, and they were the only ones to know.

Acknowledgements

I AM GRATEFUL to the team at Westland: to Ajitha G.S. for believing in the book and editing it with such care and sensitivity, to Karthika V.K. for her faith in my writing and Vishwajyoti Ghosh for his valuable suggestions. I could not have asked for a better home for the book.

To my colleagues in the Pratham programme and beyond: Rukmini Banerji, Mukut Bhuyan, Shruti Nag, Khogen Murmu, Sapna Hembrom, Dumka Tudu, Manoj Koch and the rest of the team in Kokrajhar and Chirang for their support and generosity, and for sharing their world with me. For friends and family who have allowed me through their friendship and support – at various points in the last few years – a place of rest so essential to writing. With much gratitude to Jennifer Liang, Sunil Kaul, Balawansuk Lynrah, Abo Jabsri, Jemon and the collective at The ANT; Rachna Singh, Mahesh Gopalan, Amrapali Basumatary, Xonzoi Barbora, Dolly Kikon, Bhrigupati Singh, Prerna Singh, Elli Kalita, Anu Saha, Duncan McDuie-Ra, Prashant Keshavmurty, Urvashi Butalia. And as always, to my family: Capt. K.K. Singh, Purnima, Nisha, Jai, Rotha and Vavrinec.

This book was imagined over a chance conversation with my friend and agent, Shruti Debi. Thank you Shruti and little Piya – this has been an adventure in so many ways. I am grateful to my first reader, Anahita Lee for sharing the excitement and for her invaluable suggestions. And Yengkhom Jilangamba for help with edits and revisions and for putting up with all the troubles a book brings in its wake. And Hiyang, *thank you.*